Quinn turned on her, eyes black with fury.

Suddenly his hand was at her throat. For one terror-stricken moment, Janine feared he might strangle her.

Instead, he caressed the soft flesh below her jaw, a gesture that was undeniably dangerous, yet exquisitely erotic. "I understood you didn't intrude on your guests' privacy. Was I misinformed?"

"Not at all," Janine said shakily. "I was simply curious...."

He slid one fingertip slowly down her throat—more a lover's caress than a warning. "Curiosity," he murmured. "Fatal to felines, and unhealthy for humans, as well..."

All she had to do was take a step back, and she'd be free. But she couldn't move. She was trapped by his penetrating gaze, his mesmerizing touch. She was frightened, yet the fear was not for her physical safety.

The fear was for her soul, and for the power this man had over it. Over *her*...

Dear Reader,

It's spring, and the days are getting longer, but here at Shadows we're still in the dark—and that's the way we like it. And our books this month are guaranteed to keep the chills coming, even though the days are warming up. For starters, there's Diana Whitney's *The Raven Master*. The setting is a rooming house you definitely wouldn't want to visit in real life, but for passionate shivers, there's just no place like it.

Then there's *Kiss of Darkness* by Sharon Brondos. What is there to say about a book that features a vampire, the discovery of immortality and Death himself as a main character? Only that you won't want to miss it—it's one of our scariest yet.

In coming months, look for more of the best mix of passion and peril in books by Jane Toombs, Rachel Lee and Evelyn Vaughn, to name only a few of the authors we'll be featuring.

Enjoy!

Yours,
Leslie Wainger
Senior Editor and Editorial Coordinator

Please address questions and book requests to:
Reader Service
U.S.: P.O. Box 1325, Buffalo, NY 14269
Canadian: P.O. Box 1050, Niagara Falls, Ont. L2E 7G7

DIANA WHITNEY

Published by Silhouette Books
America's Publisher of Contemporary Romance

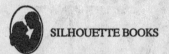 SILHOUETTE BOOKS

ISBN 0-373-27031-3

THE RAVEN MASTER

Copyright © 1994 by Diana Hinz

Printed in U.S.A.

DIANA WHITNEY

says she loves "fat babies and warm puppies, mountain streams and California sunshine, camping, hiking and gold prospecting. Not to mention strong, romantic heroes!" She married her own real-life hero twenty years ago. With his encouragement, she left her longtime career as a municipal finance director and pursued the dream that had haunted her since childhood—writing. To Diana, writing is a joy, the ultimate satisfaction. Reading, too, is her passion, from spine-chilling thrillers to sweeping sagas, but nothing can compare to the magic and wonder of romance.

To Christine Rimmer, who so generously shares
her sympathetic ear, absorbent shoulder,
unending support and cherished friendship.
Thanks pal!

CHAPTER ONE

Flames leapt toward the night sky, a devouring conflagration of carnage and death. Only a moment earlier the small frame structure had been someone's home. Now it was a fiery tomb, mocking heroic efforts of frantic volunteers.

Torrential blasts from firehoses arched into the inferno then evaporated into impotent clouds of sizzling steam. Nearby dwellings, engulfed by wind-whipped smoke and undulating waves of radiant heat, appeared to tremble in contemplation of sharing the building's grisly fate.

The steepled chapel across the street was engulfed by eerie reflections, a holy site perched on the precipice of purgatory, surrounded by the hellish flames. From the shadows an observer glanced away from the visual heresy, refocusing attention on the raging blaze. It had been so long, so painfully long. The waiting was over now. This was the place.

Dawn crept through a gray pall of lingering smoke and early spring fog that frequently shrouded the Pacific Northwest. From the kitchen of her Victorian boardinghouse, Janine Taylor parted hand-stitched gingham curtains and gazed at the pristine forest surrounding the remote village of Darby Ridge. Normally she took great pleasure from the picturesque view. On this dismal morning, however, the swirling mist smelled of burned wood and scorched earth and death.

The fact that she had barely known the victim didn't ease Janine's distress. Over the past three years she'd met relatively few of Darby Ridge's two thousand residents and knew only that Marjorie Barker had been an attractive, middle-aged woman who lived across from the Presbyterian church. When Janine had passed the house en route to the corner grocery, the woman had occasionally been outside tending her roses, and they would exchange casual greetings. Marjorie had been pleasant and soft-spoken with delicate eyes and a ready smile. Now she was dead.

Janine turned away from the window and shivered, rubbing her arms against the dampness. Upstairs, warped floorboards vibrated a warning that her guests were awakening. They'd be down soon, and they'd be hungry.

Shaking off her sad mood, she returned to the comforting breakfast routine by filling the dual-carafe coffeemaker and sliding a pan of homemade biscuits into the black iron oven. She arranged a pound of bacon in an oversize skillet, flipped on the antiquated gas burner, then methodically cracked two dozen eggs into a large ceramic bowl and beat them with a wire whisk until the mixture was fluffy enough to fly.

By the time Janine heard footsteps on the stairway, the enticing scent of brewed coffee and sizzling bacon had dispelled the chilly gloom. She felt better now, not good, but better.

Hushed voices filtered in from the foyer. A moment later, Jules Delacourt solicitously escorted his grandmother into the spacious farm-style kitchen.

They were a peculiar pair, obviously devoted yet so contradictory in appearance that it was difficult to believe they were related. Edna Fabish was a squat, bucket-shaped woman, heavily jowled, with a petite nose and saggy, blue button eyes. A ruffled mass of gray-streaked, ecru curls framed her paunchy face like the corkscrewed pelt of an ungroomed poodle.

Physically her grandson was the diametric opposite, tall and exceptionally thin, although he carried himself with the fluidity and grace of a *danseur noble*. With lazy dark eyes and meticulously groomed ebony hair slicked into classic European style, Jules was quite handsome although a porcelain-pale complexion and refined features gave him a pinched, somewhat effeminate appearance that Janine found unappealing.

This morning, as always, Jules was impeccably attired in a freshly starched dress shirt with a tasteful silk tie tucked under a V-necked argyle pullover. Janine guessed that his wool trousers, fashionably pleated and hemmed precisely one-eighth inch above the gleaming toes of his wing tips, probably cost more than the austere boardinghouse earned in a month.

Extravagant business apparel notwithstanding, Jules hadn't worked since arriving a year ago and apparently was supported by his grandmother, who held a nursing position at the town's small medical facility. Janine had always found that rather peculiar but respected the privacy of her guests and would never be so crass as to question their source of income. Edna and Jules were tidy, undemanding and, most important, paid their rent in a timely fashion. For that Janine was deeply grateful and willing to ignore their eccentric and occasionally disruptive personality foibles.

When Jules and his grandmother reached the kitchen table, Janine pasted on her cheerful hostess facade. "Good morning, Jules, Edna."

Ignoring the polite greeting, Edna dabbed her red eyes with a tissue. "God's wrath is upon us," the woman lamented, settling heavily into the ladder-back chair that her grandson held out. She blew her nose and tucked the soggy tissue into the polyester pocket of her white uniform. "Praise be to the Lord."

Jules sympathetically squeezed the older woman's shoulder. "*Grand'mère* is quite upset. She was very fond of Marjorie."

Startled, Janine laid down the spatula and looked over her shoulder. "I didn't realize that you were acquainted with Miss Barker."

Edna stoically lifted her chin. "She was a godly woman and a valued member of our congregation."

"I'm so sorry." The words sounded trite but not knowing what else to say, Janine returned her attention to the eggs she was scrambling.

"I must call the Reverend Mr. Weems about the services," Edna murmured sadly, lifting a china cup from her place mat and handing it to her grandson. "Such a horrible thing to happen."

Jules nodded somberly. "Yes, horrible." He dutifully placed a chaste peck on his grandmother's upturned cheek, then crossed the room and set Edna's cup beside the coffeemaker.

As Janine transferred scrambled eggs from the frying pan into a serving bowl, Jules glanced warily over his shoulder then whispered, "Did you see the flames?"

"Excuse me?" A spoonful of congealed egg hovered in midair.

"The flames," he repeated impatiently, his eyes glittering strangely. "They were positively immense. Did you see them?"

Unnerved, she slowly set the spoon in the bowl. "Yes, from my bedroom window."

Jules poured two cups of steaming coffee and continued in a hushed voice. "It was a magnificent spectacle, wasn't it?" Before she could respond, he'd returned to the kitchen table and set a steaming cup in front of his grieving grandmother, who patted his arm and smiled up gratefully.

Sighing, Janine shook her head. Appearance notwithstanding, Jules Delacourt was definitely an odd duck, a twenty-three-year-old man with the emotional development and bizarre imagination of a child. He seemed harmless enough, although Janine was occasionally unnerved by his propensity to read a sinister intent into ordinary events.

A raspy female voice suddenly demanded, "Who the hell do I have to kill to get a cup of coffee?"

With a glance toward the doorway, Janine set the bowl of eggs and a platter of crisp bacon on the table. "Good morning, Althea. You're up early."

The sullen woman shuffled across the linoleum and slid onto an empty chair. "One of the waitresses called in sick," she muttered peevishly. "Good old Al gets to cover the morning shift again."

Always the caregiver, Edna was instantly concerned. "The poor woman. I do hope it's nothing serious."

Althea shrugged. "Could be a case of the clap, for all I know."

Janine rolled her eyes, wishing to heaven that Althea wouldn't deliberately bait the other guests. The sharp-tongued woman wasn't likely to change tactics, however, and since she obviously enjoyed shocking people, poor pious Edna was a particularly tempting target for Althea's crude comments and tawdry wit.

Now Edna glanced quickly at her grandson, who was busily filling his plate, a crimson streak below his ear the only indication that he'd heard the coarse remark. The older woman returned her attention to Althea and frowned disapprovingly. "That was quite unkind, dear."

Ignoring the rebuff, Althea yawned and stretched luxuriously, seeming unconcerned that her silky peignoir had spread apart, exposing considerable cleavage above the lacy bodice of her gown. Unconcerned, but not unaware. The subtle tilt of her freshly glossed lips indicated that she'd noted Jules's discomfort and was amused by it.

In spite of the overbleached hair and exaggerated, chorus-girl makeup, Althea was an attractive woman. To her, however, only adjectives like stunning, gorgeous and breathtaking were acceptable.

Embittered and emotionally bruised by several failed relationships, Althea flaunted her fading assets with the terrified desperation of a woman still grieving for her lost youth. Each new crow's-foot sent a dagger into her heart; every sagging muscle was a personal tragedy of gigantic proportions. After all, she was only forty-four, still in her sexual prime. It wasn't her fault, Althea had once complained, that society valued a tight butt over the wisdom gained by experience.

And Janine suspected that Althea Miller was nothing if not experienced.

At the moment, however, Janine hoped that a caffeine fix would temporarily silence the woman's disruptive tongue, and handed her a steaming cup of coffee. Althea gurgled in delight, downed the hot liquid as though it were a shot of whiskey, then unceremoniously held out the cup for a refill. Janine complied without comment.

"Ahh." Althea took a healthy swallow, then set down the cup and lazily raked her fingers through a shoulder-length mass of brittle, strawberry-blond hair. "Nectar of the gods."

Jules, who apparently was desperately trying to avoid looking at the woman's partially exposed bosom, laid down his fork and delicately dabbed his lips. "Have you heard about last night's fire?"

Althea emitted an annoyed snort. "Damned sirens kept me awake half the night."

"Marjorie Barker died," Jules intoned, his eyes glistening with barely suppressed excitement. "It was tragic, simply tragic."

At the mention of her friend's name, Edna twisted her linen napkin. "Such a dear woman. She volunteered at the hospital, you know."

Leaning forward, Jules lowered his voice. "I heard that the authorities suspect arson."

Edna sniffed loudly and murmured an obtuse biblical quotation that seemed irrelevant to the discussion.

"What if it really *was* arson?" Jules insisted. "That means that Miss Barker was actually murdered. Think of it! A real killer loose right here in Darby Ridge. Why, we could all be in mortal danger."

Althea made an impolite noise. "Bull. The man-stealing slut got what she deserved."

Edna gasped and turned as white as her uniform.

Janine looked up from the toast she was buttering. "That was a very cruel remark, even for you."

Shifting uncomfortably, Althea fidgeted with the cup handle. "I was just trying to convince the paranoid prophets that nobody's going to skin them in their sleep, that's all. I mean, everyone knows the Barker broad wasn't particular about bed partners, and she probably ended up boinking somebody else's man."

"How dare you defile a virtuous woman?" Edna's eyes flashed blue fire. "Mark my words, Althea Miller, your evil tongue is an abomination to God, and He will have His revenge."

Jules pushed his plate aside. "Perhaps Miss Barker was mixed up with the mob."

Janine frowned. "Excuse me?"

"She could have been a gangster's moll," Jules suggested, obviously enthused by the grotesque theory. "Perhaps she was killed because she knew too much, or she might have had gambling debts, so the mob hired a hit man to, ah, off her.''

Smirking, Althea propped an elbow on the table. "You been watching the 'Untouchables' again, honey?"

Jules stiffened indignantly.

Janine pinched the bridge of her nose and moaned. The young man's macabre speculation made her skin crawl, and when the door bell rang, she was relieved to excuse herself from the unpleasant conversation.

Exiting the kitchen, Janine passed through the formal dining room to the small foyer at the base of the staircase. She absently tucked a stray strand of nondescript brown hair behind her ear, smoothed her oversize fleece top, opened the door and felt the breath back up in her throat.

A stranger was lounging lazily against the doorjamb. "I was told you might have a room for rent."

She took a step back, uncomfortable with the man's nearness and the disturbing familiarity his casual stance displayed. There was something unnerving about his gaze, a primal stare that made her instantly wary.

But the man had obviously been directed here—the antiquated Victorian manor was separated from town by a wilderness ravine and accessible only by a rickety wooden bridge—and a paying guest was always a welcome sight. Assuming, of course, that a person dressed in worn denims and black leather could afford the price of a room.

As she glanced beyond the porch, however, she noted a dusty beige minivan parked on a grass flat at the end of the rutted gravel road. If the man could afford a vehicle, he probably wasn't a vagrant.

Managing a strained smile, she finally found her voice. "You were correctly informed, Mr. . . . ?"

"Coulliard. Quinn Coulliard." He regarded her intently, with magnetic eyes the color of polished steel. "Are you the proprietor?"

"Yes. Janine Taylor." She cleared her throat and offered her hand. His palm was firm, warm and surprisingly soft. After a lingering moment, she withdrew it and clasped her hands together. "What brings you to Darby Ridge, Mr. Coulliard?"

His smile was forced, guarded. "Will my answer affect the availability of a room?"

A familiar heat crawled up her throat. "Of course not. It's just that we're so far off the beaten track that we don't receive many visitors. I was simply curious."

Without responding, he gazed over her shoulder, and as he scrutinized the spacious foyer, Janine took the opportunity to scrutinize him. The coffee-colored hair tied at his nape extended nearly to his shoulder blades, and although a bulging duffel sat on the porch by his feet, she instantly realized that Quinn Coulliard wasn't a typical drifter.

The man's purposeful gaze was tough, a stark contradiction to his surprisingly soft voice and articulate speech. All in all, he exuded a palpable aura of strength, which was unsettling, to say the least.

Suddenly he hoisted the stuffed bag and gazed deep into her eyes. "May I see the room, Miss Taylor?"

Janine hesitated. There was something about the man—and her own breathless reaction to him—that made her uneasy. His gray gaze was hypnotic, seeming to penetrate and probe the darkest recesses of her mind. For one heart-stopping moment, she wondered if he'd somehow entered her thoughts, observing the secret shame that she'd meticulously concealed from the world.

Of course that was impossible.

Mentally reprimanding herself, she shook off the disquieting notion. The man wanted a room, and she desperately needed the money. "Payment is requested in advance, Mr. Coulliard. Would you prefer the daily or weekly rate?"

He smiled and pulled out a tattered cloth wallet. "How much for the week?"

"Seventy-five dollars."

When the bills were safely tucked in her jeans, she smiled thinly and stepped back to allow him access. "Right this way."

After closing the door, Janine retrieved a key from a nearby closet, then suppressed her uneasiness and guided the enigmatic stranger upstairs to her last vacant room—the one next to her own.

"Breakfast is served at 7:00 a.m. and dinner is at six," Janine told him. "There's no television in the rooms, but a color set in the parlor is available for guest use. You may also use the stereo, although I do ask that the volume be kept down so that the other residents aren't disturbed."

Coulliard's eyes warmed, just a little. "Anything else?"

"There's a bathroom at the end of each hall." Janine handed him the key. "I hope you enjoy your stay with us."

He bounced the key on his palm. "I'm sure I will."

She licked her lips, nodded curtly, then turned and strode quickly down the hall.

When she reached the stair landing, a stain on the faded carpet caught her eye and she paused to investigate. She rubbed her fingertip over the gritty brown spot, then noticed another muddy smear a few feet from the first.

As she searched for other mud stains, a shrill voice from the kitchen distracted her. Making a mental note to add carpet cleaning to her list of projects, she hurried downstairs to referee the rest of her squabbling tenants.

After closing the door, Quinn examined the interior locking device and was annoyed to discover that the security lock automatically engaged each time the door shut. It was not an easy lock to jimmy. If the other rooms were as well protected as this one, that segment of his mission would be more difficult than he'd hoped.

The security arrangements were an unfortunate surprise. Quinn had counted on the trusting nature of rural residents to make his job easier. Although the Darby Ridge towns-folk had greeted him warmly, cheerfully answering personal questions about their neighbors without suspicion or hesitation, it appeared that his lovely landlady wouldn't be as obliging.

In spite of a polite demeanor, she'd scrutinized Quinn as though committing his features to memory and the fact that she'd also paid meticulous attention to his vehicle hadn't escaped his notice, either. He wondered if the woman would be astute enough to check the license number with the Department of Motor Vehicles. That could be a problem.

In fact, Janine Taylor herself could be a problem. The leery woman had watched him as a sparrow might watch a stalking cat, a surprising—and unpleasant—contradiction to the guileless welcome he'd received from her Darby Ridge neighbors. Apparently she wasn't a native of the area, yet she seemed rather young to have deliberately cloistered herself in such a remote location. Quinn had also noted a peculiar apprehension in those golden brown eyes, a secret fear that he might have found intriguing under other circumstances.

At the moment, however, his speculation wasn't born of idle curiosity. It was crucial that he understand exactly with whom he was dealing. A mistake in judgment could be fatal.

Dropping his duffel on the tidy bed, he glanced around the sparsely furnished room. A frameless oval mirror was positioned over a plain pine bureau, unadorned except for an ashtray and a thin stack of magazines. A gooseneck floor lamp was positioned beside the dresser and a wobbly wooden chair sat under the room's only window. There was also a narrow closet containing an extra pillow and a few bent hangers.

After a cursory inspection of the accommodations, Quinn rolled up the yellowing vinyl shade and was pleased to see that the second-story vantage point offered a clear view of the smoldering ruins several blocks away. That was an added bonus.

After reclosing the shade, he extracted a snub-nosed .357 revolver from his duffel, spun the cylinder to check load, then tucked the weapon into his jacket pocket and walked out of the room.

By late afternoon, the sun had broken the fog's gray grip, and clouds billowed like cotton mushrooms in a field of cornflower blue. The breeze was cool, not chilly, but as she walked the familiar sidewalks of the quiet residential area, Janine paid no attention to the pleasant weather. Instead she clutched the empty canvas tote, stared at cracked concrete and plodded up the hill toward the place where only yesterday Marjorie Barker had tended her roses.

The acrid smell of smoke clung to the air, becoming even more pungent as Janine crested the rise. She didn't want to look up, didn't want to see the carnage. Swallowing hard, she focused on the brisk movements of her own sneakered feet and busied her mind by identifying the various weeds that flourished between the sidewalk's concrete slabs.

Suddenly she jerked to a stop. From the corner of her eye she saw the smoke-stained pickets at the edge of the burned-out property. Hesitantly, she raised her eyes. The sight turned her stomach.

Beyond the fence, thorny stalks stood barren amid the clutter of shriveled blossoms and dead leaves—all that remained of Marjorie's beloved garden. A brick chimney rose from an elongated heap of charred and blackened debris;

everything else had been completely consumed by the raging flames.

Both repulsed and ghoulishly fascinated, she was unable to look away. That scorched skeleton had once been a home, a safe haven that had suddenly and inexplicably turned deadly. The grim scene was a bleak reminder of how fragile life was, how easily destroyed.

As Janine contemplated that sobering thought, a movement beyond the ruins caught her attention. She shaded her eyes and was stunned to see her newest tenant lurking in the shadows beyond the burnt hulk of Marjorie Barker's house.

Quinn Coulliard emerged from behind a tree not thirty feet away. Apparently unaware of her presence, he walked to the edge of the rubble and bent to examine a charred remnant. After a moment he dropped the object then stared at the cold ashes with an expression of regret and utter despair that touched Janine to the bone.

As she studied the man's jagged profile, she noted that his features appeared softer, less intimidating than she'd first thought and the subtle slump of his shoulders hinted at an unexpected vulnerability that was oddly appealing.

A breeze swirled through the site, scattering ashes and whipping the few loose hairs that had escaped the binding at his nape. Standing, he absently brushed the long strands from his face, turned into the wind and looked straight at Janine. The grief in his eyes took her breath away.

In less than a heartbeat that intense sadness dissolved into an impassive stare. He nodded an acknowledgment, ducked under the yellow police ribbon haphazardly stretched around the perimeter and sauntered toward the sidewalk. Tucking his hands in his jacket pockets, he gestured toward the fire scene with his head. "How did this happen?"

Janine shrugged weakly. "I don't know. Since our fire fighters are all volunteers, the investigation team will probably come from Eugene, which is about fifty miles west of here.''

''When is this team expected?''

''I have no idea. Why do you ask?''

''The site is unprotected,'' he replied curtly. ''When a death is involved, authorities aren't usually so cavalier about preserving evidence.''

A cold chill skittered down her spine. ''How did you know that someone died here?''

''Word gets around, even to newcomers.'' His wintry eyes held her captive. ''Some say it was arson.''

Although the last comment was issued like an afterthought, Janine was nonplussed by the intensity of his gaze. She moistened her lips, reminding herself that a man so deeply affected by a stranger's tragedy must be more compassionate than those secretive eyes would indicate. ''Small-town gossip tends to be overly dramatic, Mr. Coulliard. The fire was probably started by a spark from the fireplace or an electrical short.''

''It wasn't.''

''How do you know that?''

Without answering her question, he gazed at the burned rubble. A muscle below his ear twitched. His jaw clenched and beneath his sculpted cheekbones deep hollows suddenly appeared as though the flesh had been gouged away by demonic fingers. Shaded by a thick fringe of darkness, Quinn's eyes were as cold as frozen ponds and his sharply angled features hardened like a stone mask, revealing a leashed rage that frightened her half to death.

She stumbled backward, her heart pounding wildly.

Suddenly the fearsome expression dissipated and was replaced by one of calm concern. As Janine followed the direction of his gaze, she saw two frightened children cowering behind a tree at the edge of the burned property.

Quinn greeted them softly. ''Hello.''

A brown-eyed boy of about nine emerged towing a blond girl who appeared to be a year or two younger. Janine recognized them as Rodney and Sara Drake, who lived a few houses up the block.

The boy nervously returned Quinn's smile. "Hi."

After Janine completed the introductions, Quinn squatted down to the children's level, smiling at the girl who peeked out shyly from behind her brother.

"Sara is a pretty name," Quinn told her and was rewarded by a happy giggle. He turned his attention to the somber young boy. "I'll bet you take good care of your sister, don't you, Rodney?"

The boy nodded. "I have to, 'cause she's a girl and all."

An amused twinkle warmed Quinn's pale eyes and the transformation was stunning. As Janine watched in mute fascination, the man who had terrified her only moments ago now exuded a magnetism that shook her to the soles of her feet.

And she wasn't the only one affected. Quinn was speaking softly, gesturing toward the burnt house, and both children were listening with a rapt attentiveness that bordered on reverence. "How did you feel last night when you saw the fire?" Quinn asked.

"I was real scared," Rodney replied quickly, then jammed his hands in his jeans pockets and studied his scuffed sneakers. "Don't tell my pa, though. He says real men never get scared."

"Hmm." Quinn laid a comforting hand on the boy's shoulder. "Well, I certainly would have been scared."

The boy peeked up uncertainly. "Really?"

"It's okay to be frightened. Fear is what makes us cautious and gives us the ability to protect ourselves."

While Rodney considered that, Sara stepped forward with huge eyes. "Miss Barker was real nice. Sometimes she gave me flowers to take to my mommy." The girl's tiny lip quivered as a fat tear slid down her cheek. "Do you think she got scared when the fire came?"

"I don't know, Sara." Quinn gently touched the child's face, wiping away her tears with his thumb. "It's very sad when someone dies, isn't it?"

The girl hiccuped and wiped her nose with the back of her hand.

Quinn smoothed the child's shiny bangs. "Are you afraid that what happened to Miss Barker might happen to you?"

Sara twisted the hem of her T-shirt and nodded.

"Let's talk about that," Quinn said softly, sandwiching the child's small hand between his own large palms. To Janine's surprise, the girl responded, blurting out her feelings as though she'd known Quinn Coulliard all her young life.

After encouraging both youngsters to express their feelings, he listened intently then responded softly, calming their fears without mocking them. To Janine it seemed as though he'd actually established a kinetic mind-link with the children, and she couldn't help comparing Quinn's perceptive interaction with Charles's rigid intolerance.

Charles. Even the silent echo of her ex-husband's name brought exquisite sadness and regret. It seemed a lifetime ago that she'd been deeply in love, looking forward to starting a family with the man who had stolen her heart. During the courtship, Janine had been honest with Charles about her desire for children. In retrospect, however, she realized that he'd never specifically responded to her excited chatter about having a houseful of babies; still, she hadn't expected that Charles would deliberately deceive her.

But he *had* deceived her, and the betrayal had been shattering.

A childish voice broke into the sad memories. "We gotta go home," Rodney was saying. "Ma gets real worried if we're gone too long. Are we gonna see you again, Mr. Coulliard?''

Quinn stood. "Sure. I'll be around."

Smiling, Rodney waved goodbye, then took his sister's hand and led her up the hill toward their house.

When the youngsters had disappeared from view, Janine tilted her head, regarding Quinn with new respect. "You're very good with children."

He shrugged, avoiding her gaze. "I like kids. They haven't lived long enough to be cynical."

"Only a confirmed urbanite would be so jaded." She regarded him curiously. "Obviously you haven't spent much time outside of the asphalt jungle. Do you have friends here in Darby Ridge?" When he didn't answer immediately, she forced a teasing smile. "Was that a difficult question?"

He looked at her then, but his eyes were veiled and unreadable. "Will I be evicted unless I can provide local references?"

She flushed, realizing that her probing questions were less than subtle but was unable to quell her mounting curiosity. "Of course not. I just wondered how long you've been in town and what brought you here in the first place."

His gaze never wavered. "I was passing through yesterday afternoon and liked the scenery."

Janine doubted that. On any map of Oregon's Cascade Mountains, Darby Ridge was a nondescript dot on a winding broken line and much too secluded to be stumbled across. Besides, despite his transient appearance, the mysterious drifter's eyes seemed to reflect a higher purpose.

Still, she decided to keep her questions to herself. If Quinn Coulliard wanted to maintain his privacy, she could respect that. After all, Janine had her own sordid secrets.

Squaring her shoulders, she smoothed the canvas tote. "If I don't get to the grocery store, dinner will consist of packaged macaroni and carrot sticks."

"That sounds fine."

She laughed tightly. "Unfortunately the other tenants aren't as easy to please. Without a three-course meal and appropriate dessert, I'm afraid there would be an ugly revolt."

"You're exaggerating, of course."

"Not at all. The last time dinner was a disappointment, Edna spent the entire meal praying for my salvation, Jules sulked like a thwarted child and Althea cursed my cooking with words that could only be defined by an X-rated dictionary."

"Well, my new neighbors sound quite colorful." His eyes gleamed with sudden interest. "Tell me more."

"Words wouldn't do them justice. Besides, you'll meet them all at dinner." She glanced at her watch and groaned. "Which won't be served until midnight unless I get to the store."

"Of course." Since Quinn was blocking the sidewalk, he took the hint and politely stepped aside. "I'll see you this evening, then."

"Yes. This evening." With a weak smile, she turned away and hurried up the hill.

When she'd disappeared over the rise, Quinn's smile flattened. He wasn't the least bit pleased that his lovely landlady had caught him viewing the fire scene. The woman had too many questions, and his evasive answers hadn't fooled her one bit. He'd seen the curiosity lurking in those soft brown eyes, recognized the skeptical crease of her brow. She didn't trust him. That was too bad. A curious woman was an annoyance but a suspicious one could jeopardize his mission.

Quinn hoped that Janine Taylor wouldn't interfere with his plans, but if she did, he'd have to deal with her—and she wouldn't much care for his methods.

CHAPTER TWO

The memorial service for Marjorie Barker took place on Friday morning, two days after the fire. An overflow crowd packed the tiny chapel while the Reverend Mr. Weems delivered an eloquent if somewhat protracted eulogy. Prayer books were opened. Respects were paid. Amens were spoken. Flowers were laid on a snow-white casket. Finally the congregation spilled into the courtyard, gathered at linen-draped refreshment tables and transformed the solemn occasion into a social event.

Finding shade beneath a flowering jacaranda, Janine alternately fanned herself with the mimeographed remembrance card and sipped sticky sweet punch from a paper cup. After being forced to breathe the repugnant combination of Edna's overpowering cologne and stale body odor from an anonymous pewmate, Janine decided that fresh air had never smelled quite so wonderful. The service had droned on forever, and she hoped Marjorie would forgive her gratitude that it was finally over.

With a quick glance at her watch, Janine fretted about the chores awaiting her back at the boardinghouse. There hadn't been time to clean up after breakfast, and if she didn't tackle the mound of laundry piled in the basement, there would be no clean linens for the weekend.

Although she longed to slip away early, there was a certain decorum to be maintained, and she certainly didn't want to become fodder for the rumor mill that, if hushed whispers and shocked expressions were any clue, was already in full gear.

Shifting restlessly, she scanned the groups of gossiping matrons and blustering, somber-faced men. Some shook their heads sadly; others touched their throats or covered their mouths in wide-eyed disbelief. Janine didn't have to hear the muted conversations to know what was being said. Thanks to Jules's uncanny ability in wheedling information from "informed sources," she'd heard everything last night at the dinner table.

According to Jules, Marjorie's body had been found in bed with her hands neatly folded on her chest. Since preliminary investigation revealed that the fire had started in the kitchen, it was presumed that the woman had set a pot on the stove, then dozed off and been overcome by smoke as she slept.

The explanation, although perfectly logical, had been deeply disappointing to Jules, who was still reluctant to relinquish the notion that Marjorie had been the victim of foul play. In fact, he'd been quite annoyed that the Barker family hadn't permitted an autopsy, and he'd stubbornly insisted that a proper medical examination would have proven his theory that the woman had been murdered by the mob.

At that point Althea had called Jules a disgusting ghoul; he had retaliated by pointedly questioning Althea's lineage. Edna, having experienced a remarkable recovery from her previously inconsolable grief, had ignored the ruckus and solicitously dished a second helping of pot roast onto Quinn's plate.

Such unpleasant arguments between tenants were unfortunately all too common, although Janine silently conceded that the presence of her newest boarder had probably prevented the discussion from becoming even more volatile. Not that Quinn had said anything particularly soothing. In fact, he'd spoken very little, evading personal questions with nondescript replies and inspecting his table-mates with his trademark intensity.

The other tenants had nonetheless responded to the new-comer by displaying a restraint that for them was significant. Except for an occasional lapse, Althea's vocabulary had been uncharacteristically civil, and although Jules had basically ignored Quinn, Edna's nurturing frenzy had barely fallen short of actually tucking a napkin under the poor man's chin.

It had been an interesting evening, to say the least.

Dabbing her moist forehead, Janine considered another sip of punch, then discarded the notion, stepped behind the jacaranda and discreetly poured the nauseating beverage at the base of the tree. She patted the bumpy trunk, then glanced up and noticed a couple standing apart from the crowd, apparently engaged in an intense conversation.

Although the woman was facing away from Janine, that brittle, red-gold bouffant was unmistakable. Besides, only Althea Miller would be crass enough to wear a leather miniskirt and cropped midriff top to a funeral.

The inappropriate attire wasn't particularly surprising but the fact that Althea was attending services for a woman she'd professed to despise was a bit of a jolt, and the man to whom she was speaking seemed inordinately uncomfortable. He was a distinguished gentleman, perhaps in his mid-fifties, and would have been quite attractive but for his pained expression. Althea's spine was as stiff as a broom-stick, a desperate rigidity that was quite uncharacteristic.

Janine watched intently as Althea fumbled in her bag then dabbed at her face with a tissue. The man glanced around as if assuring himself that he couldn't be overheard before bending forward to issue a terse statement. Instantly Al-thea's head drooped and her shoulders quivered. The man said something else, then spun on his heel and strode away.

Extending her hand, Althea called after him—it sounded like "please wait"—but he didn't respond. In a moment he'd disappeared and Althea stood alone, trembling.

Janine was both stunned and alarmed by the emotional exchange, never having seen Althea so obviously upset. Before she could react, however, Edna hurried over and hustled her distressed neighbor away. After a moment's hesitation Janine followed and found the two woman conversing softly behind a screen of oleander.

"I hate the bitch," Althea murmured, ineffectually wiping at the wet mascara smudges under her eyes. "I'm glad she's dead."

Clucking softly, Edna took the woman's hands. "Satan covets the righteous and leads them astray with temptations of the flesh. 'Every tree which bringeth not forth good fruit is hewn down, and cast into the fire.'" Rolling her eyes upward, Edna added a heartfelt amen.

Althea lifted her chin defiantly and uttered a succinct oath.

The older woman paled three shades. "God forgives your blasphemy, child, as you must forgive Marjorie. She is with her Lord now and has been absolved of sin."

Janine frowned, completely perplexed by the odd exchange. Barely two days had passed since Edna had become apoplectic at the mere suggestion that Marjorie Barker might have been less than saintly, so this unexpected discussion of sin, temptation and rotten fruit was startling to say the least.

The conversation's content, however, was none of Janine's business. Even when motivated by concern, eavesdropping was unacceptable, so she quietly backed away from the peculiar scene, turned around and rammed into a male chest.

Gasping, she whirled around and laid a hand over her racing heart. "You startled me."

"So sorry," Jules replied uncontritely. "It was a lovely service, wasn't it?"

"Uh...yes, lovely," Janine murmured, still distracted by what she'd just overheard.

"And, I might add, so are you."

"Hmm?"

"You look lovely this morning."

"Oh." She self-consciously smoothed the skirt of her teal print sundress. "Thank you."

Jules dusted his immaculate suit jacket, palmed his slick hair and flashed a Continental smile. "The bonnet is quite fetching, although it seems a shame to conceal those beautiful mahogany tresses."

Janine managed to stifle a moan. The quaintly described "bonnet" was a straw sun hat with a ribboned crown, and the "beautiful mahogany tresses" consisted of nothing more than a weedy thatch of dirt brown hair cut into a blunt, Buster Brown bob.

Although she really tried to be tolerant of Jules's penchant for testing out new personalities, the peculiarity grated on her nerves. Last week, for example, the impressionable young man had watched three John Wayne movies on television, then swaggered through the boardinghouse calling everyone "pilgrim." Today, however, his exaggerated formality and jauntily tilted chin appeared to be a pitiful parody of David Niven.

Of course, lots of people enjoyed performing impersonations, but with Jules the practice seemed more an eerie transformation than a quirky party trick.

At any rate, she was considering the most expedient way to extract herself from the unwanted conversation when she glanced toward the refreshment table and saw the man to whom Althea had been speaking. Leaning to her right, she peered around Jules' slender frame, hoping for a better view.

He followed her gaze and frowned. "Who are you looking at?"

"That gray-haired gentleman standing beside the punch bowl."

"Gregore Pawlovski?"

Janine straightened. "Do you know him?"

"Vaguely." Disdainfully arching a brow, Jules brushed invisible lint from his lapel. "Althea said that he was once a European diplomat but apparently he retired last year."

"So he's a friend of Althea's?"

"Ah, much more than a friend." Jules leaned forward and whispered in her ear. "They were doing it."

Blinking, Janine stepped back. "Doing what?"

"You know." Jules smirked and offered a sly wink.

Janine frantically fanned herself and stared at the ground. "I see," she murmured, regretting that she'd ever brought the subject up and quite ready to drop the entire matter.

Jules wasn't. "Althea was quite mad for Gregore and had actually deluded herself into thinking that he would marry her. Can you believe that?"

Curiosity overcame social propriety, and she couldn't keep herself from asking what had happened. Leaning forward, Jules spoke in a conspiratorial whisper that gave her the shivers. "Pawlovski and Marjorie Barker were having an affair. It was really quite sordid, and Althea was livid, simply livid."

Janine was appalled by the lurid accusation. "How on earth could you possibly know that?"

"I have my sources."

"Well, I don't believe it. Marjorie Barker was a lovely woman."

He shrugged. "She was a whore."

"Jules!"

"Marjorie had sex with lots of men. She wanted to have sex with me, too, but I refused because she was unclean."

His dark eyes glittered strangely, as though pleased to have shocked her, yet when she showed her displeasure by turning away, he seemed genuinely grieved. "Have I offended you?"

She didn't bother to deny it. "Yes, you have."

"Naturally, a true lady would be distressed by the discussion of such indelicate matters." He wrung his slender hands. "You have my word that it will never happen again. Please forgive me."

Sighing, Janine massaged her throbbing temple. "It's all right, Jules. Let's just forget about it."

"Of course." He tugged his collar. "Perhaps it would be best not to mention this, uh, unfortunate incident to *Grandmère*. We wouldn't want to upset her."

Without further response, Janine walked away, trying to ignore the sinking sickness in the pit of her stomach. She'd always been aware that Jules was different; now she wondered if he was mentally unstable, because only a very sick person would make up such disgusting lies.

It never occurred to her that he could have been telling the truth.

Althea slammed furiously into her room. She flung her purse into the wall, threw herself across the unmade bed and beat the rumpled pillows with her fists. "Damn him!"

Clutching the bedclothes, she sobbed until the pillow slips were stained with runny mascara and soggy blotches of orange Pan-Cake makeup. Marjorie Barker had gotten just what she deserved, and someday Gregore—the two-timing bastard—would burn in hell along with his cheap whore.

Sniffing, Althea sat on the edge of the mattress and grabbed a handful of tissues from a box on the nightstand. She blew her nose and wiped melted makeup from her face, then miserably dropped the wadded tissues on the floor. She stared at her bare knees, riddled by guilt and feeling worthless.

In spite of her crude bravado, she'd been sickened by the fire's fatal aftermath. The worst part was that the Barker woman had died for nothing. It was a shame, a lousy stinking shame. A wasted tragedy. But there was no sense blubbering about something that was over and done with.

With a final wipe of her wet eyes, Althea went to the closet-door mirror and critically examined her full-length reflection. Sucking in her tummy, she turned sideways and inspected her curvaceous profile. Not bad, she decided. Her boobs didn't droop, her butt was nice and tight, she could still crack walnuts with her thighs and her legs were to die for. Of course, her waist wasn't quite as sleek as it used to be, but what the hell. All in all, she wasn't too damned shabby for a broad pushing the big four-five.

So why didn't Gregore want her any more?

Biting her lower lip, she tangled her fingers in her brassy hair and fought a renewed surge of tears. It wasn't supposed to happen like this. Now that his precious mistress was dead, Gregore should have returned to Althea for comfort. Instead he'd called her filthy names and said that he never wanted to see her again.

The rotten son of a bitch. God, she loved him.

Janine propped the basket of soiled towels against her hip and descended the narrow stairs into the damp cinder-block basement.

The cavernous space served as the manor's main storage and service area, housing tools, hardware and miscellaneous supplies along with the boiler, water heater and circuit boxes. A raft of fluorescents suspended from ceiling joists slid into the dungeonous blackness but Janine didn't bother to turn them on. The laundry corner was situated close to the stairway and cheerful shafts of sunlight from two high windows provided adequate illumination for the task at hand.

After dumping the soiled bedclothes, she absently massaged the small of her back and mentally calculated the number of loads represented by the mountainous pile. With any luck, she'd be finished by midnight. Depending, of course, on how long she chose to stand there feeling sorry for herself instead of loading the stupid washer.

After all, the first residents of this magnificent manor scrubbed sheets on a washboard, lugged wet laundry to a sagging clothesline, then crossed their fingers and prayed that a few minutes of sunshine would break through the dreary clime. From that perspective, stuffing linens into a modern machine and pushing a button didn't seem a particularly daunting task.

Smiling to herself, she dragged a length of rumpled percale from the pile and daydreamed about how life must have been at the turn of the century. There would have been hardships, of course. Still, she liked to imagine the lazy pace of those times and picture a gentle life-style unaffected by the pressures of a modern culture that espoused expectations so unrealistic that disappointment—and failure—was inevitable.

As Janine poured a dollop of detergent into the loaded machine, she considered how she'd have enjoying living in that era. She even liked the fashions, flowing and feminine, with yards of shining fabric swirling over mounds of ruffled petticoats and...

Her hand hovered over the controls. Suddenly uneasy, she glanced toward the unlighted portion of the basement and had the eerie sense that she was being watched. Something didn't feel quite right. Beyond the bright laundry area, the thickening darkness exuded an aura of charged danger, like the heavy air preceding a summer storm. Her scalp tingled. A fine mesh of gooseflesh tickled her arms.

As she moistened her lips, her nervous gaze landed on the light-switch at the base of the stairs. She flexed her fingers, eyes darting from the switch to the abysmal darkness.

A figure stepped from the shadows.

Gasping, Janine backed into the washer and froze until the silhouette emerged into sunlight. She exhaled all at once and relaxed slightly.

"I didn't mean to frighten you," Quinn said quietly. His right arm was sharply angled behind him, half-hidden by the drape of a hip-length khaki vest that seemed an odd complement to faded blue jeans and a white T-shirt.

She waited until her heart had resumed a quasi-normal rhythm. "I didn't realize there was anyone else here."

Without responding, he tucked something behind his back, then emerged into the fully lit laundry area, crossed his sculpted arms, propped a slim hip against the clothes dryer and stared in a manner that she would have considered rude had she not been rendered momentarily senseless by his mesmerizing gaze. He had the pale eyes of a snow leopard, cunning and wise, glowing with predatory intent.

Suddenly feeling like a trapped hare, Janine rubbed her upper arms. "Why are you here? In the basement, I mean."

A vague wariness clouded his eyes while he considered a response. Since Janine had already noted the enigmatic stranger's tendency to weigh words carefully, the hesitation was expected.

"My van needs washing," he said finally. "I was looking for a bucket."

"There's a stack of five-gallon buckets in the storage area across from the boiler. They're difficult to find in the dark." She took two steps and flipped the switch. A half-dozen fluorescents fluttered to life, illuminating the entire basement.

His expression remained impassive. "Thank you."

Acknowledging him with a jerky nod, Janine was unduly irritated by a nagging feeling that *she* was the intruder.

That peculiar sensation wasn't her only source of discomfort. In Quinn Coulliard's presence, she felt a heightened sense of awareness, an exquisite sensitivity that bordered on pain, as though every nerve in her body was burrowing to the surface.

There was something about him, a renegade quality that was both unnerving and strangely compelling. The wild mane of espresso-colored hair, so tightly bound yet never quite controlled, seemed a silent metaphor for the man himself.

Averting her gaze, Janine turned on the washing machine and feigned interest in sorting the remaining laundry. "There's liquid detergent in the overhead cupboard and a box of rags if you need them." She slanted a glance over her shoulder. "I imagine your van gathered a pretty thick layer of road dust during that long trip from California."

After a long moment, he responded, "Actually, I drove down from Washington."

"Really?" She straightened, still clutching the hem of a rumpled sheet. "Since your van has a California license plate, I naturally assumed—"

"Assumptions are dangerous." The softness with which he spoke belied the warning glint in his eye. Then he smiled, a vague tilt at the corner of his mouth that did little to warm his guarded gaze. "I once lived in California."

"So did I." Dropping the linens, Janine leaned against the agitating washer and regarded him curiously. "San Diego. And you?"

He stared into her eyes without blinking yet she perceived that his mind was working quickly, analyzing the ramifications of every conceivable response. Finally he slid his hand beneath his vest and hooked a thumb in the waistband of his jeans. "I've spent time in that area."

The man's evasiveness was beginning to irritate her. If he was this secretive about something as mundane as mentioning where he was from, he'd probably endure torture rather than reveal the really important stuff, like whether he preferred his coffee black or with cream.

Normally Janine would have respected such an obvious desire for privacy, but for some unfathomable reason, his deliberate attempt to embellish an air of mystery just brought out the devil in her. "So, Mr. Coulliard, may I assume that you and I might once have been neighbors?"

This time he answered with barely a pause. "It's possible."

"San Diego is a beautiful city."

"Yes."

"Most people fall in love with the place and wouldn't dream of living anywhere else." She hesitated, hoping he'd elaborate. He didn't. She posed a blunt question. "Why did you leave?"

A disturbing gleam warmed his eyes. "For the same reason you did."

She felt the blood drain from her face. God, how could he know? Her breath backed up in her lungs as she fought to maintain her composure. She told herself that he was just fishing and prayed it was true. There was no way on earth this man could know a secret that had been too shameful to share with her own family.

Clasping her hands together, she faced him squarely. "I doubt we left for the same reason."

To her surprise, his eyes warmed and he regarded her with something akin to respect. "Not specifically, perhaps, but in spirit."

She exhaled slowly. "Forgive me, but deciphering ecumenical vagaries has never been my strong suit."

The corner of his mouth twitched, as though he was faintly amused by her response. "Life is a journey, Miss

Taylor, one each of us must travel, physically and spiritually. In that context, we'd be soul mates, wouldn't we?"

Caught by his penetrating gaze, Janine heard a whispered voice that sounded very much like her own. "Yes, I suppose so."

Peculiar waves of warmth washed over her, an odd floating sensation that settled like a fluttering bird to nest in her feminine core. In spite of a cultured manner, there was a primitive quality about this mysterious man that awakened an ancient part of her own soul. Like a magnificent warrior, Quinn Coulliard exuded an aura of strength and leashed savagery that was deeply disturbing—and incredibly erotic.

Confused and unnerved, she glanced away long enough to take a deep breath and clear her fuzzy mind. She managed a tight laugh. "Well, regardless of metaphysical consequences, it seems that Darby Ridge is a gathering point for displaced San Diegans. Marjorie Barker once mentioned that she'd owned some kind of business outside of Mission Bay."

"And your other tenants, are they from Southern California?"

The underlying urgency of his question gave her pause. "I'm not certain."

His smile wasn't particularly pleasant. "So of all your guests, only I have been singled out for your intensive interrogation. Should I be concerned or flattered?"

Her face warmed. "It wasn't my intent to interrogate you, Mr. Coulliard. I was simply making polite conversation."

A victorious smile played on his lips. "So was I, Miss Taylor."

Decidedly uncomfortable, Janine fidgeted with the detergent box. He was right, of course. She hadn't grilled her other guests about their pasts. Quite frankly, she hadn't been interested, and that realization opened an entirely new area of thought. Obviously she *was* interested in Quinn Coulliard yet was unsure as to exactly why. She'd have to think about that later.

At the moment, however, she offered a conciliatory smile. "Jules and Edna are originally from Massachusetts, but from what I understand, they most recently lived in Seattle. They've been in Darby Ridge a little over a year. As for Althea, she's lived here longer than any of us."

"Ah, yes, Ms. Miller. She's quite an interesting woman." He absently rubbed his index finger along his angled jawline. "Ms. Fabish and her grandson are also...rather unique."

Janine straightened and said nothing.

Quinn pursed his lips thoughtfully. "All of your guests are so colorful, I can't help wondering what has brought them to such a secluded place."

She forced a nonchalant shrug. "I wouldn't know. Maybe they're soul mates, too."

He regarded her for a moment, then posed a blunt question. "Don't you find their peculiarities to be unsettling?"

Shifting nervously, she fingered a rusted scratch on the washing-machine lid, remembering the horrible things Jules had said about poor Marjorie and how his eyes had gleamed with perverse pleasure. "No one is perfect, Mr. Coulliard. We have to accept people as they are, not as we'd wish them to be."

"But if such wishes could be granted, what changes would you make in the people living under your roof?" The moment the question slid from his lips, Quinn knew he'd pushed too hard.

Janine's shoulders squared stubbornly. She suddenly grabbed the detergent box, shoving it in the overhead cabinet with unnecessary force. "I don't care for hypothetical questions, Mr. Coulliard, and I make it a point not to discuss my guests' personal lives."

One look at the angry spark in those liquid amber eyes and Quinn knew that he had to act quickly or he'd lose the advantage. He took her hand, ignoring her startled expression as he expertly guided the conversation to a more intimate level. "I'm concerned about you, Janine."

As her eyes widened, she touched her throat in a gesture that could have been interpreted as an expression of shock or vulnerability or both. She managed to stammer a single word. "Why?"

With slow strokes of his thumb, Quinn lightly caressed the back of her hand. "Surely you've noticed how Jules looks at you." The fear in her eyes hit him like a body blow.

She withdrew her hand. "I don't know what you're talking about."

Surprised by a visceral reaction to her distress, Quinn took a moment to compose himself and scrutinize the woman who had evoked the unexpected response. There was a purity about her, an air of innocence that he found oddly appealing. Hers was a quiet beauty, fresh and natural, her face framed by silky strands of chestnut hair cut in a simple style that complemented her dainty features. She neither used nor needed cosmetic enhancement but her exotic eyes, so delicately tinted with flecks of gold, reflected a vague sadness that he found strangely unsettling.

Quinn looked away, breaking the spell and refocusing his mind on what had to be done. After a moment, he faced her again to gauge her reaction. "Jules appears to be an emotionally fragile young man." As her perfect complexion faded, he deduced that Janine was well aware of her tenant's emotional problems.

To her credit, however, she defiantly lifted her chin and met his eyes without blinking. "To make such a denigrating statement about a man you've just met is presumptuous to say the least, and unless you have a psychology degree tucked in those ragged jeans, I suggest you keep your pompous opinions to yourself.''

Quinn arched a brow and regarded the gutsy woman with a combination of admiration and renewed wariness. Under ordinary circumstances, he'd have appreciated such chutzpah. These, however, weren't ordinary circumstances, and at the moment he'd have preferred the exquisite young lady to be less perceptive and more compliant.

To obtain what he needed, Quinn had to establish her trust, and since she could not be easily manipulated, he'd have to open his own life just far enough to gain her empathy and confidence. He hadn't wanted to do that but she'd left him no choice.

Sighing, he rubbed his forehead. ''Actually I do.''

The cryptic statement appeared to knock the breath out of her. ''Do what?''

Dropping his hand, he smiled in what he hoped was a modestly endearing manner. ''I don't keep it in my pocket, though. Sheepskin tends to wrinkle.''

She frowned, tilted her head and eyed him skeptically. ''You're a psychologist?''

''I was.''

Folding her arms, she aimed a pointed glance at his unconventional attire, dubious that a ponytailed man in torn denim could have ever held such a position. At least, that was Quinn's assumption, so her next statement took him by surprise. ''I should have guessed,'' she murmured. ''Especially after watching how you calmed those terrified children. You were wonderful with them.''

Taken aback by such unexpected praise, Quinn covered his discomfort with an impassive shrug. ''The children needed to express their fears in order to face them. I just asked the questions.''

''Perhaps, but I recognized something deeper in the way you related to them—an affinity and concern that can't be taught at a university." She smiled and a dazzling warmth settled inside Quinn's chest. "Do you specialize in working with children?"

"No. I had hoped to but . . ." He hesitated, unwilling to expose such a painful part of his life. A quick glance confirmed her interest. He took a deep breath and plunged ahead. "I couldn't afford to open my own practice, and since a depressed economy limited the number of positions available in my area of expertise, I ended up in a state clinic counseling adults with drug and alcohol problems."

"You didn't find that fulfilling?"

"At first I did."

"And something changed that?"

He shrugged. "My patients were only there because treatment had been mandated by the courts."

"But you still helped them."

"No, I didn't. When their probation ended, nearly all of them returned to self-destructive behavior."

"Oh." She regarded him thoughtfully. "That wasn't your fault, you know."

"Then whose fault was it? My patients were broken people, with lives destroyed by an addiction they were powerless to control. They wanted help—my help—and I failed them."

A dusty sadness clouded her dark eyes, an exquisite empathy that jolted him to the core. She laid a slender hand on his arm. "So you gave up your career?"

His skin tingled beneath her soft touch. "It seemed a good time to reevaluate my life and my priorities." After accepting her sympathetic nod, he offered a poignant smile. "Now that I've revealed all my innermost secrets, perhaps you'll return the favor."

Instantly wary, Janine retrieved her hand and shielded herself with tightly crossed arms. "I have no innermost secrets," she lied. "Sorry to disappoint you."

Although he returned her thin smile, his eyes were again veiled, unreadable. "In that case, I hope that you can reassure me that I won't awaken to find one of your guests hovering over me with a boning knife."

"You are quite safe," Janine said quickly, believing that assurance in spite of having been undeniably shaken by events of the past days. "It's just that everyone has been so jittery since the fire. Although frayed nerves have a tendency to exaggerate eccentricities, I can assure you that we're all quite harmless. Everything will be back to normal in a few days." She smiled brightly and fervently hoped that was true. "So you see, no innermost secrets there, either. Unless, of course, you consider the house itself."

Janine winced, wondering what had possessed her to blurt something so foolish. The words had slipped from her lips the moment she'd noticed Quinn glance toward the stairs, as though preparing to leave. For some odd reason, she hadn't wanted him to go. Now that he was watching her with renewed interest, she felt silly.

"A house with secrets?" An attractive web of laugh lines crinkled the corners of his eyes. "Should I keep an eye out for ghosts?"

"The place only looks haunted, but it does have a rather colorful history. It, uh, used to be—" she cleared her throat and smiled wanly "—a bawdy house."

He arched a brow. "Complete with red velvet wallpaper?"

"I, uh..." She coughed away an embarrassed tickle. "I wouldn't know. This has been a respectable dwelling for over sixty years."

"And before that?"

"Before that, this lovely old mansion was the highlight of Darby Ridge social life." She couldn't help smiling at his bemused expression and found herself relating the ancient gossip with considerable zeal. "Apparently, turn-of-the-century loggers were quite a rowdy bunch, and when the townsfolk finally got tired of the riffraff, they hired a marshal to clean up the town. The rumor is that the marshal took his job seriously, but after months of nightly raids never made a single arrest.''

"Why not?"

"There was never anyone *to* arrest. The deputies would stake out the place and see dozens of, uh, clients enter, but when the posse stormed inside they found no one except the ladies.''

A gleam of amusement lightened his gaze. "So where did the men go?"

"No one knows for certain, but there was whispered speculation that when the marshal came through the front door, the brothel's clients escaped through a secret tunnel leading to the ravine behind the house, then forded the little creek and crept quietly back to their homes.''

The amused twinkle faded. "Where is this tunnel?"

"As far as I know, there isn't one." Janine was surprised by his serious tone and sudden interest. "The story is just folklore.''

"Folklore is usually based on fact."

"Perhaps, but over so many decades, facts are frequently embellished to the point of fiction. Besides, I've lived here for three years and can assure you that there's not a hidden door or secret passage in the entire house.''

He considered that for a moment. "You're probably right. Still, it's an intriguing story, isn't it?" He paused. "Well, I've held you up long enough. I'll leave you to your work.''

As he headed toward the stairs, Janine stopped him. "Mr. Coulliard?"

Hesitating on the third step, he glanced over his shoulder. "Yes?"

She smiled sweetly. "You forgot the bucket."

CHAPTER THREE

After rubbing cleaning foam into the stained carpet, Janine dropped the sponge into the bucket and decided that it was a losing battle. She sat back on her heels, disgusted. Even if she got the stupid spot out, the carpet would still be ugly. The putrid color reminded her of rotten lettuce and the original sculpted contour had long ago been tromped flat.

Eventually she hoped to scrape together enough money to replace the matted mess—she'd already managed to recarpet all the bedrooms except her own—but until then there was little she could do to keep the upstairs hallway from looking like a moldy meadow.

With a resigned sigh, she protected the wet spots with colorful plastic barrier, gathered the cleaning supplies and hurried downstairs. Since Jules and Edna were doing volunteer work at the church bazaar and Althea's shift at the diner ended somewhere around midafternoon, there was little time left to complete her Saturday chores before the tenants returned.

As for the mysterious Mr. Coulliard, Janine hadn't seen him since breakfast. His van was still parked at the edge of the gravel cul-de-sac so she assumed that he hadn't gone far. But then the man was constantly disappearing and popping up in the most unexpected places. His random schedule was puzzling. None of her business, of course, but definitely odd.

As Janine replaced the cleaning supplies in the sink cupboard, she idly wondered if her newest boarder was a nature lover who enjoyed taking solitary hikes through the surrounding woods. Or perhaps he walked into town and spent long hours warming a bar stool at one of the town pubs.

That was doubtful, though, since he never smelled of alcohol and hadn't exhibited even the slightest symptom of inebriation. Besides, it seemed unlikely that a man who had once counseled alcoholics would spend his spare time in a bar—assuming, of course, that Quinn had been truthful about his background. That might be a rather large assumption but Janine believed him. At least, she wanted to believe him and at the moment she had no reason not to— except for a nagging intuition continually whispering that Quinn Coulliard wasn't precisely what he seemed.

Shaking off the disquieting notion, Janine focused on her chores by setting a package of pork chops on the counter to thaw. As she removed the vacuum cleaner from the broom closet, an agitated yowl in the backyard was followed by a peculiar rustling and a hollow wood-on-wood clunking sound. Then there was a horrible, bloodcurdling shriek.

Rushing to the kitchen window, Janine saw the source of the ruckus was a huge black raven perched on a stack of firewood. One of the bird's massive wings was fully extended; the other slanted down at an awkward angle. A stalking cat circled the woodpile, then flattened into a threatening crouch. The bird screeched, hopped to the edge of the woodpile and tried to intimidate its feline adversary with bristling feathers and a fierce hiss.

The cat was not impressed. As Janine watched in horror, the animal leaped onto the woodpile and tried to bite the bird's neck. The gutsy raven pecked viciously, forcing the thwarted feline into a temporary withdrawal. Janine feared that in spite of such bravado the injured raven would be hard-pressed to fend off another attack, so she snatched up a flimsy flyswatter and ran out the back door.

An angry male shout greeted her. She jerked to a stop, and glanced around in confusion just as Quinn Coulliard appeared and shooed the frustrated cat away. Then the most extraordinary thing happened. Quinn knelt, extended his hand and spoke softly to the terrified bird. In less than a heartbeat, the raven hopped down from the woodpile and limped toward his rescuer.

Quinn stroked the animal, smoothing the injured wing, then gently gathered up the bird and carried it toward the back porch. When he'd nearly reached the steps, he saw Janine and hesitated.

Awed by what she'd seen, Janine stared at the placid raven nestled in the crook of Quinn's arm. "How in the world did you do that?"

She hadn't really expected an explanation and wasn't surprised when he ignored the question and nodded toward the kitchen door. "Would it be all right to take him inside and tend his wounds?" he asked.

"Of course." She stepped aside and followed him into the kitchen. "Is there something I can do to help?"

When he glanced over his shoulder, a tingling sensation brushed her spine and she realized that the man's Svengali effect was not limited to feathered creatures. "His wing is broken," Quinn told her. "I'll need something to bandage it."

"I have some gauze and first-aid tape. Will that do?"

"That would be fine, thank you."

As he turned away, Janine called out, "The hall carpet is wet. Watch out for the barrier."

He acknowledged her warning with a nod, then carried the injured bird upstairs while Janine gathered the supplies.

Minutes later, she entered the open doorway of Quinn's room and saw that he'd placed the raven beside a folded newspaper on top of the dresser. He glanced up and spoke to her reflection in the mirror. "Would you mind closing the door?"

Assuming he was concerned about keeping the bird confined, she complied without comment and laid the first-aid items on the bed. "I brought antiseptic, in case you found any open wounds."

"Thank you." As Quinn tossed the newspaper onto the bed, a small scratch pad-size square fluttered to the floor.

Janine started to mention the dropped item, but became completely intrigued watching Quinn's expert examination of the injured bird. He carefully stretched the twisted wing to its full eighteen-inch span. The animal hissed a warning, parting its impressive beak to reveal a stumpy round tongue, which was as black as its feathers.

With its peculiar yellow eyes darting wildly, the raven tried to back away but Quinn laid a restraining palm on its back. "I know it hurts," he murmured softly. "Just a few more minutes." The raven cocked its head and, seeming somewhat mollified by the reassurance, displayed uncanny trust by docilely allowing Quinn to fold the feathered appendage back into place.

Janine rubbed her eyes. This was without a doubt the strangest thing she'd ever seen in her life.

"I could use those bandages now."

"Hmm?" Janine blinked. "Oh. Sorry."

He accepted the cloth roll she handed him, gently bound the injured wing to the creature's body and secured the bandage with surgical tape. Duly impressed by his expertise, Janine peered over his shoulder. "Where did you learn how to do that?"

Quinn used a fingertip to stroke the shiny black head. "When I was a kid, my dad raised pigeons. He let me help."

"But those were domestic birds."

"They weren't built any differently than Edgar."

She backed away, feeling stupid. "Well, of course not, but I've never seen a wild bird that would tolerate human contact... Edgar?"

The raven responded with a shattering screech and flapped its good wing. It cocked its ebony head, fixed Janine with a jonquil stare and emitted an ominous hiss.

Eyeing the raven's sharp beak, Janine retreated even farther. "Edgar is a fine name, just fine."

Diverted by his new surroundings, Edgar hopped around the dresser, pecked at the mirror, then turned his attention to the gooseconecked lamp a few feet away. With a hop and a flutter, he wrapped his claws around the comfortably curved stem and claimed his new perch with a raucous squawk.

Quinn slid Janine a furtive glance. "He shouldn't be released until the wing has healed."

"No, of course not."

Leaning lazily against the dresser, Quinn regarded her thoughtfully. "Are guests allowed to keep pets?"

"I've never thought about it. Actually, the subject of pets has never come up." She cleared her throat. "Perhaps if we could locate some kind of a cage—"

Edgar screeched a protest.

Frustrated, Janine folded her arms and glared at the bird. "Keep that up and you'll be headquartered in the basement."

With a shriek that seemed unnervingly responsive, Edgar pivoted on the perch and turned his back on her.

When she turned her stunned gaze on Quinn, he merely shrugged. "I think you've hurt his feelings."

"Oh, for goodness' sake." She shook her head and chuckled, willing to go along with the gag. "All right, Edgar. Forget the cage. You can stay in the room but only if you're quiet, understand? One midnight screech, and you're outta here."

On cue, Edgar turned to face her and calmly settled himself on the flexible column.

Sighing, Janine turned to Quinn. "Could you at least spread newspapers under the lamp?"

His eyes crinkled. "Consider it done."

She fidgeted for a moment. "I should get back to work."

Straightening, he gathered the remaining first-aid supplies and handed them to her. "Thanks for the help."

"You're welcome." She balanced the loose objects in the crook of her arm, shifted nervously and wondered why she was so hesitant to leave. "Do you need anything else? I mean, birdseed or something?"

He regarded her quizzically. "Do you have any birdseed?"

She nearly groaned aloud. Of course she didn't have any birdseed. What on earth was the matter with her, anyway? "Well, no, but I was planning to go to the market later..." The lie caught in her throat. She coughed it away and smiled brightly. "So I could pick some up and anything else you might need."

After considering that for a moment, he gave her the tolerant smile usually reserved for fools and small children. "Actually I'm going into town myself this afternoon. If you tell me what you need, I'll save you a trip."

"That's very nice of you." Her cheeks ached. "I'll make a list."

She backed awkwardly out of the room, wondering what it was about this man that made her feel like a clumsy adolescent. He was an enigma, unsettling, almost frightening, yet his unique abilities contradicted her own sense of uneasiness. Animals and children instinctively recognized inner kindness. They trusted Quinn; why couldn't she?

The answer was clear. Quinn Coulliard was a dichotomy—a cultured rebel with the tortured eyes of a person at war with himself. He was also the most fascinating man she'd ever met.

Balancing fresh linens on one arm, Janine used her master key to enter Quinn's room. To avoid inconveniencing the guests, she tried to schedule routine cleaning while they were away. So after Quinn drove into town—ostensibly for birdseed—Janine took advantage of the perfect opportunity to complete her chores.

As she closed the door behind her, the raven sidled along the curved lamp stem, cocked his head and eyed her suspiciously. She tossed the key onto the dresser and put the linens on a nearby chair. "Hello, Edgar. Are you feeling better?"

Edgar said nothing.

She was oddly disappointed. In his master's presence, the bird had seemed, well, almost human. That was silly, of course, but Quinn Coulliard had a knack for creating illusions of reality from the most implausible scenarios. Perhaps the man was a mystic. Or a magician.

Or a con artist.

Not that it really mattered. To Janine, he was simply another tenant. Yet as she absently stripped sheets from the mattress, she couldn't suppress a bit of curious speculation. She wondered if he was married. He wore no wedding ring but that wasn't necessarily proof that he had no wife. And if there was a woman in his life, what was she like?

Obviously the fortunate woman would have to be very special. Since nothing about Quinn Coulliard was ordinary, Janine couldn't imagine he would be attracted to someone plain, a woman with—she glanced at the mirror—mousy hair, dull brown eyes, a flat chest and a flabby bum.

Disgusted, she turned away from the mirror, angrily dragged the soiled sheets from the mattress and tossed them in a heap on the floor. The notion that a man like Quinn Coulliard could ever be attracted to her was ludicrous. After all, Janine was well aware of her physical limitations. Once, she had believed herself to be reasonably attractive—a fantasy that Charles had effectively quashed on their honeymoon. Now she no longer deluded herself and reluctantly accepted the sad fact that she had the sex appeal of road kill.

But since Quinn Coulliard had entered her life, Janine had found herself staring into the mirror with an increasing sense of disappointment. Last night she'd actually pushed her drab hair on top of her skull, wondering if a fluffier coiffeur would make her more attractive. She'd caught herself, of course, and had been both embarrassed and depressed by such futile speculation. She was a plain woman. Everyone said so. At least, everyone who mattered.

But there was something in the way Quinn looked at her that didn't make her feel the least bit plain, and she'd been bothered by strange sensations, an undefinable longing that made her restless and itchy.

Janine was still considering the implications of these odd feelings while she shook out the fresh sheets and absently continued her chore. She tucked in one side of the bedclothes then rounded the bed and accidentally bumped the goosenecked lamp, sending Edgar into an indignant flurry. Janine whirled and grabbed at the tilting perch. The bird squawked and aimed a painful peck at her wrist.

"Ow!" She yanked back her hand.

Although the weighted base kept the lamp from falling, Edgar continued to screech and frantically flap his good wing.

"Oh, good Lord." Fearing that the frenzied animal would reinjure itself, Janine attempted to calm the bird by emulating Quinn's soothing manner.

"There, there," she cooed.

Edgar cocked his head, beak ajar, and regarded Janine with an expression that could only be described as one of absolute disdain. The bird did seem calmer, though, so Janine was encouraged enough to extend a tentative hand. The creature emitted a raucous shriek and instantly attacked. Before she could so much as gasp, a flapping ball of feathered fury leaped at her face, pecking and screeching.

Folding her arms as a shield against the raven's needle-sharp beak, she stumbled backward. The bed blocked her way. "Ouch! You stupid bird. Stop it!" She swatted wildly. "Do you hear me? *Stop!*"

She finally fell onto the bed, then rolled frantically until she fell off and hit the floor with a painful thump. Panting, she rose to her knees and shoved a wad of hair out of her face. The raven gave her a hard look, apparently decided that she posed no further threat to his perch and placidly began to groom himself.

Standing shakily, she blew out a breath. If Quinn wanted the left side of his bed made, he'd damn well have to do it himself. No way was she going to get within pecking distance of that blasted bird again.

She scooped up the soiled linens, piled them in the hallway, then dragged in the vacuum and began cleaning the carpet. The nozzle struck something under the bed. After bending to investigate, she pulled out Quinn's deflated duffel, tossed it onto the mattress and finished vacuuming the room.

As she was cleaning the base of the dresser, she noticed the white square that had fallen while Quinn was tending the raven's wounded wing. After retrieving the scrap, she turned it over and took a sharp breath. It was a tattered, finger-smudged photograph of the most stunning woman Janine had ever seen.

The woman in the photograph had sparkling, ice blue eyes shaded by lashes long enough to braid and a sensual mouth puckered into the kiss-me pout favored by models in fashion magazines. As if those endowments weren't enough, a thick blond mane framed her perfect oval face. The woman was gorgeous, absolutely gorgeous.

Janine was so engrossed in studying the image that she didn't hear the bedroom door open.

"What the hell are you doing here?"

She jumped and whirled around. "I...cleaning."

Quinn stood in the doorway, taut as a gate spring with his right arm twisted strangely behind his back. After a moment, his hand emerged from beneath the loose khaki vest and he slammed the door. His narrowed gaze swept the room, lingering briefly when he noticed the floppy duffel on the bed, then moving to the oversize key ring on the dresser and finally settling on the photograph clutched in Janine's rigid fingers.

She moistened her lips and held out the picture. "It was on the floor," she explained lamely, more annoyed by her own embarrassment than by his accusatory stare. All she'd done was rescue the photo from being sucked into the vacuum yet she felt guilty enough to have been caught snooping through his underwear drawer.

With one more glance at the half-made bed, Quinn crossed the room slowly and, she thought, with forced casualness. When he was close enough that she caught the stimulating scent of pine soap, he reached out, but instead of accepting the proffered picture, he captured her bruised wrist.

Startled, she tried to pull away but he held her firmly, examining the blue welts and bloody scratches scattered across her inner arm.

Perhaps it was his nearness that made Janine's heart race wildly; perhaps it was the warmth of his strong palm encircling her wrist. The reason didn't matter. She was *aware* of him. *Acutely* aware—of his maleness, of his distinctive scent and of the radiant, almost incandescent energy that seemed to be emanating from every pore in his body.

Her lips parted, allowing more oxygen into her suddenly starved lungs. A prickling sensation from her captive wrist crawled up her arm, teased her nape like a lover's kiss, then slid down her spine with a violent shiver. Janine would have stepped away, except that her legs felt like lead pillars and her feet seemed to have been soldered to the floor.

Without releasing his grip, Quinn slid the index finger of his free hand delicately over her wounded flesh. "Did the raven do this?" There was an edge to his voice that gave her chills.

"It wasn't Edgar's fault," Janine assured him. "When I was making the bed, I accidentally hit the lamp. He . . . was upset."

"Was he?"

Quinn brushed his knuckle over an ugly puncture mark at her elbow and the look in his eyes frightened her half to death. For a brief moment, she had the horrible image of a raven roasting on a spit but she shook off the awful thought, reminding herself that Quinn had rescued the bird in the first place.

Still, this hard-eyed person bore little resemblance to the gentle man who had tended a wounded bird less than two hours earlier. The ominous transformation was unsettling.

Janine gestured weakly toward the half-made bed. "Edgar seems to be rather protective of his perch. He wouldn't let me finish."

"I don't expect you to clean up after me." To her shock, Quinn brushed his lips across the sensitive flesh of her inner wrist then released her so abruptly that she wondered if she'd imagined the sensual gesture.

Before she could compose herself, he'd plucked the photograph from her hand and stepped away. Without his comforting touch, Janine swayed slightly, and when he turned his back on her, she felt strangely bereft.

He spoke again in a voice that was cool, almost harsh. "In the future, perhaps you'd be good enough to leave the clean linens in the hallway."

Confused, Janine crossed her arms to quell an annoying tremor. "But I always clean the guest rooms on Saturday."

He replied without turning. "I don't require maid service."

The haughty remark rankled her. "I'm not a maid, Mr. Coulliard. I do, however, provide a courtesy that most of my tenants appreciate. Please understand that I did not intentionally violate the privacy that you quite obviously cherish."

A heavy silence shrouded the room. Quinn's shoulder muscles rippled as he crooked one arm. Although Janine's view was blocked by his body, she thought from the tilt of his head that he was looking down at the photograph.

After what seemed a small eternity, his arm fell to his side. "You're right. I do value my privacy." He turned slowly and laid the photograph on top of the bureau, beside the master key. "I didn't mean to be abrupt."

"And I didn't mean to intrude." Janine's eyes were drawn to the picture of the smiling blond woman.

Quinn followed her gaze but remained silent.

A small voice in the back of her mind warned against comment. She couldn't help herself. "The woman is quite lovely. Who is she?"

Suddenly the tension was thick enough to slice. Quinn's jaw twitched as he stared silently at the picture. Seconds ticked away. He closed his eyes. His chest expanded and held steady, then deflated slowly. Finally he posed an abrupt question. "Why do you want to know?"

A closer examination of his dark expression might have made her reconsider the answer. "I just wondered if she was your wife."

Quinn turned on her with eyes as black as bruises and lips flat with fury. Before Janine could do more than suck in a startled breath, his hand was at her throat. For one terror-stricken moment, she feared he might strangle her.

Instead his fingers caressed the soft flesh below her jaw, a gesture exquisitely erotic yet undeniably dangerous. "I was under the impression that you don't intrude into the personal lives of your guests. Have I been misinformed?"

Although her heart was pounding hard enough to break through her ribs, Janine managed to stammer a reply. "Not at all. I—I was, uh, simply curious."

He slid one fingertip slowly down her throat until it nested at the clavicle juncture. "Curiosity," he murmured. "Fatal to felines and unhealthy for humans, as well. The woman in the photograph never learned that lesson. But you will, won't you?"

She shivered as his palm encircled her throat so delicately that it seemed more a lover's caress than a sinister warning. He wasn't holding her, not by physical means. All Janine had to do was take a step back and she'd be free of his touch.

But she couldn't move and didn't want to. Like a doe in headlights, she was trapped by his penetrating gaze, frozen by his mesmerizing touch. She should be frightened—and she was, in a way—yet the fear was not for her physical safety. The fear was for her soul and for the power this man had over it. Over her.

He bowed his head slightly, bending so close that his hair tickled her cheek and his breath warmed her ear. "Curiosity and carelessness can be a deadly combination. Be more careful about entering a man's bedroom. You never know what might happen."

She closed her eyes, praying her rubbery legs would hold for just a few minutes longer. "I—I trust my guests."

"Trust no one." His mouth brushed her throbbing temple.

Opening her eyes, she whispered, "Including you?"

His smile was not reassuring. "Especially me."

Before she could assess that unsettling comment, he stepped away. "Good day, Miss Taylor." With that, he walked to the window and presented his back.

Janine was so flustered by the brusque dismissal that her shaky limbs threatened to collapse entirely. She grabbed at the dresser to steady herself and her hand grazed the master key. It slid off onto the carpet a few feet from the goose-necked lamp. Feeling dizzy, she cooled her face with her palm, then turned to retrieve the key ring.

The raven lifted himself like an ebony phoenix and screeched a furious warning. Shielding her head, Janine snatched up the key and stumbled quickly out of the room.

When Quinn heard her unsteady footsteps on the stairs, he quietly crossed the room and closed the door. Disgusted with himself, he absently rubbed his aching head. Damn. He'd nearly kissed her. In fact, he'd nearly taken her to bed and she would have allowed it; he knew that even if she didn't. He'd recognized the passion flaring in those lovely amber eyes, the desire she'd been too naive to conceal.

There was an inner frailty about Janine Taylor that touched something deep inside Quinn, exposed secret thoughts that he hadn't faced in a long time. He didn't like that. In fact, he hated it. That doe-eyed woman was going to mess up everything.

Quinn blew out a breath, pulled the revolver out of his waistband and laid the weapon on the dresser. He touched the photograph gently, then slipped it into his vest pocket, turned toward the bed and extracted a large manila envelope from his duffel. A meticulous examination of the taped flap assured him that the seal hadn't been tampered with. This time.

But he'd definitely been careless. It wouldn't happen again.

As he glanced around the room, his gaze fell on the raven. He smiled.

Ten minutes later, Edgar sat on the dresser pecking at a bowl of birdseed while Quinn finished prying a piece of flat steel from the bottom of the lamp base. He set aside the Frisbee-sized circle, and was pleased to note that the rounded top of the base was hollow, rather like an inverted hubcap. Satisfied, he carefully taped the manila envelope inside and replaced the flat bottom. When he tried to stand the lamp upright, however, it tilted slightly and the flat piece slid off.

Frustrated, he squatted to inspect the problem and realized that when he'd pried off the round metal, he'd inadvertently broken one of the tabs holding it in place. He sat back on his heels, contemplating the dilemma. If the bottom couldn't be snapped tight, he'd have to depend solely on the raven's protective fury to keep intruders at a distance. That wasn't a perfect solution but it would have to do.

Holding the flat metal in place with his hand, he carefully raised the lamp, then stood to examine his handiwork. When he was certain that no trace of the concealed envelope was exposed, he sat tiredly on the bed.

Although his foray into town had been an informational bust, the afternoon hadn't been a total waste. At least he now knew what the master key looked like. Unfortunately he didn't know where Janine kept it. Since she'd taken his room key from the foyer closet, that had been the first place he'd looked. He'd also checked the kitchen drawers, the pantry, every nook and cranny in both the library and parlor. That left only her bedroom and the downstairs office, both of which were secured by those damnable jimmy-proof locks.

Despite Janine's protestations to the contrary, her trusting nature obviously had limits but he already knew that from the leery way she watched him. He'd encouraged that, of course. He wanted her to be afraid of him, to keep her distance. Every time she'd gotten too close, he'd momentarily lost sight of his priorities. There was something about her...

As Janine's image floated through his mind, he was instantly aroused. Her delicate fragrance lingered in the humid air, an enticing combination of floral sweetness and musky excitement that made his head spin wildly. His fingertips tingled with the memory of her softness, the way her creamy flesh had pulsed beneath his touch. And those incredible eyes, filled with a guileless passion that probed the core of his manhood until he'd been nearly mad with wanting her.

She was so fragile, so innocent—

Quinn swore and pinched the bridge of his nose. Had he learned nothing from the past? He reached into his vest pocket and pulled out the worn photograph. He studied it again. Cynthia had had innocent eyes, too. Her betrayal had taught him the ultimate lesson—and she had paid the ultimate price.

The mattress vibrated as the raven hopped onto the bed and waddled up beside his master. Quinn absently stroked the glossy black feathers, silently pondering the quest that had brought him to Darby Ridge. The end was in sight. Soon, it would all be over. Then the killing could stop.

CHAPTER FOUR

"Here, dear. Let me help." Edna took a soiled dinner plate from Janine's hands, sympathetically eyed her bruised forearms and tutted. "Are you in a great deal of pain?"

"It's nothing, Edna. Really." Embarrassed by the attention, Janine made a production of filling the sink with soapy dishwater. "Besides, the ointment you gave me helped a great deal."

"You must use it twice daily," Edna said sternly, shaking a fistful of gloppy forks. "Infection is always a concern when wild creatures are involved."

Jules propped his elbows on the kitchen table. His dark eyes sparkled with excitement. "What if it's rabid?"

Althea smoothed the dipping bodice of her fire-engine red cocktail dress, tossed her napkin on the table and emitted a contemptuous snort. "Birds don't carry rabies, you idiot."

"But what if they did? Why, we might come to breakfast some morning and find poor Janine writhing on the floor with foam oozing out of her mouth."

Rolling her eyes, Janine roughly turned off the faucet. "I promise not to foam, Jules."

"Oh." The disappointed young man scooted his chair backward so his grandmother could finish clearing the table. "Still, the creature is dangerous. It should be taken into the woods and shot."

Janine quickly glanced over her shoulder and was relieved that Quinn's dispassionate expression hadn't changed. He was seated casually with one arm looped over the back of the chair, his lean legs extended and crossed at the ankles. Actually, he didn't appear to be the least bit concerned by Jules's threat.

In truth, neither was Janine. She knew perfectly well that all this rabies business was just part of the young man's melodramatic nature. Nevertheless, Janine felt obliged to defend her decision in allowing the raven to stay. "Edgar is not dangerous, Jules. As I've already explained, I frightened the bird and he reacted. Besides, he's safely secured in Quinn's room. There's no way for him to escape."

Althea grinned smugly. "Unless, of course, he was deliberately let out and, say, locked in Jules's room. My goodness, that big blackbird could probably peck a person's eyes out while he slept."

Jules went white. "That's not funny."

Since Janine was up to her elbows in bubbles, she suppressed an inhospitable urge to fling soapsuds in the smirking woman's face. "You're not helping the situation, Althea."

Althea instantly arranged her crimson lips in a sultry pout and patted Jules's knee. "Now you know I was just teasing, don't you?"

Jules folded his arms and stared sullenly at the gingham tablecloth. "I detest birds. They're . . . dirty."

"Every creature of God is good," Edna murmured, piling the remaining dishes on the counter.

Althea turned her attention to Quinn, leaning flirtatiously across the table. "Personally, I think it's very sweet that you rescued the poor thing." She fluttered her clumpy eyelashes. "Is it true that men who like animals make the best lovers?"

Quinn managed an indulgent smile. "I couldn't say."

Pressing her upper arms against her breasts, Althea bent provocatively forward, expertly defining the exposed cleavage. "Come up to my room later, and we'll find out."

"Really, Althea." Edna indignantly dropped a damp tea towel beside the dish drainer. "That kind of talk is most inappropriate."

Crossing her bare thighs, Althea leaned back and chuckled. "What's the matter, Edna? Did you want first crack at him?"

The older woman turned pink as a peony. "You are a sinful woman. I'll pray for your soul."

"It isn't my soul that's horny." Althea stretched, stood and crossed the room to give the dumpy little grandmother an unexpected hug. "But pray for me, anyway. I'll take any help I can get."

Edna patted Althea's thickened waist. "I will, dear. I will."

There was a scraping sound when Jules suddenly pushed back his chair. "Shall we play chess tonight, Althea?"

The rhinestone cascade dripping from the woman's earlobes glittered as her head shook. "Not tonight, hon."

Crestfallen, Jules extended a pleading hand. "Just one game? Please?"

Althea ruffled the young man's hair, an affectionate, motherly gesture that should have seemed out of character yet oddly enough didn't. "No offense, sweetie, but I look too damned good to waste time pushing carved figures around a dinky board." To prove the point, she adopted a runway stance and gestured the length of her slinky red gown. "Is this enough to knock your socks off or what?"

Jules shoved his hands into the pockets of his perfectly tailored slacks and regarded her sullenly. "You look like a tart."

Althea grinned. "Good enough to eat, huh?"

Edna's brow puckered with concern. "Jules is quite right, dear. Modest attire would be much more attractive."

Suppressing a smile, Janine dunked a soapy plate in rinse water and pretended she wasn't listening.

"Oh, sure. I suppose you want me to dress like Miss Plain-as-mud, here." Althea disdainfully eyed Janine's floppy, thigh-length top. "Now there's a fashion statement."

The dripping plate froze in midair. Janine looked over her shoulder, astounded and appalled to have become the subject of conversation. Even worse, the two women continued their ardent discussion and gave no more thought to Janine's presence than they would of any inanimate object.

With chunky fists pressed in the vicinity of her shapeless hips, Edna rose up to her full five-foot height. "Janine does not expose herself, if that's what you mean."

"At least I don't have to hide in a tent." Althea mimicked the older woman's stance. "I'm proud of my body."

Edna lifted her flabby chin. "Janine is a God-fearing woman."

"Yeah? Well, if you ask me, she dresses like a man-fearing woman."

Janine sucked in a quick breath and steadied herself on the counter.

"Look at her," Althea insisted. "No makeup. Hair that hasn't seen a comb in God-knows-when. Is this a woman out to attract men?"

Cringing, Janine absently touched her stringy bangs and wished the kitchen floor would swallow her whole. She didn't dispute Althea's brutal assessment but was nonetheless mortified by the public critique. She was considering whether she should beat a judicious retreat or ignore the humiliating ordeal when Quinn, who had been watching quietly from his seat at the kitchen table, suddenly spoke.

"Janine is a beautiful woman," he said softly. "She doesn't use cosmetics because she quite obviously doesn't need them."

Jules tilted his pinched face, scrutinizing Janine in much the same way the raven had done. "I quite agree. Natural beauty is much more appealing than an artificial, painted look.''

A red flush crawled up Althea's exposed bosom. "Excuse me while I gag.''

Now it was Jules's turn to grin smugly. "What's wrong, Althea? Are you jealous?''

"Oh, pul-eeze.'' She flipped her head so sharply that the rhinestone dangles whipped her face. "Go ahead and waste a perfectly good Saturday night singing Saint Janine's praises. I'm going to party.''

With that, Althea spun on a spiked heel and strode angrily out of the room.

When the front door slammed, Quinn gave Janine a slow smile that did peculiar things to her insides. "Was it something I said?''

Suddenly shy, Janine lowered her gaze as she returned his smile.

Edna bustled over to the table, wringing her fat hands. "You must forgive Althea,'' she told Quinn. "She wants to be a good woman. Once, I'd thought her worthy of redemption but the devil has taken her.''

There was a peculiar agitation to Edna's voice that caught Janine's attention. To her surprise, she saw that Edna was fussing with Quinn's hair, smoothing back a lengthy strand that had escaped the pinion at his nape. Her eyes, however, held an odd, faraway expression and she continued to speak in such a low, pious tone that Janine became extremely uneasy.

"Still, we must never give up," the woman murmured. "We must all pray for Althea. Only when her soul is purified will she see the kingdom of God.''

"Purified," Jules repeated dutifully. "Amen.''

Janine could have sworn Quinn gave Jules a look cold enough to freeze lava. After she blinked, there was only the impassive expression she'd come to expect from her newest tenant. Except, however, for a frustrated frown as he attempted to escape Edna's frantic grooming. Finally Quinn twisted away and captured her busy hands.

The flustered woman emitted a nervous titter. "May I pour you another cup of coffee, dear? Perhaps you'd like some dessert. I'm sure Janine has something in the pantry—"

"No, thank you. I'm fine." Quinn stood, releasing Edna's hands only when his hair was safely out of reach.

Jules took a tentative step forward. "May I have some dessert, *Grand'mère?*"

Edna's tiny blue eyes registered instant disapproval. "The Lord's abundance must not be abused with gluttony."

The young man folded his arms and stared at the floor.

At that moment, Janine felt terribly sorry for Jules. She understood that beneath the educated veneer he was emotionally childlike and easily wounded. Any rejection, real or perceived, sent the fragile young man into a sullen depression.

Edna, however, seemed oblivious to her grandson's distress. "I'll say good-night now. I must prepare my Sunday school lessons." She lifted a cheek to receive Jules's perfunctory kiss and smiled brightly at Quinn before toddling away.

Janine set the final pot in the drainer and wiped her hands on a tea towel. "Actually, Jules, you've just reminded me that I had planned to set out a plate of cookies. Not as dessert, of course, but as part of the meal."

A flash of interest lit his dark eyes. He glanced over his shoulder, peering through the open doorway until his grandmother's footsteps had faded away, then faced Janine and rubbed his slender hands together. "It would be rude to refuse, wouldn't it?"

"Of course." She smiled and went to the pantry.

"Janine?"

She rooted through the crowded shelves. "Yes, Jules?"

"Will you play chess with me?"

"I'm not good enough, remember?" Retrieving the cellophane bag of soft-baked chocolate chip cookies, Janine closed the pantry door. "The last time we played, you said—and I believe these were your exact words—'a demented chimpanzee would be a more challenging opponent.'"

"I didn't mean it." Extending his hands, Jules followed her around the kitchen pleading his cause. "I wasn't feeling well that evening. Please . . . I promise not to comment on your mental acumen."

Janine pulled a serving platter from an overhead cupboard. "I'm sorry, Jules. I have to pay bills this evening."

"Can't it wait?"

"Sure, if you're willing to give up hot water, television and cooked food."

Jules's thin shoulders drooped in defeat.

Quinn folded his arms and leaned lazily against the doorjamb. "I'll play chess with you."

Straightening, Jules regarded Quinn scornfully. "Are you any good?"

"Are you?"

Mightily offended, Jules hoisted his sharp little chin and puffed out his skinny chest. "I am a certified chess master."

When Quinn angled a questioning glance at Janine, she answered with a nod. He smiled and returned his attention to Jules. "I think I can hold my own."

Jules sniffed. "I doubt that."

Stretching, Quinn rolled his head. "There's only one way to find out, isn't there? Besides, you don't appear to have any other offers."

After considering that for a moment, the young man issued a curt nod. "I'll set up," he said brusquely, then spun and hurried out of the room.

Janine set the unopened cookie bag on the platter. "Jules really does play brilliantly. Althea is the only person I know who can stretch a game past five minutes."

"Are you concerned for my ego?"

"Of course not." She moistened her lips as he moved closer to her. "Just a friendly warning, that's all."

"A warning." He stood close behind her, so close she felt his breath on her hair. "That sounds rather sinister. What happens if I lose? Will I be murdered in my bed?"

"Don't be ridiculous." An enticing whiff of spicy after-shave enveloped her. She inhaled deeply before completing her reply. "You'll probably endure some unpleasant taunting, that's all. Jules enjoys crowing about his game prowess."

When Quinn slid his index finger up her arm, her knees nearly collapsed. "And what happens if I win?"

"I—I don't know." She gripped the table as his knuckle brushed her earlobe. "No one has ever beaten Jules before."

In a proprietary gesture so sensual it took her breath away, Quinn casually wound a strand of her hair around one finger. He bent so close that his breath warmed the sensitive flesh behind her ear. "Then this should be an interesting evening."

A cool draft brushed her back, and when she turned, Quinn had gone. Janine sagged against the table like a deflated balloon. Her heart pounded and her legs wobbled like rubber bands; the room seemed as hot as a sauna and her skin grew slick with nervous perspiration. She was scared to death.

A man-fearing woman.

God, how right Althea had been.

Janine wiped her moist brow and stiffened her spine. She had no time to mull past regrets. She had a business to run. Taking a deep breath, she headed toward her office.

As she passed the parlor, both players were hunched over a carved pedestal chessboard. When Quinn suddenly looked up, his gaze affected her like a body blow. She absently touched her abdomen and hurried down the hall, fumbled in her pocket for the key and entered the stuffy office. Propping the door open to allow air circulation, she sat at the desk and pulled out a depressing stack of unpaid bills.

After a few minutes, she was interrupted when Jules appeared in the doorway and discreetly cleared his throat. She glanced up. "Can I help you?"

"I, uh . . ." He offered a strained smile. "The cookies?"

"Oh!" She pushed away from the desk and stood. "I forgot. I'll bring them into the parlor."

Jules smiled gratefully. "You're very kind."

Janine rounded the desk and walked briskly, pausing only for a furtive glance as she passed the parlor door. When she met Quinn's quiet gaze, she quickly looked away and continued into the kitchen.

It took only a few minutes to arrange the cookies on the scrolled silver-plated platter. When she returned to the parlor, Jules was alone. She set the platter on a nearby table. "Where's Quinn?"

"A call of nature." Jules took a cookie, nibbling it delicately. He frowned.

"Is something wrong?"

"It's a bit dry." He glanced longingly toward the kitchen. "A glass of milk might be nice."

With a pained sigh, Janine trudged back through the dining room without considering the possibility that she could have told Jules to get the milk himself. She was, after all, the hostess and tried to make all of her guests feel pampered.

After she'd poured two tall glasses, she returned the carton to the fridge and went back to the parlor. Jules was chewing a cookie, staring at the chessboard as though reading the secret of the universe. Quinn was back in his seat but seemed more interested in Janine than the game.

The rubbery sensation returned to her legs.

She set down the glasses, acknowledging Quinn's thanks with a brief smile.

Jules suddenly emitted a crow of pleasure and took one of Quinn's white pawns with his own black knight. "Your queen is in jeopardy, Coulliard. I'm afraid this will be an extremely brief game."

Still staring at Janine, Quinn smiled slowly before returning his attention to the board, and without so much as a pause for thought, he slid a white bishop into position. "Check."

Jules uttered a disparaging snort. "That's a ridiculous move. My pawn will take your bishop and your queen will be destroyed on the next... What's this?" Leaning over the board, Jules carefully examined the arrangement of Quinn's white pieces, his eyes glowing. "Very clever, Coulliard. Perhaps I've misjudged you."

"Perhaps you have," Quinn murmured, staring at Janine. "It's your move."

"Yes, yes!" Jules laid the half-eaten cookie aside, rubbed his hands together and hunkered over the board. "This is delightful, simply delightful."

Janine quietly backed out of the parlor and returned to her office, struck by a disquieting notion that Jules might not be the only person who had misjudged Quinn Coulliard.

It was nearly ten that night when Jules returned to his immaculate room, feeling more alive than he had since the night of the fire. He had won the chess game, of course. The outcome had never been in doubt but the thrill of the chase had been exquisite.

Naturally, Jules had outwitted Coulliard at every turn yet had to admit that the man had proven to be a worthy opponent. He had fought a brave battle, then given up his life—his king's life—without simpering or pleading for mercy. Jules admired that. It wasn't any fun when they begged. That made him feel impotent; nothing was ever gained by winning over weakness. The defeat of the strong—that was what empowered him.

Throwing back his head, Jules laughed out loud, a primal roar of pleasure that emanated straight from the gut. The strength of the vanquished flowed in his veins. Life was good.

His chest heaved with masculine pride as he opened the closet and extracted a pair of freshly pressed pajamas, carefully hooking the padded hanger over the doorknob so the garment wouldn't wrinkle while he undressed. Even in slumber, it was important to be tidy.

As Jules removed his clothing, he arranged each piece on a hanger specifically designated for that item, then polished his shoes before placing them on the closet floor, toes out, heels together like disembodied soldiers. Socks went into the laundry bag at the rear of his closet, as did his expensive cotton briefs. Such intimate items could never be worn for more than a few hours. Jules fastidiously changed them several times a day.

Straightening, he averted his eyes from the dresser mirror—observing his own nude body would be unseemly—then reached for his sleepwear and was startled when the bedroom door suddenly opened.

Using a key she'd secretly duplicated for the purpose of checking up on her grandson, Edna entered without comment and quietly closed the door.

Jules held the pajamas in front of his body and stared at the carpet while a shameful heat crawled up his naked belly. "Good evening, *Grand'mère.*"

"Good evening, dear." She held her cheek up for the perfunctory kiss, then perched on the edge of his mattress. "Have you said your prayers?"

"Not yet." He licked his lips and stated the obvious. "I haven't finished preparing for bed."

"There is time for that. First, we must pray."

Since argument was futile, Jules held the concealing garment and started to kneel.

Leaning over, Edna roughly pinched his bare shoulder. "Are your thoughts pure?"

He winced. "Yes, *Grand'mère.*"

"Then why do you hide yourself?" She looked pointedly at the cloth shield he clutched.

Jules stiffened, holding his breath as his grandmother's disapproving gaze focused on the rumpled garment. The pride that had only moments ago swelled joyfully in his chest was replaced by burning shame and humiliation. Finally she emitted a haughty snort and pointed to the floor beside the bed.

Still covering himself, Jules knelt awkwardly and bowed his head, not in prayerful reverence, but to conceal the rage that burned behind his eyes. He uttered the familiar words, a lifeless monologue that no longer held meaning but which he'd been forced to repeat every night since his mother had deserted him.

When he'd finished speaking, Edna patted his head as though he was an obedient puppy. "Now finish dressing so *Grand'mère* can tuck you in."

Jules stood stiffly and complied, trying not to hurry or his grandmother might suspect vile thoughts and insist on an even more humiliating inspection process. When he'd secured the final button, he slid between the sheets and waited tensely.

Edna smiled lovingly as she smoothed the bedclothes around his body. She caressed his forehead, then brushed her wrinkled lips over his cheek. "Good night, my sweet boy."

"Good night, *Grand'mère*."

Edna turned off the nightstand lamp and left quietly.

Jules stared at the dark ceiling until he heard his grandmother's bedroom door close. Then he threw off the bedclothes with a murderous fury.

The wrinkled old bitch enjoyed emasculating him, making him feel less than human. He despised her and he despised his slut of a mother for having abandoned him to such a dismal fate. Women were all the same. Heartless tramps with ice water in their veins and honey between their legs. He hated them all.

But he knew how to get even.

After propping a chair beneath the doorknob, Jules tiptoed to the closet and retrieved a flat box hidden beneath a neatly folded pile of blankets. He sat cross-legged in the center of the room, fingering the edges of the closed box. His heart pounded in anticipation. He licked his lips, then carefully lifted the cardboard lid and removed a flashlight.

He took a shuddering breath and shone the light beam inside the open box, illuminating a color photograph of an anonymous nude woman. Sweat beaded his brow. He caressed the picture, running his fingertip over the glossy image of perfect, rose-colored nipples. Slut. Tramp. Whore.

And silently chanting that sacred mantra, Jules envisioned all the things he would do with the woman in the picture and smiled as his body responded to the impure thoughts.

CHAPTER FIVE

With a choked cry, Janine bolted upright. As she stared into the midnight darkness, her throat was paralyzed, each wheezing breath a painful struggle. Slowly the cobwebs of slumber dissipated and she realized that she wasn't in San Diego. Charles was gone. He couldn't hurt her anymore.

She threw off the covers and palmed cold sweat from her face. It had been a dream. A nightmare, really. Familiar yet with a twist. A frightening twist.

Janine swung her feet to the floor and took two steps before tripping on the rag rug beside her bed. She stumbled, caught herself, then knelt to straighten the colorful oval mat. One of these days, she'd break her neck on the stupid thing; still, she was hesitant to discard it because the braided fabric provided some protection from the drafty hardwood floor.

After smoothing the rug, Janine opened the window and allowed the moist breeze to caress her sweaty skin. She closed her eyes, remembering the disquieting dream in which she'd been awakened by a man bending over her bed. Even asleep, such a threatening event should have frightened her. But it hadn't.

Instead of fearing the intruder, she'd opened her arms to him. He'd slid between the sheets, embracing her, kissing her, igniting her senses with white-hot passion. And she had responded wildly, with a rapture she could never have imagined.

Suddenly, they'd both been naked. When the stranger had moved over her, a thick mane of silken hair had swept her bare breasts. With a moan of pure ecstasy, she'd gazed up into Quinn Coulliard's crystalline eyes.

A fluid heat formed in her belly, spreading outward like ripples in a still pond until her entire body had arched and shuddered. Then her body had turned to ice and it had been Charles looming over her, his face contorted in rage. She'd screamed, over and over and over, until the nightmare had finally ended.

Now she was as limp as a wrung dishrag. The sensation had been so vivid, so real—so terrifying. During the first part of the dream her body had reacted in such a peculiar manner. She'd actually been thrilled, wanton, desperately anticipating a more intimate touch. The feelings had been wonderful, of course, but they made no sense. To Janine sex had always been a degrading, painful ordeal. Naturally that had been part of her problem, or so Charles had repeatedly told her.

Throughout the course of their marriage, Janine had been harshly judged and found deficient. Her husband had accused her of being frigid, only half a woman, unworthy and unwanted by real men. She'd had no reason to doubt that brutal assessment. Until now.

Now things had changed—Janine had changed—and although she wasn't certain exactly how that monumental feat had been accomplished, she knew without doubt that Quinn Coulliard had been the cause. There was something electric about the solitary stranger who made her heart race wildly with no more than a sensual glance. No man had ever affected her this way, not even her husband.

And yet Janine couldn't shake a feeling of foreboding, nor could she forget Quinn's clouded warning—*Trust no one ... especially me.*

She shivered. Turning away from the window, she absently rubbed her upper arms and stared at the rumpled bed. She knew that she should at least try to get some sleep but was not yet ready to re-call demons of the night.

A peculiar sound caught her attention. Listening, she cocked her head and heard a muffled noise. When she cracked open the bedroom door, illumination filtered into the hallway as if a downstairs lamp had been left on. A glance at her watch confirmed that the town pubs were closed so she assumed that Althea must be stumbling around in another drunken stupor.

Stepping into a pair of worn terry scuff slippers, she pulled on a floppy bathrobe and padded downstairs. When she reached the foyer, she followed the light and a series of soft tapping sounds, both of which were emanating from the parlor.

She moved quietly to the doorway and jerked to a stop. After rubbing her eyes, she squinted into the dimly lit room and briefly wondered if the stunning sight was the wild hallucination of a sleep-deprived brain.

It wasn't. Quinn Coulliard was no mirage, although Janine couldn't for the life of her figure out why he had one ear pressed against the maple paneling and was tapping the wall with his knuckle.

She cleared her throat.

Quinn jumped as though shot, spun around and sagged back against the wall, obviously not pleased by the interruption. He cleared his throat and spoke brusquely. "I'm sorry to have disturbed you."

Janine didn't bother to mention that the mere thought of him had awakened her long before she'd noticed any downstairs noises. Instead she closed the parlor door so that the other guests wouldn't be disturbed. "I thought Althea was down here."

Rubbing the back of his neck, Quinn settled on the rosewood arm of her flowered Queen Anne sofa. "She hasn't come in yet."

Janine frowned, wondering why he was so certain, before noticing that he wore the same clothing he'd had on at dinner time. "It's past two in the morning. Have you been down here all night?"

"I don't require much sleep."

"How convenient. That allows so much more time to, uh, practice tapping Morse code on the parlor walls." She smiled at his pained expression. "Are you CIA or something?"

With a resigned sigh, he massaged his forehead. "If I say that I am, will you stop looking at me as though I'm certifiable?"

"Are you?"

"CIA?"

"Certifiable."

His lips curved, just a little. "That's a matter of opinion, I suppose."

"Since you're a psychologist, I'm sure you have a professional opinion about a man who slinks through the dead of night probing walls." Clutching the drooping lapels of her chenille robe, she seated herself a safe distance away. "Are you some kind of ghostbuster?"

"Excuse me?"

She laughed softly. "Were you trying to communicate with spirits?"

"Why, is the place haunted?"

"Not to my knowledge." She slid him a teasing glance. "If I didn't know better, I'd think you had taken rumors about this Victorian's colorful history to heart and were searching for secret passageways."

He smiled weakly but his eyes held no amusement.

Janine propped an elbow on her knee and leaned forward. "That's it, isn't it? You were actually looking for the brothel tunnels?"

"Sorry to disappoint you." Stretching, he rolled his neck and extended his arm across the sofa back. "Actually, the house is infested with rodents, not ghosts."

She sat upright and stared in disbelief. "I beg your pardon."

"Mice. In the walls." He looped a lazy thumb toward the paneling against which his ear had been so recently pressed. "I heard them rustling around in there."

"That's impossible!" She was horrified even by the mere suggestion that such dirty little beggars could be scurrying inside the walls of her immaculate establishment. "The exterminator comes every month for routine maintenance, and besides, I've never seen the slightest evidence of rodent infestation."

"Then I must have been mistaken." His gaze dropped to her crossed knees, where the chenille had parted to reveal a sliver of creamy satin. "Unless, of course, the house really *is* haunted."

Suddenly uneasy, Janine rearranged the robe over her legs. A slow heat spread from her belly and crawled up her throat. "I don't believe in ghosts, Mr. Coulliard."

He stared at her without speaking.

Cheeks burning under his intense scrutiny, she moistened her lips and plucked loose lint from the fuzzy tail of her tied belt.

The silence was deafening. Quinn stared. Janine fidgeted. Finally she swallowed and raised her chin. "Do I have dirt on my nose?"

After a long moment, he spoke without breaking the visual stalemate. "Your nose is fine. Perfect, actually." Smiling slowly, his gaze traveled the length of her in a manner she normally would have considered insolent. Now, however, her skin tingled beneath the sensuous scrutiny that constricted her lungs as effectively as an embrace. She felt strange and wondered why Quinn didn't seem to notice that the room was undulating.

Pinned by his magnetic eyes, Janine was vaguely aware that a peculiar transformation was taking place. Suddenly his dark hair broke free and flowed wildly around his handsome face as though blown by a savage wind. He became the man of her dream, the man who had taken her with such erotic sensuality.

Emotions lumped in her throat—joy, anticipation... fear.

When she blinked, the image evaporated. Quinn stood beside the sofa, his hair tightly leashed and passions confined behind a cool, transparent gaze. She vaguely realized that he was speaking, but before she could respond he bade her good-night and left.

Cursing his rotten luck, Quinn ascended the stairs and strode briskly down the hall. As he entered his room, the raven rose with a warning hiss. "Quiet," he whispered. The bird calmed and settled down on the lamp.

Quinn sat tiredly on the bed, not believing for one minute that Janine had fallen for the ridiculous mouse story. The woman was naive, not stupid. He rubbed his face in frustration. A few uninterrupted minutes and he might have found what he'd been searching for. He knew that he was on the right track. From now on, it would be just a matter of time, a precious commodity that grew scarcer by the day.

Still, the evening had been quite productive. Reaching into his jeans, he pulled out the guest-room master key. Talk about perfect timing. Jules's sweet tooth and their lovely landlady's forgetfulness had provided the perfect opportunity for Quinn to slip into her office, find what he sought, then return to the chessboard without missing a beat.

Repocketing the key, Quinn realized that he couldn't continue to count on such fortuitous moments. Tonight's interruption had been a prime example. He certainly hadn't expected Janine to be prowling around in the wee hours, particularly since she was always up before dawn. But then, Janine Taylor frequently surprised him.

He shrugged off the concealing vest, flipped the garment over a nearby chair, took the revolver from his waistband and absently set it aside. As his thoughts returned to Janine, he wondered if she understood the power of her own beauty. He decided that she probably didn't. That lack of self-awareness was part of her charm.

The woman intrigued him. Her covert glances and sensual shyness conveyed a chasteness that seemed peculiar for a woman in her twenties. Quinn briefly considered that Janine might actually be a virgin, discarded the notion, then instantly reconsidered it. Those curious eyes, the naive passion she so guilelessly displayed—all were obvious signs of a woman who had never experienced pleasures of the flesh. Yet she was too beautiful, too inordinately lovely to have remained unscathed.

Quinn did know that Janine was single—Edna had made a comment to that effect—yet he'd initially assumed that she must have had previous involvements. A woman so desirable would have been rigorously and repeatedly pursued, although he conceded the remote possibility that Janine, like himself, had managed to evade the sweet trap of marital bliss. It was unlikely, of course, since most females were humming the wedding march in their cradles. Still, it was possible.

That interesting consideration caused him to reevaluate his original assumption, and the erotic speculation that she might never have known love did peculiar things to his insides. Someday she would choose a man to teach her those sensual secrets. Quinn wished to hell that it could be him.

* * *

It was midmorning on Sunday when Janine drove her sullen passengers home from church. Jules and Edna had been strangely tense during the service and the strained atmosphere had continued during the trip back to the boardinghouse.

After Janine parked in the gravel drive, Jules quickly exited from the passenger side and opened the rear door for his grandmother. Janine stepped out and walked around the vehicle just as Edna emerged.

The older woman offered a thin smile. "Thank you for driving, dear. Next week, Jules will drive, won't you, dear?"

"Yes, *Grand'mère.*" After closing the car door, Jules released his grandmother's hand and discreetly wiped his palm on his slacks.

Edna's sharp gaze caught the subtle movement and her tiny eyes clouded. "The sermon was excellent, don't you think?" she asked of no one in particular. Clutching her handbag, she nervously kneaded the worn tapestry with her knobby fingers. "The Reverend Mr. Weems was most inspirational this morning. I was moved, truly moved."

Averting his eyes, Jules clasped his hands behind his back and stared sullenly into space.

To break the tense stalemate, Janine mumbled that the service was indeed inspirational, then started up the walkway, anxious to remove herself from the unusual tension between Edna and her grandson. In spite of the older woman's desperate attempts at cheerful small talk, Jules had quite pointedly remained silent. He'd sulked all morning, responding tersely only when asked a direct question. The entire situation had been unbearable.

Janine was completely baffled by the strange behavior. She'd never seen poor Edna quite so agitated, nor had Jules ever treated his grandmother so coldly. It seemed that everyone in the boardinghouse had been acting weird lately.

Janine herself was as edgy as a treed cat, and it occurred to her that no one had been quite the same since the night of the fire—the night Quinn Coulliard had appeared.

As the three of them entered the foyer, Jules walked briskly toward the stairs, pausing only when Edna called his name. Without turning, he laid a hand on the balustrade and waited.

Edna twisted her purse strap. "Jules, dear, it's such a lovely morning I thought we might walk down to the river."

His slender fingers tightened around the smooth wooden grip. "I'm rather tired."

Poor Edna looked positively distraught. "Then perhaps we could share a nice cup of hot tea."

"I don't want any tea."

"It will make you feel ever so much better."

Intensely uncomfortable, Janine moved discreetly toward the downstairs hallway. "If you'll excuse me, I have some work to finish."

Neither expecting nor receiving an acknowledgment, Janine quickly went to the rear of the building. As she unlocked her office door, the muffled sound of Edna's pleas and Jules's resistance reverberated through the hallway.

Once inside her private domain, Janine switched on the desk lamp and settled into her comfortably worn leather chair. She rolled her head, massaged her aching neck and, after idly wondering who would win the battle of wills, finally decided that she quite frankly didn't care. Whatever unpleasantness was going on between Edna and her grandson was none of Janine's business.

But even though she wanted to ignore the stressful situation, she couldn't shake an unsettling premonition that if the tension between them ever exploded, the resultant blast would annihilate everyone in its path. Something strange was happening around the boardinghouse. Janine didn't like it one bit.

At the moment, however, there was nothing she could do except complete her monthly bill-paying so that she and the rest of her guests didn't end up on the streets. Janine extracted the album-size checkbook from the neatly arranged center drawer and plucked a blue ballpoint from the section where writing instruments had been arranged by color and tip size. She frowned at an empty space in the segmented plastic organizer. The master key was missing.

Swallowing a surge of panic, she quickly scanned the desktop, then opened and searched the remaining drawers. She sat back, pressing her palms over her temples as though the gesture could jump-start her brain. Could she have left the key in one of the guest rooms? No, that was impossible. Janine was a fastidious person who always paid meticulous attention to details. Although she had to concede a certain mental distraction since Quinn Coulliard had entered her life, she was nonetheless certain that the key had been in its proper place last night.

Janine pushed away from the desk and quickly scanned the room. Perhaps she'd absently taken the key from the drawer and laid it on the bookcase or the file cabinet or had dropped it into her pocket without thinking. What had she been wearing last night?

Before she could answer the silent question, the front door slammed with enough force to vibrate the walls. Janine peeked into the hallway, heard an angry barrage of loud voices and went to investigate.

"You dare defile the Lord's day?" Edna demanded shrilly.

Still wearing her slinky red cocktail dress, Althea sagged against the wall and pressed both hands against her temples. "Cripes, give it a rest, will you?"

Janine stepped from behind the stairwell. "Are you all right, Althea?"

A pair of bloodshot eyes squinted in Janine's direction. "Yeah, sure. It's just this damned freight train roaring through my head."

A shadow fell from the top of the stairs. Janine knew without looking that Quinn was there, watching. She suppressed a sensual shiver and forced her attention back to the activity in the foyer.

Although Jules folded his arms and regarded Althea with a silent smirk, Edna was beside herself with righteous indignation. "You reek of alcohol and sin," she proclaimed. "You mock the Sabbath, and He is mightily offended."

"Bull." With a derisive snort, Althea waved the woman away, then nearly fell over trying to pull off one spike-heel shoe. "Besides, I haven't had a drink since midnight, so the way I figure it I haven't mocked a damned thing."

Janine reached out to steady her. "Where have you been, Althea? What happened to you?" Since the frazzled woman looked like she'd been ransacked, the questions were issued out of concern rather than curiosity.

With a nonchalant shrug, Althea tried unsuccessfully to comb her tangled hair with her fingers. "I had a wee bit too much cheer and spent the night in my car." She smiled sweetly at Edna. "I never drive while intoxicated."

"God sees through your lies, Althea," Edna intoned. "I heard you moving in your room last night."

Startled, Janine glanced up at Quinn and saw his knowing smile. Believing that he was thinking the same thing, she felt her face warm and quickly looked away. Mice. Disgusting rodents. The place must be crawling with them. Janine shivered then returned her attention to Althea, who staunchly continued to defend her position.

"I don't care what you heard," the disheveled woman replied tiredly. "Where I was and what I did is none of your freaking business."

"It's God's business."

"Then I'll take it up with Him so you can stay the hell out of my face."

Jules's smirk widened. "What's the matter, Althea? Was Gregore so good last night that you had to have him again this morning?"

"On the Lord's morning," Edna whispered. Tears sprang to her eyes.

Althea's cheeks reddened. Ignoring the older woman, she responded snappishly to Jules. "Now why would I want a washed-up old man like Gregore Pawlovski? What I want is some hot young stud with enough stamina to keep my furnace stoked." When Althea slid Jules an appraising glance, his smug grin faded.

Instantly Edna stepped in front of her grandson, shielding him with her squat little body while her tiny eyes flashed with zealous fury. "You are an evil woman, beyond redemption. I have prayed that *ekpyresis* would be your eventual salvation but you are unworthy. You are doomed, Althea Miller, doomed to eternal damnation."

Janine blinked. *Ekpy* what? The foreign word was vaguely familiar, but at the moment Janine's main concern was keeping a heated situation from getting totally out of hand. "Please, Edna, that kind of talk will only make matters worse."

Althea, however, simply stared in stunned silence before clutching her abdomen and emitting a raucous laugh. She wiped her eyes and addressed the curly-headed gnome who was quivering with righteous indignation. "Don't get your girdle in a twist, Edna. When I said young, I didn't mean I was going to rob a damned cradle." Grinning, she cocked her head and eyed the stiff young man. "No offense, hon. You're cute as hell but you could be my own kid, you know?" Her smile warmed as she added, "You're a good boy, Jules. If I had a son, I'd want him to be just like you."

At the last comment, Janine steadied herself on a credenza. If Althea wanted a son like Jules, the poor woman must be further gone than anyone realized.

Still chuckling to herself, Althea swept up the stairs like ascending royalty. When she reached the top, Quinn stepped aside and the woman paused, scrutinizing him with a lusty leer. She poked an enameled fingernail in the center of his chest, gave him a smoldering look, then glanced over her shoulder. "Now *this* is what I had in mind," she told the gaping group gathered at the base of the stairs.

Returning her attention to Quinn, Althea moistened her lips with her tongue, growled deep in her throat, then presented her backside and walked away with an exaggerated hip-roll.

Quinn watched dispassionately, then glanced downstairs and arched a brow before sauntering back into his own room.

"Shameful," Edna murmured, waddling upstairs. "Simply shameful."

Looking completely perplexed, Jules wandered toward the kitchen talking to himself.

Janine shook her head, pondering indefinable threats of doom, mysterious sounds emanating from empty rooms and the inescapable sensation that somewhere along the line, the old Victorian was evolving from boardinghouse to asylum.

Then she went into her office and called the exterminator.

Clutching a Bible, Edna arranged burning candles on the altar, then knelt in silent prayer to beg forgiveness for having failed in God's blessed work. She had tried to save Althea but had been too late. The blasphemous woman would never know the joy of true redemption. Her sin was too great; Althea must burn in purgatory.

With a heavy heart, Edna prayed for mercy on the woman's wretched soul, then requested divine guidance for her own troubled life. Jules was turning against her, as he'd once turned against his own mother. Edna didn't know what to do. When the devil had pursued her beloved daughter, God had stepped in, guiding the lost woman to his kingdom.

But Satan had been angered by the loss and now sought vengeance through her grandson's weakness. The lust had returned to Jules's eyes, first for poor Marjorie, now for Althea. His immortal soul was in danger. Edna needed God's help to protect him.

In fact, Edna needed God's help to protect everyone for whom she cared deeply. Everyone, that is, except Janine, who consistently refused Satan's temptation and lived in celebration of the Lord's holy word. The embodiment of purity and grace, Janine was the sweet, celibate daughter of God and had assured her own place in the Kingdom of Heaven. Edna loved her fiercely.

But it was the failure with Jules that tore Edna's heart out. Her beloved grandson had repeatedly broken the Lord's commandments and for that he must answer to God. Until then, Edna must continue to protect the sinful child and conceal his crimes from the mortal world.

Quinn leaned back, scrutinizing Jules's worried expression as he studied the chessboard. "We can declare a draw, if you like."

Jules waved away the suggestion without glancing up. "Another moment," he murmured.

Since the young man was preoccupied with the game board, Quinn allowed his stiff smile to flatten. In the corner, a grandfather clock ticked rhythmically, counting each passing second. Since everyone else had retired hours ago, the rest of the house was silent.

Quinn decided that he'd had enough quiet observation. Now it was time to delve behind the black curtain of Jules Delacourt's fragile psyche and see what demons could be unearthed. "Your time is up," he announced harshly.

Startled by the gruff tone, Jules stiffened. "Ah...yes, of course. Sorry." Seeming suddenly disoriented, he wiped his palms on his slacks, eyes darting between Quinn and the chessboard.

Quinn had expected confusion and momentary loss of concentration. He was, however, taken aback by the child-like fear in the young man's eyes and his own pang of regret at having caused it.

Jules stuttered something unintelligible, flexed his fingers over the board, then castled his king and again nervously rubbed his palms on his trousers.

Expressing deliberate scorn, Quinn encompassed the board with a derisive gesture. "A rather noncommittal move, wouldn't you say? I expected better of you."

The young man flinched as though struck. "I, uh..." He scanned the board anxiously, suddenly unsure.

"You can't take it back," Quinn told his quavering opponent. "That would be against the rules. You wouldn't want to break the rules, would you?"

Sweat beaded Jules's upper lip. "No...I...of course not."

Quinn watched quietly, absorbing how quickly Jules's cocky confidence had dissolved when he was faced with the merest hint of disapproval. That was interesting. Not unexpected, but interesting.

Propping his elbows on his knees, Quinn leaned forward, feigning interest in the game board. He slanted a furtive glance across the table. "Didn't your mother teach you how to play by the rules?"

Jules stared sullenly at his knees. "It's your move, Coulliard."

Quinn smiled slowly. "Another moment."

Allowing the silence to thicken, Quinn waited until Jules was squirming in his chair before sliding the white bishop into position. Leaning back, he hooked his thumbs in his jeans and inspected his worried opponent.

Jules furrowed his moist brow, hovered over the chessboard like a starved hummingbird and stared at the inanimate pieces as though expecting they, too, would sprout wings and fly.

"You must miss your mother very much," Quinn said smoothly. "Do you think about her often?"

Jules looked up quickly. "I never think about her."

"Why not?"

"Because she's gone. It's foolish to think about someone who's gone."

"Where did she go, Jules?"

"She ran away with the devil."

"How do you know that?"

"*Grand'mère* told me."

"Why would your mother do that, Jules? Why would she run away and abandon her only son?"

Jules's voice dropped to a barely audible whisper. "She . . . was a wicked woman."

"Was she disappointed in you, Jules? Is that why she left?"

The young man's jaw sagged. "No—"

"Time's up," Quinn interrupted roughly. "It's your move." Near panic, Jules licked his lips and tried to focus on the game. At that moment, Quinn didn't like himself very much but there was no choice. He had to find out who he was dealing with. Taking a deep breath, he waited until Jules reached out to make a move, then questioned him roughly. "How old were you when your mother left?"

The disoriented man's hand froze above the board. "I—I don't remember."

"Time's up, Jules. Move or forfeit."

"I, uh..." Blinking frantically, Jules stared dismally at the scattered pieces, made a hurried move, sagged back in his chair and mopped his brow.

Quinn steepled his hands. "I'll bet you think about your mother all the time. When you go to bed at night, you smell the pillow and dream of her sweetness, don't you?"

As more color drained from his wan face, Jules balled his skinny fists and stared at his lap. "Shut up, Coulliard."

"Is she dead, Jules?"

"No!" He scoured his face with his palms. "She went away, that's all."

"I think you're lying. You were with her when it happened, weren't you? You watched the final breath slide from your mother's lips..."

Jules shook his head violently. "That's not true—"

"And saw her body shudder as the life drained away—"

"*No!*" The chair fell backward as Jules leaped to his feet. "You don't know anything, Coulliard, nothing at all!"

Impassively noting that Jules's face was now a rather odd shade of purple, Quinn glanced absently at the board and slid the white rook into its final position. "Checkmate."

Jules went totally rigid, staring at the chess pieces in stunned disbelief. Tears splashed from his flashing black eyes and his thin lips contorted in rage. "You bastard." He lurched to the doorway, shaking his fist. "You'll regret this, do you hear? You're going to *pay!*" Then he spun around and dashed up to his room.

Quinn stared coldly at the vacant doorway and whispered to the empty room. "I've already paid, you sick SOB. Now it's your turn."

CHAPTER SIX

The cursed mist enveloped the forest like a death shroud. Bundled against the damp chill, Janine knelt on the cold earth and tended her pitiful garden. Limp sprouts scattered along the wet furrows attested to her inexperience with the dismal climate.

It wasn't completely her fault, of course. A lack of consistent sunshine resulted in a shorter growing season than she was used to. Still, this was her third failure in as many years and she was becoming increasingly frustrated.

She dropped her spade and shivered. God, she hated the fog and the constant, bone-chilling dampness. Secretly she longed for the warmth of Southern California, the cloudless sky and crystal blue ocean. Of course San Diego had its share of fog but only in the winter. From April on, one could count on the weather to be mild and hospitable to plants as well as people. Janine's vegetables had flourished, and she'd harvested the bounty well into October.

The sweet memories made her heart twist. She wanted to go home. She wanted to, but she couldn't. Not yet. Someday, perhaps, she'd gather enough courage to face the demons that had driven her away. In the meantime, she had no choice but to battle root fungus, pray for sun and take whatever solace she could in the beauty of her picturesque surroundings.

A child's voice startled her. "Whatcha doing?"

Turning, Janine pulled off her muddy gloves and smiled. "Good morning, Rodney...Sara. You're a long way from home."

"Ma said we could ride down to the ravine." Rodney kicked the metal stand and propped his battered mountain bike beside the garden plot. Behind him, his sister watched shyly and clutched the handlebars of her own bicycle, a smaller and considerably shinier version of her brother's.

Janine spoke to the bashful little girl. "That's a lovely bike, Sara. Is it new?"

"Uh-huh." She hooked a finger over her lower teeth and stared at the ground. "Yesterday was my birthday."

"It was? That's wonderful, sweetie. How old are you now?"

Sara held up six fingers.

"Well, that definitely calls for a celebration." Janine stood and brushed off her jeans. "What would you say to some chocolate chip cookies and a big glass of milk?"

"I'd say yeah," Rodney replied without hesitation.

Tugging her brother's sleeve, Sara whispered, "You're supposed to say thank-you."

"That's *after*," the boy explained with exaggerated patience. "First you gotta *get* the cookies, then you can say thank-you."

Sara's nose wrinkled adorably. "Oh."

Because she couldn't help herself, Janine caressed the little girl's soft blond hair. "Why don't you park your bikes by the picnic table and I'll see what kind of birthday goodies I can scrounge up?"

With a grin and a giggle, the children steered their bicycles across the emerald lawn. Janine watched, smiling. They were so precious she could have hugged them both until they squeaked.

As she considered how lucky their parents were to have such wonderful children, a sudden stab of envy shocked her to the core. Shaken, she turned away and touched her belly, feeling empty. Cheated.

She thought back to the betrayal that shattered her trust and nearly destroyed her sanity. After three years of marriage without a pregnancy, Janine had been elated to discover a fertility specialist who, she had heard, could perform miracles. And she had so desperately wanted that miracle, a child of her own to love and to nurture always.

So she'd scheduled an appointment. After her own examination, the doctor had been so encouraging that Janine had nearly exploded with excitement. There was no reason she couldn't get pregnant, he'd told her, but before a treatment could be determined, Charles had to be examined.

Only Charles had adamantly refused to go. In fact, he'd been furious with her for having seen the specialist without his permission. In the midst of their bitter argument, he had angrily admitted that he'd had no intention of ever becoming a father. That was why he'd secretly had a vasectomy the month before their wedding.

Janine had been devastated by her husband's cruel deceit and by the realization that there would be no babies: not then, not ever. She had turned to her parents for consolation but they'd been more concerned about the disgrace of divorce than by their daughter's shattered dreams. Charles's family was old-money, the social elite. As long as Janine had been his wife, her parents had enjoyed an elevated status not otherwise possible for their middle-class life-style.

Since Janine's decision would have a decidedly adverse effect on their own social position, they'd berated her angrily, denouncing her pain as a petty grievance and consistently pointing out the material advantages of continuing the marriage. Although deeply hurt by her parents' attitude, Janine had quietly gone through with the dissolution. Then, ostracized by her family and feeling completely alone, she'd gathered her few possessions and moved north.

Three years later, the pain of betrayal was as acute as the day it had happened, and her empty womb still longed for fulfillment.

Shrugging off the familiar yearnings, Janine reminded herself that her young guests were waiting for cookies, so she entered the kitchen and went to work.

After placing three glasses of milk on a hand-painted tea tray, she pulled a fresh bag of cookies out of the pantry. A couple of test tugs didn't budge the stubborn cellophane so she opened the utensil drawer and reached for her scissors. Instead she came up with the missing master key.

Stunned, she stared from key to drawer. "How on earth did it get in there?"

The answer was obvious. She must have put it there during a preoccupied moment. That conclusion was unsettling. She realized that she'd been distracted—she just hadn't understood *how* distracted. Apparently she'd fallen victim to whatever unknown mental virus was responsible for the increasingly bizarre behavior of the other tenants.

Vowing to be more careful in the future, she pocketed the key, finished fixing the children's snack and carried the heaping tray out to the delighted youngsters.

While they enjoyed the chewy treat, she slid onto the bench to chat with them, laugh at their childish jokes and brush the occasional crumb from a smiling little mouth.

Since Janine was thoroughly enjoying herself, she was disappointed when Rodney announced that they had to leave. "So soon?"

The boy straddled his bike and nodded. "Ma wants us to bring home some bread and stuff from the store."

Sara smoothed her bibbed overalls. "Maybe we can come back tomorrow."

Janine touched the girl's flushed cheek. "I'd like that."

"We'll ask, okay?" Sara waved goodbye, climbed onto the padded banana seat of her birthday bike and pedaled madly to catch up with her sprinting brother.

When they'd disappeared from view, Janine traced the rim of the empty cookie plate and sighed.

A male voice startled her. "It looks like we're too late."

Janine whirled, pressed a palm over her racing heart and exhaled, all at once. "If you don't stop sneaking up on me, I'm going to chain a cowbell around your neck."

Quinn smiled without apology. Not until a fluttering black wing caught her attention did she notice the bandaged bird perched on his forearm.

The raven sidled to his master's cocked elbow, tilted his head and emitted a rasp that could have been interpreted as a greeting. Quinn idly stroked the glossy black head and glanced toward the gravel road. "Since Edgar needed some fresh air and exercise, I thought the children might have enjoyed meeting him."

"I'm sure they would have." Clasping her hands safely behind her back, Janine warily eyed the obsidian beak. "From a distance, of course."

"He's really quite docile." As though to prove that point, Quinn reached into his pocket and extracted an apple slice. The bird cawed with excitement, then ripped away a jagged hunk of juicy white flesh. "Would you like to pet him?"

"I'd rather stick my hand in a drill press."

"He won't hurt you."

"I have bruises that say otherwise."

With an indulgent smile, Quinn laid the apple slice on the redwood table, then extended his arm, allowing the raven to hop beside the treat. "A territorial instinct is natural for birds. He was protecting his perch."

"And quite effectively at that," Janine murmured, cringing as the raven's razor-sharp beak sheared off another piece of apple.

Edgar cocked his head and stared up at her, then hopped across the tabletop to investigate the plate of cookie crumbs. The bird emitted a delighted screech and settled down to dispatch the remaining morsels.

Janine couldn't help smiling at its antics. Despite misgivings about Edgar's volatile temperament, she had to concede a certain admiration for the determined creature. In spite of its handicap and constraining bandage, the plucky little fellow had displayed undeniable courage.

She sighed. "I suppose that as birds go, Edgar isn't so bad."

"So you *are* an animal lover." Quinn sat on the bench, extending his long legs and resting his back against the tabletop. "I suspected as much."

After a moment's hesitation, Janine sat on the same bench a reasonable distance away. "I respect animals but I certainly don't have the instinctive rapport with them that you do."

"I think you're confusing instinct with experience."

She disagreed and said so adding, "There isn't one person in a thousand who relates to wild creatures the way you do."

His eyes crinkled. "Do you think I'm a reincarnated Dr. Dolittle?"

Feeling her face heat, she avoided his gaze and feigned interest in removing a splinter from the weathered wooden seat. "I believe that animals recognize inner kindness."

From the corner of her eye she saw him cup his hands behind his head. After a moment, he replied tersely, "You're mistaken, Janine. I'm not a kind person."

Startled by the unexpected change of tone, she responded without thinking, "Of course you are."

He considered her assertion for a moment. "I chased off a hungry cat. Don't read anything else into it."

"It's more than that," Janine insisted. "I've seen your kindness every day, in your tenderness with Edna, your tolerance for Althea's brazen behavior, allowing Jules to win at chess even though you're obviously the better player—all these things prove that you are caring and...and..." The words dissipated under the force of Quinn's probing pewter gaze.

"I'm flattered that you hold me in such high regard," he said slowly. "Unfortunately, you're wrong."

Janine would have responded but her tongue glued itself to the roof of her mouth.

"You should be more cautious," Quinn told her. "When offered too freely, trust empowers one's enemies and provides a dangerous weapon. The fact that I won last night's chess game should quash any idealistic notion you have about the purity of my motives."

"Jules lost?" Janine was so surprised by that news that the veiled warning about enemies and weapons slipped quietly to the back of her mind. "So that explains his foul mood." When Quinn lifted a brow, she explained. "Jules refused to come down for breakfast this morning. Poor Edna was beside herself. It was all she could do to coax him out long enough to drive her to work."

"Edna doesn't drive?"

Janine considered that. "Come to think of it, I'm not sure. She has a license, but as far as I know, Jules does all the driving."

"How do you know she has a driver's license?"

The blunt question startled her. "I requested identification when she and Jules first moved in. It's standard procedure when the rent is paid by check rather than cash."

"Was it a Washington license?"

"Excuse me?"

"You mentioned that Edna and Jules came from the Seattle area. Was her driver's license issued by the state of Washington?"

"No. Actually it was from California. I remember commenting on it because their car had Washington license plates." She interpreted Quinn's half smile and responded, "So you see, when I made note of your van's license plates, it was nothing personal."

"I didn't presume that it was." He turned sideways, cocking one knee over the hard bench. "Was there an address on the license?"

"Only a P.O. box."

"Didn't you think that odd?"

"Not really." Janine frowned. "Why the interrogation?"

"Just making conversation." Quinn smiled without depth and gazed up at the gloomy sky. "Is Jules still in his room?"

"I suppose so." She chose not to mention that after taking his grandmother to work Jules had made a brief telephone call before stomping upstairs and slamming his bedroom door. Quinn's intense interest in Jules's schedule didn't make much sense considering that he had followed the young man and his grandmother out of the driveway. Moments after Jules's return, she'd noticed Quinn's van parked in its usual location. At the time she'd assumed the timing to be sheer coincidence. Under the barrage of pointed questions, however, she was beginning to wonder.

As though sensing her discomfort, Quinn suddenly switched subjects. "Do the Drake children visit you often?"

"No. I've seen them hiking through the ravine once in a while but this is the first time they've stopped to chat."

"You seemed to be enjoying their company." He responded to her quizzical expression by gesturing toward an upstairs window overlooking the yard. "I couldn't help overhearing."

"I hope we didn't disturb you."

"Laughter is never a disturbance." He folded his arms, regarding her. "I like seeing you happy."

She looked away. "I'm always happy."

"Are you?"

"Of course," she lied. "Why wouldn't I be? I have everything I want."

"Do you?"

She fidgeted with the metal tab on her jacket zipper. "Are you going to charge for this session?"

His startled expression melted into one of bemusement. "I didn't mean to make you uncomfortable."

"But you did." Propping her elbow on her thigh, she nested her chin in her open palm and gave him a Freudian stare. "How do you feel about that?"

He chuckled softly. "How would you like me to feel?"

She shifted sideways on the bench and faced him. "So you do have a sense of humor."

"Occasionally." He casually tapped the tabletop, bringing the curious raven's attention to a wayward cookie crumb. "Unfortunately, cynicism is a pitfall of my profession. To the vast majority of people I worked with, life wasn't a particularly pleasant experience. People frequently equate unhappiness with failure and refuse to acknowledge sad feelings. It was my job to recognize what my patients denied."

She stiffened indignantly. "I'm not one of your patients, Mr. Coulliard...or do you prefer *Dr.* Coulliard?"

He regarded her thoughtfully. "Actually I prefer Quinn."

"*Are* you a doctor?"

"I have a Ph.D. in psychology so technically I am but I've never cared much for titles."

Somehow that didn't surprise her. "Well, then, Quinn, I'll dispense with formalities and say simply that I don't appreciate being psychoanalyzed in my own backyard."

"That wasn't my intention." With a sigh, he rolled his head and massaged his neck. "When I saw how uninhibited you were with the children and how filled with joy, I found myself wondering why you'd never married and started a family of your own. It's none of my business, of course."

"No, it isn't." Janine stared at the tightly curled fists in her lap. "What..." She cleared her throat. "What makes you think that I've never married?"

A strange expression crossed his face. "Have you been?"

She moistened her lips. "Yes."

After a strained silence, he said simply, "I'm sorry."

Startled, she glanced up. "Sorry that I was married?"

He took one of her hands and gently unfurled her bent fingers. "I'm sorry that the marriage ended. You must have been deeply hurt."

"It was my choice," she said defiantly. "I divorced Charles."

"Divorce is usually a painful process."

Her confident veneer cracked. "It's worse than dying."

Still holding her hand between his strong palms, he gently stroked the back of her hand with his thumb. "Sometimes there are no other options."

Quinn's quiet acceptance warmed Janine to the core. "You're the first person I know who has acknowledged that. Most people treated me as though I'd committed a cardinal sin."

"Why?"

She shrugged. "In our social circle, marriage is big business, more of a company merger than a human relationship. A divorce is considered a kind of boardroom mutiny, financial treason of the most dastardly sort."

He considered that a moment. "So your family didn't support your decision?"

A lump rose in her throat. "They were horrified."

"That must have hurt you very much."

Swallowing hard, she managed a curt nod. "It wasn't entirely their fault. Charles's family was third generation La Jolla elite but my parents had worked hard to get where they were. Acceptance meant everything to them. When Charles and I married, they felt as though they finally belonged. The divorce humiliated them. They were outcasts. That nearly killed them."

Quinn squeezed her hand. "Most parents would be more concerned for the happiness of their child. Perhaps your guilt has exaggerated the extent of their disappointment."

She emitted a dry laugh. "To my parents, money *was* happiness. As to exaggeration, I was informed that if I filed for divorce, they no longer had a daughter."

Unable to meet his gaze, Janine inspected the strong fingers encircling her own thin hand. Where his flesh touched hers, a peculiar energy flowed through her body and radiated into her very soul. She felt strangely comforted, cared for, understood. She was telling him things that she'd never revealed before and there was a sense of relief in exposing the pain that had been locked inside for so very long. The man had a way about him, an uncanny ability to draw out a person's most intimate secrets.

Now he simply observed her quietly, stroking the sensitive pulse point at her wrist. When he spoke, his voice was soft, soothing, hypnotic. "You must have been very unhappy to risk losing your entire family."

She looked up. It was a mistake. She was instantly enraptured by the empathy in his eyes, a tenderness that was mesmerizing. "Yes," she whispered. "I was."

"Do you want to talk about it?"

"Yes." Was that her voice? She blinked, unable to believe that, even now, the forbidden words were forming in her mind. "When you wondered why I hadn't started a family, I felt sick inside. Even when I was a little girl, being a mother was the only career I ever wanted. I dreamed of having babies, a dozen of them, all healthy and beautiful and filled with the joy of knowing that they were deeply loved. But it didn't work out that way."

His eyes filled with silent sympathy. "You weren't able to conceive?"

Using her free hand to massage her eyelids, she took a shuddering breath, then slowly, methodically, she revealed how Charles had deceived her. She spoke carefully, withholding the most intimate details of their marital problems, yet with each whispered word the pressure eased until she felt oddly buoyant and free.

Quinn listened intently, with a sincere interest that satisfied her secret emptiness. She saw no disapproval or judgment in his eyes, only a genuine concern that touched her to the core. By the time she'd finished speaking, Janine believed him to be a kindred spirit, a man who understood her feelings of betrayal. She felt deep gratitude and something more.

Quinn delicately brushed a wispy strand from her cheek. "So that's why you left San Diego?"

"I couldn't stay as a pariah, disowned by my family, snubbed by my friends." A weak smile turned into a twitching cheek. She cleared her throat and shrugged. "Someday I'll go back."

"To make amends with your family?"

She frowned. "No, I don't think so. My feelings for them have changed."

"That's understandable." He regarded her thoughtfully. "They've hurt you. There's no reason for you to trust them

again. The important thing is how you feel about yourself.''

"What do you mean?''

"Do you still blame yourself for what happened?''

"I never blamed myself." But her annoyance melted as
the truth sank in. She looked up in surprise and awe. "I did
blame myself, didn't I? Maybe I thought that if I'd been a
better person, Charles would have wanted to father my
children.''

"Is that what you believe now?''

"No." She shook her head vehemently. "In all the ways
that count, Charles was a child himself. He took no responsibility for his own actions, and now that I think about
it, he never could cope with a situation in which he was not
the center of attention.''

"Then leaving him was vital to your own survival. If
you'd have stayed, part of you would have died and your
dreams for the future would have been destroyed.''

"Yes," she murmured, amazed. "It was the right thing
to do, wasn't it?''

He smiled. "What do you think?''

"There you go again." She swatted his arm and laughed.
"Honestly, I'm going to have to wear an emotional flak
jacket when you're around. I can't believe that I've told you
all this . . . this stuff.''

He released her hand, folded his arms and leaned back.
"The first step in healing is to recognize the wound. You
didn't say anything that you weren't ready to reveal.''

A cold breeze chilled her unprotected palm. Without his
touch, she felt oddly vulnerable and exposed. "Yes...well,
thanks for listen— Ow!" Her hand flew to her head as she
spun around and stared into Edgar's beady yellow eyes.
Several strands of brown hair hung from his beak and when
he again advanced toward her sore scalp, she shook her finger. "Don't even think about it.''

The raven tilted his head, then hopped across the table and laid the wispy prize on his master's shoulder. Quinn pinched the hairs between his thumb and forefinger and held them up for examination. "Ah. Just what I need for my voodoo doll."

"Very funny." Janine rubbed her head. "Is he nesting or something?"

"Actually I believe this is supposed to be a gift."

"Edgar has a crush on you? How sweet."

She chuckled and Quinn couldn't help smiling in response. "You have a delightful laugh."

A pink glow spread over her cheeks along with a shy expression he found most appealing. Odd, he mused, how this gentle woman could affect him. As the thought crossed his mind, he glanced down at the strands in his palm and felt a peculiar warmth crawl up his arm. Janine Taylor was a very special person, and he was unaccountably angry at those who had hurt and betrayed her.

As he'd listened to her story, a strange thing had happened. Quinn had identified with Janine's suffering, recognizing the self-imposed stigma, the bonds of guilt that strangled a person's soul. He'd felt sympathy, yes, but he'd also felt something deeper, something that had struck a sensitive chord deep inside him.

Before he could ponder that unexpected development, a noise caught his attention. He looked toward the walkway just as Jules strode into view. Without so much as a glance in their direction, the young man climbed into his grandmother's car and drove away.

Quinn tensed but forced a casual tone. "I didn't realize Edna's shift ended so early today."

Janine shrugged. "As far as I know, she won't be off until late this afternoon."

"Really?" He slowly gathered the bird into his arms, preparing to make a move. "Jules seemed to be in quite a hurry. I hope nothing is wrong."

"I doubt it. He frequently gets bored and drives into Eugene for the afternoon."

"Does he?" As Quinn posed the bland question, he glanced idly around the yard to indicate that he neither expected nor was interested in a reply. He stretched, then stood without rushing. "I'd better put Edgar away while you still have some hair left."

"Of course." Janine stood, too, smiling awkwardly. "I have to finish weeding."

Quinn hesitated. "I enjoyed our talk."

Her smile relaxed. "So did I."

He allowed his gaze to linger a moment before moving casually toward the back porch. Once inside the kitchen, he glanced out the window, and after reassuring himself that Janine had gone back to her gardening, he hurried upstairs and returned the raven to its perch.

Five minutes later, Quinn was driving on the winding road away from Darby Ridge. He pushed the speed limit, scanning the road ahead. Once Jules hit the Highway 58 cutoff, there wouldn't be much chance of catching up with him. The last thing Quinn wanted was another wasted opportunity, so when he finally spotted the faded blue sedan in the distance, he breathed a sigh of relief and eased off the accelerator. All he had to do now was hang back and keep the car in sight, as he'd done since arriving in Darby Ridge. So far his clandestine surveillance had provided little information.

A search of the guest rooms, however, had been more interesting. As expected, Althea's closet had been stuffed with tacky, sexy clothing more appropriate for a svelte twenty-year-old than a middle-aged woman. Edna, bless her, had converted her bureau into a religious shrine flanked by a large family Bible complete with inscriptions that had been enlightening, if not surprising.

In Jules's room, however, Quinn had stumbled onto a hidden cache of pornography that had given him a real jolt. The magazines hadn't been locker-room stuff or the run-of-the-mill nudies favored by hormone-pickled adolescents. The stuff Jules had tucked away could only be described as hard-core, with scenes that had literally turned Quinn's stomach.

Tightening his grip on the steering wheel, he continued his furtive pursuit to the Eugene city limits, following the blue sedan past the train yard and through crowded downtown streets into the parking lot of the Lane County Mental Health Clinic.

When Quinn watched Jules enter the building, an icy numbness settled into the pit of his stomach. No amount of psychiatric help could cure the perverted bastard who kept such pornographic filth. As far as Quinn was concerned, the gesture was too little, too late.

Jules's fate had already been sealed.

CHAPTER SEVEN

Slumped on the overstuffed leather sofa, Jules contemplated the abstract shapes littering the faded Oriental carpet. His jaw ached from constant clenching. His fingers twitched into a constant blur of scratching, plucking and picking. An uncomfortable dampness coated his skin. He felt sticky. Unclean.

Across the plushly appointed room, Dr. Aaron Orbach watched quietly from an armless French Provincial intimately situated beside a gleaming cherry desk. On the desktop sat a small black machine. The doctor pressed a button, and when the recording tape whirred softly, he steepled his hands. "You sounded upset on the telephone, Jules."

Without responding, Jules stared at his manicured hands and was horrified. One of his fingernails was chipped, uneven. It looked like the claw of an animal. He was disfigured, flawed, unworthy. He panicked, desperate to repair the damage immediately. Clutching his wrist, he brought the offending hand to his mouth and gnawed at the broken nail.

Dr. Orbach crossed his legs and maintained an impassive expression. "Tell me what has happened since our last appointment."

Jules bit off a nail sliver, spit it on the floor, then held up his hand to inspect the ragged repairs. This wouldn't do at all. He trembled violently, eyes darting like trapped prey. The doctor silently reached into his desk drawer and extracted an emery board. Jules snatched it eagerly and roughly sawed at the jagged fingernail.

Dr. Orbach watched quietly for a moment before resuming the annoying inquiry. "Are you still upset about Miss Barker's death?"

"I dream about her sometimes," Jules mumbled, still engrossed in his vital task.

"What happens in those dreams?"

"She cries."

"Why does she cry?"

"Because I won't have sex with her." Holding up his hand, Jules noted an unacceptable imperfection on an adjacent nail and used the emery board to effect repairs. "My mother used to cry, too."

The doctor leaned forward. "And why did your mother cry, Jules? Did she want to have sex with you?"

The emery board slipped from Jules's rigid fingers. He was too outraged to reply.

"Did my question upset you, Jules?"

"How dare you imply something so vulgar?" he snapped, glaring at the doctor with undisguised revulsion.

Dr. Orbach offered a conciliatory gesture. "I didn't mean to offend you."

But Jules would not be mollified. He leaped to his feet and paced the spacious office, fearing he might explode from the heat of righteous fury.

"Did you love your mother?" Orbach asked.

Jules stopped pacing as an image floated through his mind, the memory of being a small boy nestled on his mother's lap. Her dark eyes had been filled with love as she'd rocked him gently, crooning the sweet lullaby that he still hummed when surrounded by frightening darkness. Deep inside, his heart still ached for her tender touch, the comfort of her soft, maternal bosom—

"Jules?"

He blinked numbly.

Orbach leaned back in his chair. "I asked if you loved your mother."

Turning away, Jules blinked back tears. "She was a wicked woman," he whispered. "It would have been wrong to love her."

Nodding dispassionately, the doctor casually rearranged his spectacles and peered over the shiny brass frames. "Why do you believe your mother was wicked, Jules?"

Jerking to a stop, Jules looked up in disbelief. "Because she did disgusting things."

"With men?"

"Yes," Jules whispered. "When the men came to see her, she made me go outside but I looked in the window and saw the things they did. It . . . made me sick."

"Did you ever discuss those feelings with your mother?"

"No." Jules pinched the crease of his trousers to eliminate a bothersome flaw in the otherwise perfect edge. "She wouldn't have cared."

"What makes you think that?"

"Because if she'd really loved me, she wouldn't have gone away and left me all alone."

"You weren't completely alone, were you? You still had your grandmother."

Grand'mère. A cold anger settled in the pit of his stomach every time Jules thought about his grandmother and the horrible day that he'd been called to the principal's office at Boston High. His grandmother had been there, eyes bright with phony grief, barely suppressing a smile as she informed Jules that his mother had run away.

Jules hadn't been surprised—he couldn't remember why—but he had been terribly upset, particularly when his grandmother told him he couldn't go back to Boston High, nor was he allowed to retrieve his possessions or even return to the apartment he and his mother had shared.

Grand'mère had told Jules that his things were tainted by evil. Jules had hated her for that. Seven years later, he still did.

But Jules hadn't revealed any of those feelings to his psychiatrist, fearing *Grand'mère* would find out. The thought of incurring his grandmother's wrath—and subsequent punishment—was frightening enough but the fear of being abandoned again was more terrifying than death itself. Jules didn't know what he would do without *Grand'mère*. She was all he had; he needed her desperately.

Shuddering, Jules returned to his seat and wiped his moist brow, vaguely aware that the doctor was speaking again. "Excuse me?"

Dr. Orbach propped his chin on his hand. "I asked what you meant when you telephoned this morning and said that the devil was chasing you."

"Yes, the devil," Jules repeated in a dull monotone. "He calls himself Coulliard."

"Ah. The new tenant you told me about last week. What has he done to frighten you, Jules?"

Frighten. The word circled his brain. A man must never be frightened. Charles Bronson was never frightened. Clint Eastwood was never frightened. Closing his eyes, Jules envisioned the movie he'd watched last night and how the hero had stood tall in the face of his enemies. As the images sharpened, his shoulders automatically squared and his chin rose defiantly.

And while the pitiful Jules Delacourt watched from a distant corner of his own mind, the essence of Charles Bronson suddenly spoke with harsh clarity. "Coulliard said that my mother is dead."

The doctor's eyes widened slightly. "Why do you believe he said that?"

Slipping one hand into his pocket, Jules swaggered across the room and slouched casually on the couch. "The reason is obvious." He smiled coldly. "Coulliard must have killed her."

That evening Althea made the rounds of Darby Ridge nightspots—two beer joints and a bowling alley—and Edna dragged her grandson to an evening church function. Quinn left without comment shortly thereafter.

Now, with the strains of her favorite symphony floating through the parlor, Janine settled onto the sofa to reread a Dickens classic and enjoy the rare evening of solitude. Except for the moaning wind announcing a coming storm, the boardinghouse was deliciously quiet.

Since a cozy fire would perfect the ambience, she gazed longingly at the massive river-stone fireplace, then at the book in her hand. The book won. With a contented sigh, she parted the pages and indulged herself by reading the first line aloud: " 'It was the best of times, it was the worst of times...' " God, she loved this story. It never failed to bring tears to her eyes.

She kicked off her sneakers, tucked her feet under her thighs and had barely finished the first page when the front door opened. Her heart sank as she hurriedly removed her feet from the cushions and sat like a lady.

Quinn leaned against the parlor doorjamb. "It's only me," he said pleasantly. "You can get comfortable again."

She smiled and laid her book on the table. "I didn't expect anyone back so soon."

"Disappointed?"

"Of course not," she murmured and was surprised to realize that it was true. "Would you like some coffee?"

He sat on the other end of the short sofa. "Is there some made?"

"There will be in a minute."

When she started to stand, he laid a restraining hand on her arm. "You don't have to wait on me. Sit down. Enjoy your book."

"But—"

"I can make coffee."

The image widened her smile. "Perhaps, but would it be drinkable?"

"Possibly." He released her arm and leaned back against the sofa cushion. "Actually it's too late for coffee, anyway. Caffeine keeps me awake."

"Well, how about some chamomile tea? It's wonderfully soothing." When he politely refused, Janine smiled. "Another time," she murmured, then stood and absently smoothed her wrinkled skirt.

Quinn frowned. "Where are you going?"

"To turn down the stereo." She shrugged nervously. "I have a tendency to hike the volume past most people's comfort level."

"It's fine." Quinn cocked his head. "Brahms's Fourth Symphony, isn't it?"

She brightened. "Yes. *Allegro non troppo.*"

He listened another moment. "No, I believe it's *Andante moderato.*"

"You like classical music?" She sat down, instantly enthused. "Who is your favorite composer? I love Mahler myself, and Mussorgsky—I adore *Pictures at an Exhibition*—and Stravinsky and Brahms, of course and..." Suddenly aware that she was babbling, she clamped her lips together and studied her hands. "Sorry. I so rarely have the opportunity to discuss music that I guess I got carried away."

He didn't bother to disguise his amusement. "It's a shame you can't muster more enthusiasm."

She smiled, unembarrassed. "You never answered my question."

He feigned surprise. "There was a question buried in that verbal barrage?"

This time she laughed out right. "Do you have a favorite composer?"

"As a matter of fact, I do." He regarded her pensively. "Liszt."

Her smile faded. "Franz Liszt?"

"Are you familiar with his work?"

"Of course. The *Mephisto Waltz*." She swallowed hard, remembering the wild, pagan beat of the Faust-inspired score. Somehow it seemed an eerie irony that Quinn would admire Liszt, the mesmerizing virtuoso rumored to have had a sorcerous power over the hearts of women.

As though sensing her discomfort, Quinn added, "I also enjoy Ravel and Tchaikovsky. Is their work more to your liking?"

Feeling a bit silly to have read so much into a man's choice of music, Janine laughed at herself. "Yes, I'll admit that it is. As a matter of fact, I have a complete collection of Tchaikovsky including his Sixth Symphony, the *Pathétique*."

"Really?" Quinn sat forward, eyes glowing. "I haven't heard that in years."

He seemed lost in thought, his wistful smile offering an unexpected glimpse behind the barrier he'd so diligently erected to hide his emotions. Janine was delighted by the tantalizing peek and intrigued to have made yet another exhilarating discovery about this provocative, mysterious man. "Would you like me to play it for you?"

He looked up eagerly. "If it wouldn't be any trouble."

After assuring him that it was no trouble at all, she crossed the room and knelt beside one of her many CD carousels, acutely aware that Quinn had followed. Her heart raced as he sat on the floor beside her. She tried to focus on each title and forced a light tone. "Actually I don't play the *Pathétique* often. It's such a somber, moody piece."

"That's what makes it so memorable," Quinn murmured, close enough that his breath lifted the fine hair around her ears. "It's the master's final symphony, an ode to the spiritual hunger of man."

"That's an interesting hypothesis, considering that the riddle of the *Pathétique* has been the bane of musical theologians for over a century." Enveloped by his musky scent, Janine felt slightly dizzy. Somehow she managed to locate and extract the proper disc. "I once read that although Tchaikovsky wanted the piece to be heard by the entire world, he intended for it to be understood by himself alone."

"Yes, I've heard that, too." Quinn seemed pleased, and somewhat surprised, by the depth of her knowledge on the subject. His gaze warmed. "You really are an extraordinary woman, Janine."

The unexpected praise startled her. "Because I've studied the classics?"

"No, because you are yourself." He touched her cheek—a sensual caress that sent shivers down her spine. "The more I know about you, the more amazed I am at the depths lurking just behind those guileless eyes."

Completely nonplussed, she fiddled with the flat plastic case in her hand. "Even a hollow tube has a certain amount of depth."

He took hold of her chin, turning her face firmly, almost roughly. "Never do that."

She was stunned by the anger in his eyes. "Do what?"

"Put yourself down." His fingers slid sensually down her throat. "You are a very special woman. You deserve to be valued and cherished. Whoever told you otherwise was a fool."

Her breath caught in her throat. "How...did you know?"

After a lingering look, he averted his gaze downward and removed the CD from her convulsive grip. "People tend to view their own worth through the eyes of others. The result is a self-esteem that has either been nourished or completely destroyed."

Massively relieved that the observation had not been based on personal knowledge, Janine exhaled slowly. "Psych 101, right?"

"But nonetheless true." Extracting the silver disc from its plastic case, Quinn slid the CD into the stereo unit. He eyed the impressive array of buttons and frowned.

"Everything is set up," Janine said. "Just press play."

"Ah." He did so.

As the room was shrouded by the dulcet strains of the first movement, Quinn closed his eyes to relish the impact. He was utterly still, except for the hand resting on his thigh and the index finger twitching like a maestro's baton.

Since he was engrossed in experiencing the symphony, Janine took the opportunity to examine him more closely and was struck by how relaxation had softened his sharp features. He was entranced by the music, entirely at ease. There seemed nothing fearsome about him now. In fact, he was suddenly so appealing that it was all she could do to keep from reaching out and stroking the fine stubble along his jawline.

Lord, but he was a beautiful man.

Yet he was also a paradox, a person who seemed capable of either expressing great tenderness or exacting a harsh revenge with unsettling equanimity. And she was helplessly drawn to him. That shocked and frightened her.

As the passage throbbed to a crescendo, Quinn's head nodded in cadence with each mournful chord. His hand rose, forcefully conducting the fevered finale of the music—and Janine's pulsing heart.

The tempo quickened. The blood throbbed in her veins. Her ears rang, the floor vibrated, goose bumps slid down her spine.

Suddenly the room was silent and Quinn was staring straight at her. The power of that gaze affected her more deeply than any symphony ever written. She couldn't speak, couldn't breathe and was only vaguely aware that the gentle strains of the second movement had begun.

The atmosphere thickened, charged with sexual static that raised the hairs on her arms. He reached out slowly, enticingly. She closed her eyes, shivering as his knuckle brushed her cheek. Then something tickled her lashes.

When she looked at him again, he was smiling. He lightly touched the sensitive skin just above her eye. "What's this?"

She blushed without response.

He traced the contour of her brow. "You don't need makeup to be beautiful."

Curling her fingers, she averted her gaze, embarrassed that she'd yielded to a sudden urge to experiment with mascara and eye shadow. "It makes me look silly, doesn't it?"

"You could never look silly." His fingertip rested at the corner of her glossed mouth. "The colors are lovely, and your eyes seem even brighter than usual."

She peeked up shyly. "Really?"

"Really," he murmured. "In fact, I find you almost irresistible."

A shocking boldness surged from some spot hidden deep inside. She met his gaze directly. "Only almost?"

He hesitated, probing her eyes for what seemed an eternity, then he slowly, exquisitely, brushed his lips over her mouth in a touch so delicate she wondered if it had been real. His hand slid down her throat, paused, then moved to cup the back of her head. "You are the most incredible woman," he whispered. Before she could even think to breathe, his mouth covered hers in a kiss that shook her to the soles of her feet.

If her brain was numb, her body was not and she responded with an instinctive fervor that was both shocking and thrilling. She melted against him, her breasts seeming to fuse with the sculpted muscles of his hard chest. Without conscious command her trembling fingers clutched his shoulders, frantic to hold him closer—and closer still.

When he urged her lips apart and tasted her deeply, something inside her cracked. Something was happening, something she didn't completely understand, but for the first time in her adult life, she realized that she wasn't dead inside. Part of her cherished that knowledge; part of her recoiled from it.

A frightened whimper bubbled from her throat. Quinn swallowed the tiny cry, then slowly, almost painfully, released her. Gasping for air, she crossed her arms like a shield, staggered by the stunning force of what had just happened.

Cursing himself for having lost control, Quinn laid a steadying hand on her shoulder. "Are you all right?"

She nodded but appeared pale and shaken.

He reluctantly took his hand away. "I'm sorry. That shouldn't have happened."

A strand of hair fell across her cheek. She pushed it away and laughed nervously. "That symphony is more powerful than I remembered."

"It had nothing to do with music, Janine. You're a desirable woman." He managed a thin smile. "But I had no right to take advantage of you."

"You didn't take advantage. We were both—" she wiped her palms on her skirt "—affected."

Quinn took a deep breath. *Affected.* That was certainly an understatement, considering the fact that his hands were still shaking. The weakness annoyed him.

Suddenly Janine stood and brushed her skirt. "It's getting late," she announced.

"Of course." Somehow Quinn got to his feet, but as he reached to turn off the stereo, she stopped him.

"Please, feel free to stay and enjoy the music."

"I don't want to disturb you."

"You won't." She rubbed her upper arms, looking so vulnerable that he wanted to sweep her into his arms and kiss her senseless. Then she forced a bright smile, bade him good-night and was gone.

After her footsteps had faded, Quinn muttered a sharp oath as his fingers furrowed the top of his head. He was furious. Kissing her hadn't simply been a matter of giving in to temptation. That implied that one had a choice in the matter, and Quinn couldn't have stopped himself if he'd wanted to. Which he hadn't. Janine's haunted eyes had touched something deep inside him, a secret place he hadn't allowed anyone to see in a very long time.

But he simply couldn't permit it to happen again. Emotional entanglements turned a man into a pawn of his own heart, blinded by love and ripe for betrayal. Love exposed weakness, and weakness exposed was weakness exploited. That had been a crushing lesson but Quinn had learned it well.

Now he rubbed his face and tried to get a grip on himself. He had to proceed cautiously. No distraction—no matter how sweet—could be allowed to jeopardize the mission. There was too much at stake.

The thunderous crack would have awakened Janine had she not already been watching the advancing storm from her window. Rain came in torrential sheets that pelted the glass with projectile force. Tongues of lightning licked the ground, illuminating the turbulent clouds with brilliant bursts that made her eyes ache.

As the storm grew closer, the wind screamed like a terrified child. Beside her window, oak branches whipped and bowed, frantically scratching the glass with leafy fingers. The raspy sound grated on her nerves.

She stepped over the curled binding of the braided throw rug, slid between her mussed covers and stared into the darkness. Three hours ago she'd left Quinn in the parlor. Within moments, the music downstairs had ceased and he, too, had returned to his room. Since that time she'd done nothing but toss, pace and memorize shadows.

Before the storm moved in she'd been aware of every sound, every minute whisper outside her door. After Edna and Jules had returned from church, they'd spent a few minutes in the kitchen before coming upstairs. A bit later, Althea had stumbled through the front door. Everyone was home now. Everyone was asleep.

Everyone except Janine.

Frustrated, she wondered if she would ever sleep again. Her lips still tingled from Quinn's kiss. The man had invaded every nerve, every cell in her body. She ached. She throbbed. She was on fire.

With a muffled cry she threw off the covers, swung her feet to the floor and sat on the edge of the bed feeling empty. When she closed her eyes, Quinn's image floated through her mind. She could feel his body heat permeating her flesh, smell the dizzying scent of his lush hair. And her mouth still savored the taste of him.

The man was driving her insane. She rubbed her eyes. Maybe hot milk would help—anything to get Quinn Coulliard out of her mind.

Slipping her feet into her terry scuffs, she pulled on her robe and loosely tied it as she descended the stairs. When she reached the foyer, a flash of lightning guided her before a blanket of darkness again smothered the room. As Janine felt her way through the dining area she heard a muffled clunk in the kitchen.

She froze, suddenly feeling exposed, as though silent eyes were watching. Touching the pounding pulse point at the base of her throat, she listened. Rain pounded on the cedar roof, all but obscuring the wailing of the wind. She exhaled slowly. It was the storm, she told herself. Only the storm.

But as she reached the doorway a hushed scuffling emanated from the other side. Frightened now, she glanced down and saw no light spilling from beneath the kitchen door; yet undeniably someone or something was in there.

She licked her parched lips. Quinn was right. The house was infested with rodents. The mere thought made her shudder.

Mustering her courage, she slowly pushed open the door and cautiously peered into the darkened kitchen. She saw nothing, not even a dim shadow—which was to be expected on a stormy, moonless night.

As she stepped inside, her heart beat like a frantic drum. She touched the wall, groping for the switch. Lightning flashed. A silhouette loomed by the table.

With a terrified gasp, she flipped the switch and almost fainted in relief. "Jules. You nearly scared me to death." Her shoulders sagged and she took several shallow breaths before realizing that he hadn't responded. She regarded him cautiously, suddenly aware that he looked rather strange. "It's very late. What are you doing down here?"

He stared at the cleavage exposed by her thin gown. "Waiting for you."

Stiffening, Janine clutched her robe at the throat, unnerved by the peculiar glow in his black eyes. "I don't know what you mean."

He took a step forward. "You wanted to be alone with me, didn't you?"

"That's absurd." The wall pressed against her back. "I thought you were upstairs asleep, which is exactly where you should be."

Jules licked his lips, his glittery gaze sliding the length of her body. "You look pretty," he murmured. "And you smell good."

Somehow she managed not to flinch. "Please return to your room before you wake the other tenants."

He seemed confused by the request. "I don't want to."

"I insist. It's late, and you must return to your room immediately."

His perplexed expression dissipated and was replaced by one that raised goose bumps on her spine. His mouth warped into a twisted line and his eyes flashed with sudden rage. In less than a heartbeat, he grabbed hold of her arm, his furious face only inches from her own. "You're trying to seduce me."

"W-What?"

"You're just like the rest of them," he hissed. "Flaunting yourself, tempting men into your bed."

She twisted against his cruel grip. "Jules . . . you're hurting me."

"My mother is a whore, too. Did you know that?" He laughed unpleasantly. "I saw her bring men into her bed. I watched what she did with them."

The pain of his bruising fingers nearly brought Janine to her knees. When he hauled her back up, she bounced off his chest and barely managed to turn her face away from Jules's sloppy kiss.

His wet mouth moved to her ear. "I thought you were different, but you're not. You're evil just like she is, and you'll both suffer the damnation of eternal hell—"

"*Jules!*" Edna rushed through the doorway and soundly slapped her grandson's shoulder. "Let go of her this instant!"

Releasing his grasp, Jules stumbled backward, blinking at his grandmother as if she were an unwelcome mirage.

Obviously distressed, Edna addressed Janine anxiously. "Are you all right, dear?"

Janine rubbed her sore wrist and managed a shaky nod. "Yes. I'm fine."

The woman's blocky shoulders drooped. She squeezed her tiny eyes closed, opened them again and spoke quietly to her grandson. "Please go back to bed, Jules. *Grand'mère* will be up to tuck you in."

To Janine's shock, the young man suddenly panicked. His pinched mouth flattened and his Adam's apple bobbed frantically. When Edna reached up to caress his cheek, he flinched and shielded himself with his hands.

"There, there," Edna said soothingly and stroked Jules's hair until the fear melted from his dark eyes. "That's a good boy. Now go upstairs, dear, and wait for me."

Janine was amazed by the young man's transformation. Plucking at his clothing, Jules seemed completely bewildered by the situation and incapable of the terrifying rage he'd displayed moments earlier. He looked at Janine with callow confusion, then bowed awkwardly and left the room.

Instantly Edna grasped Janine's hands and squeezed them painfully. "I'm so very sorry, dear. Sometimes he does things . . . in his sleep."

"He's a somnambulist?"

Edna brightened, just a little. "Yes, that's it. Please forgive him, dear. He won't remember any of this in the morning."

Somehow that information gave Janine little comfort. "Does this happen often?"

"No, no." The poodle curls vibrated with a vehement head shake. "Only when he's extremely stressed." Edna lowered her voice to a conspiratorial whisper. "The fire, you know. Jules has been most upset."

"I, uh..." Extricating her hands from the woman's compulsive grip, Janine nervously clutched her robe. "He seemed distraught about his mother."

Moisture swelled in the older woman's eyes. "God in His infinite wisdom has given Jules a mighty cross to bear."

Janine cleared her throat. "Jules...spoke harshly of her."

With a sob, Edna crossed herself and gazed heavenward. When she faced Janine again, tears were sliding down her wrinkled cheeks. "It's true. My daughter was—" she choked back a sob "—a loose woman."

Stunned by the woman's emotional admission, Janine could only stammer, "I'm so sorry."

The sympathy was acknowledged with a weak nod. Edna dabbed her wet eyes and spoke in a quavering voice. "As a child, Jules was exposed to his mother's sinful behavior. It disturbed him deeply."

Janine exhaled slowly. "So it would seem."

"But he's a good boy, truly he is."

"I don't know what to say." Janine massaged her throbbing temples. "I realize that somnambulists have little control over their activities but his behavior tonight was... bizarre." She cleared her throat. "I'm sorry, Edna, but I have other guests to consider—"

"Oh, no. Please." Edna clutched Janine's arm. "My grandson will never bother you again. I know you were frightened but I swear on the blood of our Lord, Jules never would have harmed you. He's not capable of violence."

Although the bruises on her wrist indicated otherwise, Janine was nonetheless moved by the woman's poignant plea. She considered her options. After all, there had been no other incidents during the fifteen months that Jules and Edna had been tenants, and Janine had to admit that the entire town had been jittery since the night of the fire. Besides, evicting Jules meant evicting poor Edna and there simply was nowhere for either of them to go.

Janine sighed. "All right, Edna, but if Jules's nocturnal activities become a problem—"

"They won't, dear. I can promise you that." Eyes shining with gratitude, Edna squeezed Janine's hands, more gently this time. "Bless you. You are a saint." With a damp smile, the older woman waddled out of the kitchen and headed upstairs.

Janine sat heavily at the table, unable to shake the memory of Jules looking at her with such murderous rage. But a moment later he'd behaved like a perplexed child, which supported Edna's contention that he hadn't known what he was doing.

Sighing, Janine propped her head on her hands and tried to be philosophical. Maybe Jules had fallen asleep watching an old James Cagney movie, and she should consider herself fortunate that he hadn't shoved a grapefruit in her face. She hoped that this unpleasantness had been an isolated incident as Edna insisted and that she wouldn't regret the decision to let them stay. At this point, the only thing she knew with any certainty was that she felt more like a sucker than a saint.

Edna felt her way through the dark corridor to her grandson's room. She was surprised to find the door locked because she'd told Jules to expect her.

With trembling fingers, she extracted the secret key from her robe pocket, still shaken to the core by the evil scene she'd witnessed. Jules had put his hands on Janine—had actually touched that sweet, God-fearing woman as though she'd been one of his slutty harlots. Edna shuddered in revulsion. Jules must be punished, of course. It was God's will. Afterward, Edna would hold his dear head to her bosom, stroke his soft hair and explain in great detail that sinful lust could only be drained into the unpurified flesh of whores.

Having reached that decision, Edna relaxed slightly and managed to manipulate the key until the lock clicked. But the door still wouldn't open, and she was stunned to realize that Jules had propped a chair under the knob. To keep her out?

No. That was unthinkable.

She stumbled back a step, numbed by shock, then realized that the poor, confused boy was simply trying to escape Satan's wrath. That was it, of course. Her pathetic grandson had come to his senses, realized that he'd been demonically possessed and was desperately trying to block the devil from entering his room.

Tears stung Edna's eyes at the futility of such a pitiful barricade against the monstrous power of evil. Only prayer could turn back Satan. Prayer and purification of the immortal soul. Closing her eyes, she savored the memory of her beloved daughter's serene face. Marie Louise. How Edna had cherished that beautiful girl. Satan had nearly stolen her but Edna had prevented that final sacrilege. A mother's love is powerful, as powerful as the Almighty Himself.

Edna's lips moved in an inaudible whisper. "I shall save your son, my dearest one. He is flesh of your flesh and the devil shall not have him."

Slipping the key back into her pocket, Edna returned to her own room and knelt piously before the makeshift altar. In the morning, God would exact His punishment on her fallen grandson using Edna as His holy tool. She folded her hands, bowed her head and prayed.

CHAPTER EIGHT

As Janine crossed the ravine bridge, she gazed at the sky and marveled at its clarity after having been washed clean by last night's storm. Thousands of stars glittered like sequins on an obsidian gown and the air smelled freshly scrubbed. It was an invigorating end to the tense and stressful day.

As the weathered planks squeaked under her feet, she recalled that Edna's prediction had been correct. Jules had appeared at breakfast with no apparent memory of what had transpired during the night. In fact, he'd been rather somber, but considering the young man's recent moodiness that wasn't particularly unusual.

Janine had initially been concerned about a discolored puffiness on his left cheek but Edna had explained the minor injury by insisting that her grandson had bumped into a wall while in his somnambulistic state. Although that didn't quite ring true, Janine knew little about sleep disorders and had been reluctant to dispute the theory.

Later, however, Edna had pulled Janine aside with a request that had been startling, to say the least. To prevent future sleepwalking episodes, the woman had actually suggested installing a chain lock on the *outside* of Jules's bedroom door. Janine had adamantly refused, citing safety reasons.

The older woman had been untenably disappointed and, Janine thought, a bit frightened. The entire incident had left a peculiar taste but she'd eventually convinced herself that, however misguided, poor Edna probably had everyone's best interests at heart.

Still she couldn't help fretting. After all, Edna knew her grandson better than anyone. If *she* was worried about what Jules might do...

Janine ignored the disquieting thought and decided that Jules wasn't the only one who watched too much television. As for her own reading material, she silently swore off spine-tingling thrillers until she managed to get a leash on her nerves and her imagination.

Hoisting the grocery bag, she crossed the rear yard and headed toward the kitchen door, pausing to gaze up at Quinn's bedroom window. The room was dark but the outline of a man was dimly illuminated in the moonlight. It was Quinn, of course, with the raven perched on his shoulder.

As always, the sight of him made Janine's heart beat a little faster. She stopped in the shadow of a towering birch and watched in abject fascination. He shifted slightly, resting his hand against the window frame. A glint caught her eye. She realized that he was holding something metallic.

Janine shivered, cold to the bone.

Suddenly his silhouette turned sharply, as if he'd been startled by a sound. He leaned over, and when he straightened, the metallic glint was gone. Then he moved away from the window and turned on a lamp.

A moment later, Janine saw two silhouettes in Quinn's window. One belonged to a woman.

She blinked, stunned. The outline of the backlit female was unfamiliar, having sleek, tightly wrapped hair and wearing loose, flowing garments. Apparently Quinn had made at least one friend during his lengthy absences from the boardinghouse. That was natural, of course, although she had to admit that the idea of Quinn pursuing romantic interests had never entered her mind.

Swallowing a sudden lump, Janine turned away and quietly entered the kitchen. A dull ache spread through her chest. The house had no rules about nonresident guests although even Althea had been discreet enough to conduct her liaisons elsewhere.

Feeling sick and surprisingly angry, Janine put down the grocery bag and leaned against the counter. Tomorrow she'd issue the edict that guests of tenants were not allowed upstairs. Since her other boarders were entitled to their privacy, the rule was certainly reasonable. In fact, she was extremely disappointed that Quinn had breached an unspoken courtesy with such a tawdry display of poor manners. Surely his cheap bimbo could have supplied her own bed—

Cheap bimbo? Janine's hand flew to her face. Good Lord, she didn't even know this person. How could she be so pompous and judgmental?

The answer struck with startling clarity. She was jealous. The very thought of Quinn's strong hands caressing another woman's body made her crazy inside. If Quinn's lover had been within grasp, Janine would have snatched her baldheaded without a qualm.

She sat numbly at the table. Jealous. This was a new and admittedly unpleasant sensation, one she seemed helpless to control. And that was frightening.

Quinn barely recognized the woman who was provocatively stretched across his bed. The modest gown of white chiffon flattered her tanned complexion, and her red-gold hair, brushed to a high gloss, had been twisted at her nape into a demure, schoolmarm bun. Although her delicate gray-green irises were more appealing without the usual globby black outline, they held smoldering promise, a telling characteristic Althea apparently had been unable—or unwilling—to revamp.

Quinn moved the raven to its perch, then folded his arms and regarded his visitor with detached disinterest. "Was there something you wanted?"

After a luxurious stretch, she raised on one elbow, her shiny lips curved into a sensual smile. "It's my night off. I thought you might be in the mood for a game of chess—" she paused, slowly running her pink tongue over her lips "—or something."

"No," he said simply.

Undaunted, she rolled onto her stomach, eyeing him hungrily. "I hear you're good." Her throaty whisper rankled him, as did her obvious double meaning. "Surely you wouldn't begrudge a lady the opportunity of finding out for herself."

"I'm not in the mood for chess."

Althea smiled. "Neither am I."

And Quinn wasn't in the mood for her pitiable seduction, either. He was exhausted, barely able to keep his eyes open. Not surprising, considering that he spent several hours each night pursuing his quest. Last night he'd set his clock for 1:00 a.m. and had barely gotten an hour's sleep when he'd been awakened by voices.

He'd looked into the hallway and seen Edna at her grandson's door. She'd seemed totally distraught but, after a few moments, had gone quietly to her room. A little later, he'd heard Janine come upstairs.

When he'd questioned Janine this morning, she'd said only that Jules had a bad night. No amount of coaxing would pry any more information from her lovely lips. The woman was nothing if not loyal to her tenants' privacy, even when that loyalty was dangerously misplaced.

At any rate, it had been after three in the morning before the sounds from Janine's room had faded so that Quinn could venture out. By the time dawn broke, he'd been so damned close to success that he could actually taste the

sweetness. Tonight his search would be over—the beginning of the end of the madness.

First, however, he had to deal with another problem.

Rubbing his neck, he leaned against the closet door and
eyed Althea warily. "I'm rather tired tonight. Perhaps your
usual partner will be more accommodating."

Her forehead puckered. "Gregore?"

Quinn smiled. "Jules."

"Oh. You mean for chess."

"Is that the only game you and Jules play?"

For a moment, Althea seemed too stunned to move. Then
she suddenly reared into a sitting position, eyes flashing.
"Do I look *that* desperate?" She waved her hand and swung
her feet to the floor. "Never mind. I don't want to know."
Obviously embarrassed, she smoothed her hair and chewed
her lip. The room was silent for a moment. She cleared her
throat and added, "Jules is a child."

"He's twenty-three."

She emitted a derisive snort. "To me, that's a child."

"So Gregore Pawlovski is more your type?"

An expression of pure misery clouded her eyes but she
recovered quickly and angled a seductive glance that seemed
somewhat forced. "*You're* my type, big guy. How about
it?"

He regarded her thoughtfully. "No, thanks. I wouldn't
want any of my friends to end up barbecued."

Althea's eyes darkened ominously. "You've got all the
answers, don't you?" She stood angrily and flounced to the
door. With one hand on the knob, she glared over her
shoulder. "You smug SOB. I hope you rot in hell."

She ripped open the door and stomped into the hall just
as Janine ascended the stairs. "He's all yours," Althea told
her coldly. "You deserve each other."

With that, Althea brushed past the startled landlady and
slammed into her own room. She fell back against the door,

panting. At least the tears wouldn't smear her mascara because she wasn't wearing any. She blinked at the frumpy, middle-aged woman reflected in the mirror and moaned. God, she looked like a freaking nun—bland, dull, sexually vapid.

It had been ridiculous to believe that omitting makeup would add to her appeal. All that blab about Janine's fresh-faced, natural look being so-o-o attractive had been nothing but a big fat joke on Althea. She'd been deliberately duped, coerced into making a blithering fool out of herself. At this very moment, Quinn and Janine were probably tittering their heads off over how gullible she was, how pathetic.

But it would be the last laugh they ever had at her expense. Sex was only one of the things at which she excelled. The other was revenge.

Thirty minutes after Althea slammed out of the house, Janine finished stoking a lovely fire in the parlor fireplace. She carefully closed the screen, laid the poker on the hearth and rubbed her hands in front of the crackling flames, wondering if her residual chill was due to unseasonable weather or the memory of Althea's icy stare. Even thinking about the woman's undisguised hatred gave Janine goosebumps.

She suppressed a shudder, then left the comforting fire to prepare a snack in the kitchen. After setting a pot of water to boil, she pulled a box of crackers from the pantry and retrieved a fat chunk of cheddar from the fridge. As she shaved thin cheese slices, tossing them onto a platter without attention to aesthetics, her mind was elsewhere.

When she'd seen Althea emerge from Quinn's room, she'd almost fainted from shock and relief. Shock because, without the blowsy hairdo and concealing cosmetics, Janine had barely recognized her longtime tenant, and relief because Quinn had quite obviously sent the deflated woman away. For reasons Janine chose not to explore too closely, she was immensely pleased by that.

She was not, however, pleased by the accusation in Althea's angry eyes or the silent inference that somehow Janine was personally responsible for whatever had transpired with Quinn. Although Janine and Althea had never been bosom buddies, their relationship had always been pleasant, almost cordial. Lately, however, Althea had become downright hostile, and Janine didn't have a clue as to why.

It was bizarre but so was everything else that had happened over the past few weeks. Sometimes Janine wondered if she'd fallen down Alice's magical rabbit hole because life around the old Victorian was definitely becoming a perplexing wonderland.

The kettle whistled. With a quiet sigh, she filled the ceramic teapot and then dropped in several tea bags to steep. She lifted the snack platter and headed toward the parlor, planning to calm her nerves with cholesterol and lose herself in a good book, since she now had most of the house to herself. Quinn hadn't appeared since the incident with Althea so Janine assumed that he, like Jules and Edna, had retired early. As for Althea, the poor woman was probably drowning her sorrows somewhere in town, which suited Janine just fine. Unfortunately, Janine was too financially strapped to evict the foul-mouthed woman.

As she entered the parlor, she was surprised to find Quinn staring into the crackling fire. She started to speak but was silenced by his mesmerized expression as he stared into the fireplace, unblinking, transfixed by the dancing flames. The flickering orange glow reflected from his eyes, an eerie, supernatural effect that gave her chills. The rational part of her wanted to back away, dash upstairs and lock herself in her room. The instinctive part simply couldn't leave.

She gently cleared her throat, alerting him. He blinked and looked up, slightly dazed. With the trance broken he was momentarily vulnerable, and his eyes revealed an inner sadness that touched her heart. "Are you all right?" she asked softly.

He frowned, massaging his forehead. "Yes, thank you. I'm fine."

She regarded him silently. He didn't look fine. In fact, he looked like hell, as though he hadn't slept in a month. Now that she thought about it, Quinn frequently appeared tired. Perhaps Jules wasn't the only somnambulist in the house.

After a moment's hesitation, she set the platter on the coffee table. "Do you have a headache? I have aspirin—"

He waved away the offer with a weak smile. "Actually I'd hoped to try some of that chamomile tea you've been touting."

She clucked sympathetically. "Are you having trouble sleeping?"

"Yes, oddly enough." He scoured his eyelids. "As tired as I am, you'd think I'd be out when my head hit the pillow."

She started to ask why he was so tired but thought better of it. That was, after all, prying. Instead she gestured to the platter. "Perhaps the tea will help, and as you can see, you're in luck."

He smiled weakly. "So it seems."

"I'll just get another cup from the kitchen. Help yourself to cheese and crackers."

He touched her arm as she moved toward the door. "Relax. I'll get the cup."

"It's no trouble—"

"Please. You don't have to wait on me, remember?"

She returned his smile. "All right, then. They're in the cupboard over the sink."

As Quinn left the room, Janine watched until he was out of sight, then collapsed onto the sofa breathing hard enough to have run a four-minute mile. Her heart was racing, her mouth was as dry as a desert and even her palms were damp. Physically, she hadn't been so deeply affected since an ill-fated trip to Yosemite when Charles had insisted that Janine take her first—and thankfully last—rock-climbing lesson.

There was no doubt about it. Quinn Coulliard's Lisztian power over women had woven a spell to which even Janine was not immune. Oddly enough, that wasn't particularly upsetting. She was, in fact, secretly thrilled by the unfamiliar sensations coursing through her body. They made her feel—alive.

Janine was so engrossed in thought that she was startled by Quinn's footsteps in the foyer. She barely managed to straighten before he entered the parlor carrying the chipped mug he always used for his morning coffee.

Still rattled by her peculiar reaction to the man, she emitted an uncharacteristic giggle, promptly covered her mouth and stared up in horror.

He looked at the cracked cup in his hand. "Is there some kind of unspoken social rule about using a coffee mug for chamomile tea?"

"No, no. Of course not." Mortified, she cleared her throat and reached shakily for the pot.

Quinn beat her to it. "Let me serve you, for a change."

Considering her sudden attack of nerves, she probably would have dropped the dumb pot, anyway, so she gratefully accepted his offer.

Actually, she rather enjoyed watching a man in torn denims tipping a porcelain pot embossed with delicate pink roses. His muscular forearms were fascinating, and she shamelessly scrutinized the sculpted contours emphasized by a handsome smattering of dark hairs.

The first time she'd touched his arm, she'd been surprised by how soft the hair was, like silken webs spun over solid steel. And his lean hands exuded undeniable strength yet held the fragile china saucer with such infinite care that she found herself wondering if they would caress a lover with the same tenderness.

Hypnotized, she stared at the strong, masculine fingers, the deeply corded wrist, the muscled—

"Janine?"

She blinked and looked up stupidly.

"Your tea."

When she realized that he'd been patiently holding the filled teacup while she'd been fantasizing about his body parts, she was mortally embarrassed. Mumbling her thanks, she took the proffered cup and steadied the saucer on her knee.

Quinn filled the fat mug, then sat beside her and propped an ankle on his knee. The heat emanating from his body rivaled the glowing fire. She averted her gaze, staring at the teacup in her lap and wondering if she dared try to lift it. Since her hands were trembling like windswept leaves, that was probably a bad idea. The last thing she needed at this point was to spill the scalding contents into her lap.

She took a deep breath, slid a covert glance to her left and saw that Quinn was again staring into the flames with that same mesmerized expression. And the same sadness.

She hesitated before lightly touching his wrist. "Is something wrong?"

"Hmm?" He seemed startled by her presence. "I'm sorry. Were you speaking to me?"

"What is making you so unhappy?"

He regarded her for a moment then looked away. "Why do you think that I'm unhappy?"

After retrieving her hand, she set the tea cup on the table. "The look in your eyes. You were a million miles from here."

"Was I?" He smiled weakly. "Perhaps I was. Sorry. I didn't mean to be rude."

"You weren't rude." She turned sideways, bringing her knee up to the cushion. "Do you want to talk about her?"

Tea sloshed over the rim of his mug as Quinn's head jerked around. "I don't know what you mean."

Janine moistened her lips, staring at the wet stain spreading over his denim-clad knee. "The only thing I can think of that would cause the kind of pain I see in your eyes is love...or perhaps the loss of it." She squirmed under his hard stare. After a long moment he set the mug on the coffee table and stubbornly crossed his arms. Janine sighed. "I apologize. Your personal life is none of my business. It's just that—" Biting off the words, she rubbed her face and started to stand. A warm hand settled on her shoulder. She settled back onto the sofa, glancing up expectantly.

Quinn looked at her for a moment. "It's just what?" Apparently she must have looked confused because he questioned her further. "What were you going to say?"

"Oh." Acutely aware that his hand still rested on her shoulder, she fidgeted restlessly. "I'm concerned about you, that's all."

"Why?"

The blunt question surprised her. She glanced up quickly and responded without thinking, "Because I care about you."

Something strange happened then. Quinn's eyes softened as he lifted his hand from her shoulder and lightly caressed her cheek. She closed her eyes, reveling in the exquisite sensation.

Suddenly the warmth of his touch disappeared, and when she looked at him again the glow had drained out of his narrowed gaze. He spoke with a sharpness that stung. "Strays and strangers aren't worth your concern. They're just passing by, and if you get attached you'll be hurt."

She winced at the warning. "That's a rather harsh assessment."

He moved his hand to the back of the sofa. "But nonetheless true."

Without his comforting warmth, a chill swept over her shoulder, and she was unnerved by how quickly he'd re-erected his emotional shields. Somehow she managed to lift her chin and face him directly. "Are you still a stranger, Quinn?"

He had the grace to avert his gaze. "Yes."

"That's unfortunate, considering the personal information I've shared with you." She suppressed a shudder when she recalled all she'd revealed about her life with Charles, then issued a fervent prayer of thanks that she hadn't disclosed everything. "I'd hate to believe that I've opened my heart to someone who has no feelings of friendship for me."

Their eyes held a long moment, his gray gaze probing, searching for something and apparently finding it. "I care deeply for you, Janine. I think you know that."

Her breath slid out all at once. "I care for you, too. That's why I'm concerned."

"Don't be," he whispered miserably. "I'm not worth the effort."

Instantly she touched his jaw, turning him to face her. "A friend once told me that I should never put myself down. I think that's good advice, don't you?"

His eyes widened, sparkling with undisguised amusement at having his own words tossed back in his face. "Yes, it is. Your friend sounds like a smart cookie."

She smiled. "Oh, yes. Sometimes I actually believe that he's brilliant."

Quinn feigned shock. "Only sometimes?"

She managed a nonchalant shrug. "No one is perfect."

"You are." The warm glow returned to his eyes. "In fact, you're the most perfect woman that I've ever known."

Her heart fluttered at the praise. "And have you known a lot of women?" When his gaze narrowed, she could have kicked herself for having blurted such an insensitive question.

To her surprise, however, he answered, "No, not many."

She hesitated, not wanting him to withdraw again yet intrigued by the small vulnerability that he'd revealed. "Are you—" the word momentarily stuck on her tongue "—married?"

With a poignant smile, he slowly shook his head.

If a person could drown in relief, Janine would have died on the spot. Instead she slumped back against the buttoned cushion. "Have you ever been?"

"No." He gazed absently across the room as though weighing something in his mind. Finally he spoke so softly that she barely heard. "I was engaged once."

The sadness in his eyes nearly broke her heart. "The woman in the photograph?"

Without acknowledging her question, he stared into space, rubbing his fingertips with his thumb. A stifling silence fell over the room. Janine had decided that he wasn't going to answer when he finally spoke in a voice that broke only a little. "Her name was Cynthia Zabrow."

That name and the reverence with which he spoke it struck Janine's heart like a dagger. "She's a very beautiful woman."

"Yes."

Focusing on her own wrinkled slacks, Janine wondered what kind of extraordinary woman this Cynthia person must be to ignite the passions of such a special man. A lump wedged in her throat. "You must love her very much."

He blinked, turning his gaze to Janine. "Why do you say that?"

"The look on your face, the softness of your voice when you spoke her name." Frustrated by an unexpected tightness in her own chest, Janine took a deep breath and reached for her teacup. "It's obvious how deeply you care for her."

"Is it?" He considered that for a moment, then answered his own question. "Yes, I suppose it would be. At one time I was very much in love with her."

A small spark of hope ignited when he used the past tense. "The relationship didn't work out?" Wincing under his quizzical stare, she absently twirled the cup around the saucer and stammered an explanation. "It's just that . . . you seemed so sad, I . . . I assumed, well, that you were no longer together. I didn't mean to be insensitive."

"It's all right. I understood what you meant." Quinn laid his palm over her hands to still her fidgety fingers. "Cynthia and I haven't been together for a long time."

"Oh." She managed not to smile. "I'm sorry."

His philosophical shrug seemed a bit forced. "It happens."

"That doesn't make it any easier."

When he didn't respond, Janine took advantage of the silence to take a sip of cold tea. At least she thought it was cold. As she nested the cup in its saucer, she couldn't recall if she'd actually tasted the beverage or had simply gone through the motions.

A million questions peppered her mind. Had Cynthia shared Quinn's love of animals? Of classical music? In other words, had she been *worthy* of being loved by such an extraordinary man? And how could any woman in her right mind have let him go?

It was none of her business, of course. Still, her inquiring mind wanted to know. She cleared her throat. "Were you and Cynthia high school sweethearts?"

His pained expression indicated quite clearly that the subject was as raw as an exposed nerve, yet he answered calmly, and the emotion in his eyes never reached his flat voice. "I met her at the rehabilitation center. She was a patient."

Stunned, Janine moved the rattling cup and saucer from her lap to the table. "Isn't that against some kind of ethical code? Doctors dating their patients, that is."

"Cynthia was under the care of another counselor so she wasn't actually my patient." Leaning back, he slid his arm along the sofa back and stared thoughtfully into space. "That's a technicality, I suppose, but it was enough to rationalize any qualms."

"Did you have qualms? About becoming involved with her, that is."

He considered that. "In retrospect, perhaps. At the time, I was too enamored to consider the consequences."

"What consequences?" Instantly alarmed, she blurted, "Were you fired?"

"Excuse me?"

"For becoming involved with a patient?" She blushed at his astonished stare. "I mean, you mentioned that you weren't working there anymore and I just thought that..." Unable to dig herself out of the verbal mess, she simply allowed the words to die naturally.

"I didn't lose my position because of the relationship," he said finally. "Cynthia had completed the rehabilitation process before our engagement was announced. At least, I'd hoped that she had."

Janine didn't understand the vague statement and said so.

Quinn massaged his eyelids. "Cynthia's parents had both been alcoholics. The addiction was genetically ingrained in the family. She had a difficult time in treatment."

"What happened?"

"Eventually Cynthia decided that life was unbearable without a little whiskey to soften the edges. She couldn't cope with sobriety. When she was forced to choose..." His voice broke and he shook his head. "I couldn't compete with her addiction."

Janine tried to imagine how any woman could have ever chosen a bottle of booze over a man who quite obviously adored her. The rejection must have wounded him deeply. Janine saw the raw hurt in his eyes and was touched by it.

She laid a consoling hand on his thigh, oblivious to the intimate nature of her touch. "Cynthia was a fool. You deserve better."

Quinn glanced up, startled. Then his lips curved in a slow, sensual smile that warmed Janine to her toes. "That was a nice thing to say."

"I mean it," she insisted fervently. "Any other woman would have given all she owned to be in Cynthia's place. I can't sympathize with anyone who could throw away a chance for love and spurn the man who had offered it. It's inconceivable to me."

"Yes," he murmured. "I can see that it is." He lifted her hand and lightly brushed his lips across her palm. "Perhaps only those who have experienced loss and betrayal can understand the true value of love."

Her hand tingled under his touch. When he pressed his lips to the sensitive pulse point at her wrist, she sucked in a sharp breath and hoped she wouldn't faint. With a boldness that shocked her, she touched the side of his face. His skin was warm and slightly rough where a day-old beard shadowed his jaw. The pleasant, scratchy sensation made her fingertips itch for more.

When he lifted his mouth from her wrist, his eyes darkened with sensual awareness. There was a hunger in his gaze that took her breath away. He touched her face, caressing her brow with his thumb before moving his hand around to cradle her head. "There's something about you, Janine. When I look into your eyes, it's like seeing sunshine after an arctic winter. You make me feel things that I haven't felt in a very long time."

His voice was so seductive, his gaze so intense that Janine feared her insides would simply melt away. When his lips finally took hers, the dull throb in her belly exploded, igniting sparks hotter than the crackling blaze. Her lips parted, an invitation he accepted with a searing passion that affected her more deeply than anything she'd ever experienced.

For the first time in her life, she wanted a man. This man.

Even in the fuzzy recesses of her passion-drugged brain, she realized that Quinn alone had the power to make her feel like a whole woman. He made her feel beautiful and cherished. Locked in his embrace, Janine believed that she was special—that what they shared was unique only to them. Quinn Coulliard was her soul mate, the man who shared the passions of her spirit, who could breathe new life into her traumatized body.

Suddenly she was gasping for breath and vaguely aware that his lips were generating a moist trail of heat down her throat. She moaned softly, arching her neck to allow him greater access.

"Lavender and lilacs," he murmured against her pulsing skin. "The pastel scents of spring. You smell so sweet it makes my head spin."

A sharp female voice shattered the moment. "Oh, gag me."

With a gasp, Janine looked over her shoulder just as Quinn's head jerked up.

Althea stood in the doorway, with one hand propped on her hip, snapping her gum and eyeing them both with exaggerated disgust. "Since you've obviously gone into heat, the least you can do is rut privately so the rest of us don't have to watch."

Janine was mortified to the bone.

Quinn, however, simply leaned back and smiled lazily. "Makes you hungry, does it?"

Althea flushed to her roots. "It makes me sick."

"In that case, maybe you'd better close the parlor door on your way out." Although Quinn's smile remained frozen in place, his eyes issued a warning that brought Althea's hand to her throat.

"I'm not a servant. Close the damn door yourself." Fixing Janine with a final malevolent stare, Althea spun and headed up the stairs with every vile name she'd ever heard rolling through her furious mind. She'd show them. They'd regret this humiliation.

Panting, she went straight to Jules's room, and after a quick glance to insure that no one had followed, she tapped lightly on the door. "Jules," she whispered thickly. "Open up. It's Althea." A frantic rustling emanated from inside the room. She heard his closet door snap shut, and after a moment the knob turned. She spoke to the dark eyeball peering through a crack in the door. "We have to talk. Let me in."

The eye widened, rolled to the right and to the left, then the door opened. Althea breezed in, raking her fake fingernails through her ratty hair.

After a final peek down the hallway, Jules closed the door. Obviously uncomfortable with the unexpected invasion, he self-consciously smoothed the crisply ironed lapels of his pajama top. "You seem distressed," he said finally.

Althea threw her head back and laughed.

"Shh!" Jules's panicked gaze spun around the room. "Someone will hear."

Since alienating the frightened young man wouldn't be to her advantage, Althea apologized with a pretty pout, then slid him a shifty glance. "You haven't seemed too happy lately. What's happening?"

Jules sighed dramatically. "Things haven't been going well."

"I've noticed." She folded her arms. "Actually, life around here soured the minute Coulliard arrived. I mean, no one is paying any attention to you anymore. Your grandmother's always fussing over *him,* filling up *his* coffee cup, smoothing *his* hair...." She paused while the young man nodded glumly. "If I were you, hon, I'd be pretty peeved about our new neighbor."

"Coulliard has spoiled everything," Jules replied somberly. "I wish he'd drop dead and blow away."

"Maybe we can arrange that." Smiling broadly, Althea tossed a chummy arm around his thin shoulders. "Auntie Althea has a plan."

CHAPTER NINE

Janine slowly opened her eyes, vaguely aware that the heat in her belly was slowly draining away. A peculiar emptiness settled over her, a disappointment to have been awakened. She'd had that dream again, the one about Quinn. It had been glorious. It had been frightening.

Moistening her lips, she squinted at the red LED numbers on her clock radio and moaned. It wasn't even two in the morning. She flopped back onto the pillow wondering if she'd ever sleep again. The fire was easing from her body, but her mind was alive, tormented by sweet memories, not only of the dream but of what had happened in the parlor—before she and Quinn had been so crudely interrupted.

Janine didn't even try to suppress her resentment of Althea. The woman was vulgar and malicious and quite obviously jealous as sin. Having recently encountered the green-eyed monster herself, she could at least understand what had driven Althea to behave so badly. But that didn't excuse such crassness, and Janine was still upset that, after the cantankerous woman had left, Quinn's demeanor had changed markedly. He'd instantly withdrawn and become distant, acting as if the closeness they'd shared had meant nothing.

Then he'd chastely kissed Janine's cheek, thanked her for the tea that he hadn't even tasted and said good-night, leaving her frustrated, stunned and emotionally bereft.

Even the memory of how she'd stood there staring at the empty parlor for God knows how long was embarrassing to her. What had she expected Quinn to do—take her right there on the sofa?

And was that what she'd really wanted?

Sighing, she turned over, beat the feather pillow into submission and rammed her head into the resultant dent. She squeezed her eyes shut, waited a moment, flipped over, waited another moment, then threw off the covers and fanned her face with her hand.

It was going to be a long night.

A sound in the hallway caught her attention. She sat up, listening. She heard one soft click follow another as Quinn's door opened and closed.

Sliding out of bed, she tiptoed to her door, cracked it open and peeked into the hall. She saw nothing except the dim shadows cast by the tiny stair lights. After several seconds, she'd nearly convinced herself that she'd been hearing things when Quinn's door suddenly opened again.

Janine quickly closed the crack to a mere sliver, twisting awkwardly to peer through the narrow opening. Quinn emerged fully clothed and carrying a flashlight. He fiddled with the battery compartment, tapped the tapered handle on his palm, then flipped the switch and tested the beam.

Apparently satisfied, he moved stealthily down the hallway using the flashlight to illuminate his way. When he reached the stair landing, he swept the beam around the wall. Janine opened her door a bit wider to get a better view and was completely baffled by the odd sight.

As she watched in fascination, the circular light beam rotated from ceiling to floor then settled on the enameled wainscoting that paneled the lower third of the wall. Quinn's hand slid smoothly along the cap molding. To Janine's utter shock there was a faint creaking and an entire section of wall suddenly yawned open. After glancing furtively around, Quinn slipped inside the opening and disappeared. A moment later, the wall segment swung back into place with a soft click.

Janine blinked, rubbed her eyes and stared out into the deserted hallway. Unless this was the world's most realistic dream, the old bordello really *did* have a secret tunnel. And Quinn Coulliard had located the entrance.

Excitement, anticipation and a hint of dread mingled together and slid down her spine. Entering the hall, she moved stealthily toward the landing and inspected the segment behind which Quinn had just disappeared. Considering the original purpose of the tunnel, the entrance location was perfect, easily accessible from the upstairs bedrooms or from the downstairs community areas. Janine didn't know how in the world Quinn had ever found the perfectly concealed doorway, but he'd obviously spent considerable time searching for it. She wondered why.

Without a flashlight her vision was limited, but she ran her fingers over the molding as Quinn had done and to her shock found a spot where the wood felt mushy. Her heart leaped like a triumphant trout. She'd found the latch.

Now she should go directly back to bed and confront Quinn about his discovery in the morning. That's exactly what she should do.

Of course, *should* was the operative word, as common sense argued with a newly discovered sense of adventure. She wanted to pull the covers over her head and ignore what she'd seen, but she also wanted desperately to follow him. The mental discussion was foolish. Janine had always done the right thing, the safe thing. It was her nature.

So when she returned to her room, she didn't have a clue as to why she was suddenly pulling on a pair of jeans and lacing up her sturdy hiking shoes. After shrugging into a warm sweatshirt, Janine was halfway down the hall before she snapped her fingers and returned to her room.

Two minutes later, with flashlight in hand, Janine pressed the hidden lever and the panel swung aside to expose a five-foot-wide space concealed behind the wall.

Gingerly moving inside, she held the panel open with one foot and used the light beam to explore the area. She was surrounded by exposed studs from which a few rusted nails were protruding. An oil lantern hung from one of the nails. The antique was dusty but not coated with the thick, grimy film she would have expected from an item supposedly undisturbed for the past ninety years.

Tucking that observation away, she continued to inspect the tiny enclosure and saw that, as expected, the plank floor was dirty with dried mud clods scattered about. A trapdoor had been propped open, exposing an antiquated wooden ladder descending into the bowels of the house. She eyed it with considerable trepidation. Of course, if Quinn had climbed down the rickety thing, then she could certainly manage it. But that meant releasing the door panel and she wasn't about to close herself in until she'd figured how to get back out.

That didn't take long. She spotted a wooden latch attached to a stud beside the opening. Closer scrutiny revealed that the lever was directly linked to the locking mechanism. She tested it several times, assured herself that it was indeed the lock release, then tested it again.

After a reluctant moment, she took a deep breath, pulled the panel closed and carefully descended the ladder. Claustrophobia tightened her stomach. Feeling nauseated, she moved lower, testing each splintered rung with her foot before daring to put her full weight on it. Because of her death grip on the flashlight, only one hand was free to hold the side rail, making the descent even more precarious.

By the time Janine stepped from the rotting ladder into a horizontal passageway, she was well below the Victorian's basement level. Like an old mining tunnel, the underground alley was reinforced with two-by-fours and extended well beyond the scope of Janine's vision. It was damp and cold and smelled musty.

The ground was littered with junk from another era—a rusty snuff tin, bent nails, a couple of dented food cans and another antique oil lamp—along with evidence of more recent visitations. She spotted a pair of rubber galoshes caked with dried mud, a couple of discarded flashlight batteries and a wadded plastic grocery bag.

As she moved farther into the passageway she noticed an odd reflection from a broken piece of hard plastic half-buried in the damp earth. She picked it up, noting that it was a smooth white tube about an eighth of an inch in diameter with no recognizable function. Extruded plastics had only been available for the past few decades, so she considered the shattered tube as a good indication that the tunnel had been traversed in modern times.

After tossing the broken plastic aside, Janine continued to pick her way through the darkness with considerably more empathy for the plight of the world's gopher population. She didn't like the closed-in feeling of being surrounded by earth. It was unnatural, spooky and definitely not for the faint of heart—like herself. Each breath seemed more difficult than the last, and after several long minutes, she was assaulted by an almost overwhelming desire to claw the packed dirt with her fingers. She had to get out. She had to—

Then she saw it, a shaft of dappled moonlight marking the tunnel's exit. With a massive sigh of relief, Janine hurried forward, anxious to emerge from the confining corridor and taste fresh air.

The opening was obscured by bushes and, she assumed, nearly invisible from the other side. Getting through the brush might be a bit tricky. Although she probably should have spent a few minutes searching for a neater exit, the stagnant passageway felt like a grave so she thrashed clumsily through the leafy barrier and stumbled outside.

Janine managed one gasping breath before something hard and warm covered her mouth. Instantly she was yanked backward with stunning force and dragged into the woods like struggling prey.

Kicking and clawing, Janine realized only vaguely that her fingernails were digging into the flesh of a human arm. A steely hand was muffling her screams, and she wondered if the slab of granite pressed against her back was her assailant's chest. Doubling both fists, she struck backward at a point above her own head and pummeled at what she hoped was a skull.

A yelp of pain indicated that she'd hit her mark.

Before she could take satisfaction from that, she was released and spun around so quickly that her teeth rattled. "What in hell do you think you're doing?"

She squinted into the angry face looming inches above her own. "Quinn?"

"You were expecting someone else?" He gave her shoulders a final shake, then let go. When he stood back, his unfettered hair flowed in the soft wind giving him a frightening, almost savage appearance. "You little fool. You could have been killed."

She eyed him sullenly. "Isn't that a bit melodramatic?"

Without responding, he tucked something shiny in his waistband and swore under his breath.

When Janine recognized the handgrip of a weapon jutting from beneath his leather jacket, she stiffened. "Is that a gun?"

He silently rubbed his temple.

"It *is* a gun. My God, why do you have a gun, Quinn? What are you planning to shoot?" Stumbling a step back, Janine clutched the neck of her sweatshirt, realizing that anything could have crept from the woods into the tunnel.

Lord, she could have run into a mountain lion . . . or worse. "Wild animals? Is that it? Were you expecting to run into a bear or something?"

"Right. An animal." Obviously disgusted, Quinn wiped his face with hands and peered over his fingertips. "Unless you want to wake up the entire town, I'd suggest that you lower your voice."

"The town?" She blinked, glancing around the unfamiliar woods. "Where are we, anyway?"

"In the ravine just below the lumberyard."

"You must be joking. That's over a mile from the house."

"It is if you cross at the bridge but the tunnel cuts a path straight through. If we were to ford the creek and climb that embankment, we'd be within spitting distance of downtown."

"I don't believe it." The weak denial was perfunctory, of course. In point of fact, Janine did believe what Quinn had told her because it made perfect sense. For the brothel's clients to have consistently escaped undetected, the tunnel would have to lead nearly to the center of town. And it did.

Of course, the embankment in question was a couple hundred feet high and so thickly wooded that visibility in any direction was limited to a few dozen feet. That concealment, however, would have been a real boon to red-faced residents attempting to slink away from the naughty recreation facility.

Janine sighed. "All right. You've proven that the old legend was true. But I don't understand why you had to be so . . . so covert about it."

"That should be obvious. I didn't want anyone to know." His jaw tightened. "And you aren't to say a word about this, do you understand? Not one word."

"But why not? The tunnel has no significance now except for historical interest. In fact, the town librarian will be ecstatic when she finds out ab—"

"No!" Frustrated, Quinn took hold of her arms. "Listen to me, Janine. It is crucial, absolutely crucial that you tell no one about the tunnel."

Even in the moonlight she recognized fear in his eyes and something else she couldn't quite identify. "If secrecy is so important, then you'd darn well better explain why."

"I can't." Obviously agitated, Quinn raked the waterfall of hair cascading down his back. "You'll have to trust me."

Her breath caught as echoes of an earlier warning reverberated through her mind. *Trust no one . . . especially me.*

When he unexpectedly touched her face, she jumped away and his hand fell to his side. "I don't enjoy frightening you, Janine."

She stepped warily back, her gaze automatically dropping to the weapon tucked in his waistband. He seemed different tonight. With that untamed mass of hair flowing free, he was a magnificent warrior, a throwback to another time. Wild. Dangerous. Exciting.

"You do frighten me," she whispered, realizing even as she spoke that her alarm was caused more by her own burgeoning desire than by him. But then, he had caused that desire. He was responsible for the slow heat spreading through her, turning her knees to jelly. Yes, he *did* frighten her. Almost as much as she frightened herself.

He watched her silently, intently, as if gazing deep inside her and finding the unspoken message etched on her quivering heart. Then he reached out to caress her cheek with his fingertip. "Perhaps that's best," he murmured. "Fear breeds caution. Always be cautious, Janine. Trust is the great betrayer."

She swallowed hard, shivering as his touch slid along her jawline. "Yet you ask me to trust you."

"I know." His eyes closed for a moment. "Everything will be clear to you in a few days. Can you give me that?"

She considered his plea. "And if I don't give you that time? If I tell about the tunnel, what will happen then?"

"You will be in grave danger," he said simply. "I may not be able to protect you."

That got her attention. "Protect me from what? From whom?"

He slid a fingertip along her jaw. "From those who would take advantage."

"Advantage—" she gasped as his knuckle skimmed the side of her neck "—of what? And why must the tunnel be kept secret?"

But even as the murmured question emerged from her quivering lips, the answer didn't matter as long as Quinn was touching her, stroking her throat with hypnotic tenderness.

Her muscles turned to butter. She took a shuddering breath, then did something so bold she wondered if she'd been possessed. Turning her face, she rubbed her cheek against the back of his hand and touched his wrist with her lips.

Quinn stiffened but made no move to stop her as she turned over his hand and kissed his palm. There was such strength in his hands, she thought dreamily, a sense of security that was an odd paradox to his aura of mystery. His scent surrounded her, an erotic mingling of masculine fragrances—soap and forest and maleness—a heady combination that made her head spin.

Suddenly Quinn framed her face with his hands and questioned her with his eyes. When he finally spoke, his voice was husky. Broken. "Janine...do you understand what you're doing?"

Oddly enough, she did. "Yes."

He lowered his gaze, just for a moment, then looked at her so softly that her breath caught in her throat. "I should send you away."

A tiny panic sparked in her chest. "Are you going to?"

After a lingering silence, he sighed. "I haven't got the strength."

Standing on her tiptoes, she brushed her lips over his, tentatively at first, then again with more confidence. His mouth was warm, moist, enticing. He returned her kiss without demanding more, empowering her to set the pace. It was a new sensation, one that both thrilled and perplexed her. She'd expected him to take over. Instead she was suddenly in control, and *he* was responding to *her*.

This was certainly an unexpected development. She chewed her lower lip and stared at his chest. "What should I do now?"

"What would you like to do?"

Her gaze narrowed. "Don't you dare psychoanalyze me."

"That is the last thing I had in mind."

Feeling silly, she touched his collarbone with her fingertips and stated the obvious. "I'm not very experienced with this kind of situation."

"I know." He tipped up her chin and smiled gently. "That's what makes you so appealing."

Before she could respond, Quinn took her lips in a kiss so deep, so completely shattering, that her knees nearly buckled. Embracing her tightly, he parted her lips and explored the softness beyond until she was whimpering and writhing against him.

The slow heat building in her core ignited into an erotic inferno, melting her inhibitions and making her wild with need. When his mouth moved to her throat, she clutched at his shoulders, gasping for breath, making tiny mewing sounds that she barely recognized as her own. Electric sparks encircled her ribs, and she vaguely realized that he'd slipped his hand beneath her loose sweatshirt.

Her lips parted in a silent cry as his fingers massaged the soft flesh beneath her unbound breasts. She was on fire, burning with a passion she'd never experienced. Every nerve in her body screamed, and without conscious permission her back arched an invitation for a more intimate touch.

When his palm teased her sensitive nipple, she moaned aloud. He took her breast in his hand, kneading the soft flesh, rolling the hardened tip between his fingers, caressing her so sweetly she thought the sheer ecstasy would kill her.

Then he stepped back, lifted her shirt and cherished her with his eyes. "You're beautiful," he murmured. "So very beautiful." He kissed each breast reverently, using his lips to expand the exquisite torture.

With her fingers tangled in the silken mass of his hair, Janine emitted a strangled sound and realized that her legs would no longer support her. As she collapsed under the sweet assault, Quinn caught her and gently lowered her to the leaf-strewn ground.

She lay there, taking air in broken gasps, watching, waiting, wondering how she could have lived for twenty-six years without ever having experienced such rapture. As Quinn knelt beside her, she trembled in awe and anticipation. He gazed at her as though she was the loveliest creature alive, and for that moment, for that blessed moment, Janine actually felt like a beautiful, desirable woman.

Murmuring her name, Quinn slid his thumb down her cheek, allowing his touch to linger at her lips. Suddenly he pulled off his jacket, then cupped her head, urging her to turn so he could spread the leather garment beneath her. After he'd removed his T-shirt and jeans, he arranged them to shield her hips and legs from the forest clutter.

To Janine, the small act of kindness was chivalry of gigantic proportions. No man had ever treated her so gallantly, with such tender consideration. The gesture moved her to tears.

Instantly concerned, Quinn touched the dampness on her face. "Have I hurt you?"

"Oh, no." She wiped her eyes, and suddenly noticed how beautiful his bare chest was. Reaching out, she touched him, marveling at the strength hidden beneath the smooth, warm skin. "I—I love the way you touch me."

He brushed a strand of hair from her face. "Do you?"

"Yes." The word was more a sigh than a whisper.

Her fingers found their way to his furred thighs and delicately traced a path to his knee. His muscles trembled and she was thrilled to realize that he was as affected by her touch as she was by his.

Finally he lowered himself to the ground, ignoring the sharp twigs and prickly leaves as he stretched full-length beside her. Propping himself on one elbow, he bent to kiss her. His lustrous hair swept her face and pooled around her bare breasts. Like in her dream, she thought groggily and wondered if it was really happening.

Then Quinn's kiss deepened and she knew without doubt that this was no dream. His hands caressed her more boldly, sliding down her belly and over her thighs until his heat permeated through her jeans into the marrow of her bones.

Her head moved from side to side, slowly at first, then thrashing wildly as primitive instinct took control. Moaning frantically, her fingers curled into fists, and she lifted her hips in response to his whispered request. Air brushed her thighs as he slid off the denim barrier. Then her lacy panties were swept smoothly away.

Except for the fleece bunched under her arms, Janine was completely exposed yet too drugged by passion to feel vulnerable as Quinn explored her body with gentle strokes, arousing her into a crazed frenzy of desire. With a soft cry, she pulled at his shoulders until he moved over her.

Somewhere in the deepest recesses of her brain, a joyous voice cried out that she wasn't dead inside, that she was a real woman, with a woman's body and a woman's needs. Charles had been wrong.

Charles.

The memory hit like ice water as a throbbing pressure moved between her thighs. She went rigid. Her eyes flew open and she nearly cried out in terror. It was Charles's face looming over her, mouth contorted, eyes glowing with perverse pleasure.

She remembered the pain, how he'd enter her roughly and berate her sexuality between grunting thrusts. *Like making love to a corpse,* he'd snarl. *Ice between your legs.* Then he'd slap her face. *Move, bitch. Cry, so I know you're alive.* The insults would continue until his final, shuddering release.

Afterward he'd push her away and leap from her bed as though contaminated by her ineptness. She could still see the disgust and condemnation in her husband's face. He'd called her frigid and worse, telling her that she'd never be a whole woman, never be able to pleasure a real man.

Quinn was a real man. She couldn't bear to disappoint him, to experience his contempt. Panic surged up like a bitter bile. Terrified, she tried to twist away and beat wildly on his chest. "No, stop! *No!*"

Stunned by the sudden attack, Quinn stared at her for a moment, then quickly moved away.

Freed, Janine rolled onto her side and pulled up her knees. "I—I can't. I j-just can't." With a broken cry, she started to sob uncontrollably.

"What is it, Janine?" Quinn sounded distraught. He laid a comforting hand on her shoulder. "Who's done this to you?"

All she could do was shake her head miserably and try not to choke on her own tears. Suddenly Quinn gathered her in his arms, murmuring soothing words and rocking her as though she were a wounded child. "It's all right, honey. No one is going to hurt you ever again."

Janine hiccuped and covered her face with her hands. Quinn continued to hold her until her sobs had receded into silent humiliation, then he gently pulled down her sweatshirt and helped her on with her clothes.

Once dressed, she scooted under a tree, hugged her shins and laid her forehead on her knees, wishing she would die on the spot. She felt like a fool. She *was* a fool. How could she have put herself in such a vulnerable position?

A cracking twig alerted her to Quinn's movements, and as footsteps crunched across the thick blanket of dried foliage on the forest floor, she stiffened without looking up. From beneath her folded arms she saw his sneakers and the bottom of his jeans, then his denim-clad thighs as he knelt in front of her.

He stroked her head. "Are you feeling better?"

"No." She wiped her face on her sleeve. "I'm so ashamed."

"You have nothing to be ashamed of." His palm slid around to cup the back of her neck. After a moment, he spoke with a hesitation that seemed strange for such a confident man. "Are you upset about something I did?"

The statement was so ludicrous that her head snapped up. "You? Of course not. It's me. It's always been me."

He frowned. "Always? I don't understand."

Chewing her lip, she absently brushed a dried leaf from his T-shirt. "I warned you that I...wasn't very good at this sort of thing."

He pursed his lips thoughtfully. "What sort of thing are you referring to?"

A covert glance confirmed that he wasn't making fun of her. She fiddled with a twig that had tangled in her shoelaces. "You know. Sex."

"Ah. Is that what we were doing?"

Her face flamed. "It's what we were *trying* to do."

"I think not." He urged her to look at him. "We were sharing an intimacy, exploring each other, preparing to make love. That's a great deal different, to my mind, than simply having sex."

Since the two phrases had been used interchangeably during her marriage, Janine couldn't see any definable difference and said so.

"Who told you that?" Quinn asked.

"Charles."

"Your husband."

"My *ex*-husband."

"Of course." He regarded her thoughtfully. "Let me guess. You married quite young, and although your husband was considerably older and more experienced, you went to him as a virgin. Am I close?"

If her face grew any hotter, Janine was certain that she'd start to glow. Since she couldn't choke out a word, she simply nodded.

Quinn rubbed his chin. "I would also guess that during the course of your relationship, you didn't enjoy intimacy very much."

"I don't want to talk about this." She started to stand but he stopped her with a light touch.

"I think you do. I think something is eating you up inside, and you want desperately to talk about it."

Folding her arms, she leaned back against the rough bark and stared at her knees. "I've already apologized to you. I don't know what else to say."

"You have no reason to apologize to me or anyone else. Lovemaking is a very special experience but only if it's mutually enjoyable. No one is entitled to the use of your body." He studied her reaction then added, "Not even a husband."

She averted her gaze.

"Is that what happened, Janine? Did your husband rape you?"

The word horrified her. "Certainly not! I mean, that's not even possible, is it?"

"If you didn't consent to intercourse, then it was rape."

"Of course I consented. Charles was my husband. I wanted to please him. I wanted to be a good wife but... but..." Her throat closed up.

Quinn covered her trembling hand with his palm. "But what?"

She looked away miserably. "There was something wrong with me."

Since Quinn looked like he'd been gut-kicked, that obviously wasn't what he'd expected to hear. "What do you mean, something was wrong with you?"

"I, uh..." Her gaze darting, she searched for escape. Finding none, she slumped in resignation. "I'm frigid."

He sat back on his heels and stared in disbelief. After what seemed like an eternity, he sat on the blanket of crisp leaves and started to chuckle softly.

Janine's head snapped up. "Do you think that's funny?"

"Funny? God, no." Biting away his smile, he took her hands. "Listen to me, Janine. You're not, I repeat, *not* frigid. You are, in fact, the most passionate woman I've ever known. I have the scratches to prove it."

She would have blushed had she not been so stunned. "You don't understand. Charles said—"

Quinn interrupted roughly. "I don't give a damn what 'Charles' said. The man was obviously a sadistic boor who got some perverse sexual gratification out of tormenting you."

The entire concept was just too much for her. She couldn't cope with the sudden flood of emotions, the confusing quagmire of horror, denial, shame and hope all rolled together in a jumbled mass. All she could feel was numb disbelief, a complete unwillingness to accept that a man who'd professed love would have deliberately used her in such a vile way. She stared straight ahead like a shell-shocked soldier. "That's not true. Charles had normal, healthy needs just like any other man. I . . . simply couldn't fulfill those needs."

"What makes you think that?"

Wincing at the memory, she closed her eyes and shuddered. "B-Because other women could."

A warm arm slid around her shoulder. "Did your husband have an affair?"

Squeezing her lids even more tightly shut, she managed a curt nod.

"More than one?"

Her head drooped in response. When he gave her shoulder a comforting squeeze, she found the courage to speak. "Charles had lots of women."

"How do you know that?"

She made an unpleasant sound. "Everyone knew. He wasn't very discreet. At first, people used to tell me that he was at this restaurant or that hotel, always with a different woman. Eventually he flaunted his affairs so openly that it wasn't news anymore. People just accepted it. In that society, an affair was okay. A divorce wasn't."

"And you accepted it, too."

She shrugged. "At the time, I thought it was my fault."

"Why?"

"Because those women would . . ." The disgusting words clogged in her throat. She shook her head miserably.

Quinn caressed her face, offering gentle encouragement. "What would the women do, Janine?"

"I can't say. It's too . . . sordid." Tears slid down her cheeks.

She couldn't talk about what had happened, yet she couldn't *not* talk about it. After so many years of humiliating silence, the anger festered just below the surface, threatening to explode if she didn't relieve the pressure. Quinn's gentle questions had opened the floodgates. She couldn't hold back the emotional deluge.

"Charles would tell me everything," she suddenly blurted. "He'd come home smirking and force me to listen to the lurid details of what his 'real' women had done for him. Then he'd try to make me do the same things. I—I wouldn't." A sob caught in her throat. "I wouldn't...I wouldn't...I would—"

"Shh, it's all right." He caught her wrist in midair.

Janine stared at him stupidly before realizing that she'd been pounding her legs with her fists. With a shocked whimper, she fell into Quinn's arms and cried.

He stroked her tenderly. "Don't you see what he was doing, honey? None of it was about sex. It was about domination and control. Your husband simply used sex as a tool for degradation because it made him feel powerful."

Even through her choked sobs, his words impacted like a sledgehammer. *Power.* Dear God, it was true. She looked up, searching Quinn's soft gray gaze and realizing that he was right. The emotional abuse she'd suffered had been nothing more than the cruel manipulation of a brutal man. It had been insidious and painful, yes, but it had never been an accurate reflection of her femininity. She moistened her lips as the potent revelation hit home. "So there's nothing wrong with me?"

"Nothing about you is the least bit wrong." His lips brushed her forehead. "You are a beautiful, desirable and passionately *real* woman."

Overwhelmed by sensations she couldn't identify, she caressed his cheek. "If I had any doubt that my hormones are healthy and functioning normally, what happened between us seems proof that they are."

Quinn averted his gaze, and when he looked at Janine again, she was stung by the desolation in his eyes. "You've been through a lot. It's only natural that you're feeling a bit mixed up right now."

"Mixed up about what?"

"Don't confuse gratitude with something deeper. I'm no good for you, Janine. I'm no good for anybody." Releasing her, he abruptly stood. "The sun will be up soon. We have to leave."

After a hesitant moment, Janine took his proffered hand and allowed him to help her up. As they entered the tunnel, her mind was elsewhere. Quinn's brusque warning had taken her by surprise because she knew that her feelings for him had evolved beyond mere gratitude. In fact, she wondered if she was falling in love with him yet was nonetheless plagued by doubt.

In spite of his soft-spoken manner, Quinn Coulliard exuded an aura of danger that was both chilling and thrilling. Janine was playing with fire and she knew it.

After shushing Edgar's noisy greeting, Quinn sat heavily on the bed and rubbed his aching head. For the most part, his plan had gone beautifully. Once he'd remembered seeing muddy splotches on the upstairs carpet, his search had narrowed considerably. The mud—which he'd ascertained to be a smeared footprint—had appeared the day after the Barker fire, and since there had been no stains on the stairway or anywhere else in the upstairs hall, the tunnel entrance had to be within a few steps of that footprint. And it was.

After that small victory, though, things had unraveled fast. He certainly hadn't expected Janine to follow nor had he expected the raw passion that had suddenly exploded between them.

With an angry grunt, he slammed his fist into the mattress, ignoring the raven's startled screech. The rage still burned in his gut, a white-hot fury at the filthy snake who'd so cruelly defiled such a sweet, trusting woman. At that moment, Quinn would have given ten years of his life for one hour alone with that cowardly worm.

Frustrated, he stood and paced the small room, fingers raking through his long hair. His anger wasn't limited to Janine's ex-husband; he was also furious with himself. Not only had he been powerless to heal her pain, but he was also disgusted by his own weakness in wanting to. The woman was getting to him, and Quinn simply couldn't allow that to happen. He had to control himself, to focus on what must be done. It was a matter of life or death.

CHAPTER TEN

Janine fiddled with the switch on her ancient vacuum, greatly annoyed that the stubborn thing refused to work. Only the painful memory of the toe she'd once broken prevented her from giving the recalcitrant machine a swift kick.

This was a frustration she didn't need. A new vacuum was beyond her pitiful budget, and the cost of repairs would probably exceed what the dismal old unit was worth.

Muttering irritably, she dragged the useless vacuum back to the kitchen and shoved it into a closet. There was nothing she could do with it at the moment, and besides, if she didn't start cooking, dinner would be delayed and her guests would be even crankier than usual. If that was possible, of course, which she doubted. All of her tenants had been so testy Janine was beginning to wonder if there were grump germs in the well water.

As she hauled a bag of potatoes from the pantry, the telephone rang. After hoisting the lumpy sack onto the counter, she tucked the wall phone receiver under her chin. "Taylor's Boardinghouse."

An agitated female voice greeted her. "Is Jules there?"

"Edna?" Janine dropped a wet potato in the sink and glanced at the clock. "No, he's not. I assumed he was on his way to the clinic to pick you up."

The woman clucked in dismay. "I've been waiting for half an hour. Jules is never late, never."

A quick look out the kitchen window confirmed that Edna's car was still parked outside, although Althea's vehicle—and Quinn's—were both missing. "I guess they're not back yet."

"They?" Edna's voice rose to a squeak.

"It's all right, Edna. Jules is with Althea."

A horrified gasp filled the receiver. "Are they...alone?"

Although baffled by Edna's sudden apprehension about Jules and Althea being alone together, Janine sought to calm the agitated woman. "When Althea works the early shift, she and Jules frequently spend the afternoon at the video arcade. They must have lost track of time, that's all."

Obviously that tidbit of information was news to Edna. "The devil's victory," she whispered ominously. "God will punish all who forsake Him. *Ekpyresis.*"

That peculiar word again. Janine stared at the receiver, perplexed by the woman's continued overreaction to a harmless afternoon diversion. "It's just a video arcade. Althea probably took Jules to the ice-cream store afterward. You know, for all their squabbling, they're really quite close."

Actually the paradoxical duo were more like battling siblings than true friends; still, there was an emotional attachment between them and an obvious affection that Janine found rather touching. Since Edna had never shown any prior concern about her grandson's relationship with Althea, Janine couldn't understand why the woman was so distressed.

"Edna...? Please stop crying. I'll pick you up in ten minutes, okay?" Janine took the muffled sob as an affirmative answer, mumbled a quick goodbye and hung up the phone. She sagged against the counter envisioning the unpleasant confrontation that would doubtless take place when Jules and Althea finally returned.

With a pained sigh, Janine grabbed up her car keys, wondering why the comfortable environment that had once been her refuge had turned so ugly and hostile.

* * *

Twenty-five minutes later Janine drove back across the wooden bridge while her distraught passenger clutched a dime-store cross, warned of God's wrath and prayed for divine intervention. The pious moaning grated on Janine's nerves, and as she reached the gravel drive, she twisted the steering wheel with more force than necessary.

Edna bounced off the passenger door, righted herself, smoothed her white polyester uniform, then resumed her zealous prayers about sin and Armageddon without missing a beat.

When Janine spotted Althea's dumpy little import parked in the driveway, she was instantly relieved. "Now you see, Edna? I told you there was nothing to wor— Oh, no."

At the same moment, Edna spotted the sheriff's vehicle parked beside Althea's car and started to wail. "It has begun again! God save us all!"

"Oh, for heaven's sake." Janine hit the brake and flipped off the ignition. "The sheriff is probably selling tickets for a department fund-raiser or something." That reassurance was lost on Edna, who had jumped from the car and was rushing up the walk.

Grabbing her purse, Janine hurriedly followed, and her heart sank with every pounding step. This time she had the sick feeling that Edna's prognostications of doom might not be so far off the mark. Something was terribly wrong. She felt it in her bones.

When Janine entered the foyer, she immediately saw that Jules and Althea were standing beside the parlor sofa. Edna was in the doorway with her knobby knuckles pressed on her brow, swaying faintly. Suddenly she blurted, "Praise the Lord," and waddled into the room with open arms. She ignored her grandson but fervently clutched Althea's waist and sobbed into the startled woman's bosom, "I've been so worried, dear, so dreadfully worried."

Althea's jaw dropped. Staring over the top of Edna's curly head, she met Janine's astonished gaze and shrugged in confusion.

Edna stepped back, wiping her wet face. She slid an apprehensive glance at her grandson, then took Althea's hands. "Are you all right, dear?"

"Well...sure." Althea gave Janine a questioning look, to which Janine could only spread her hands helplessly. When she turned a perplexed gaze on Jules, he simply sat down on the sofa, folded his arms and stared sullenly at the floor.

At that point, a movement caught Janine's eye, and she realized that a flat-faced man wearing a taupe uniform and a polished brass badge was standing beside the stereo. He dropped a pair of aviator-style sunglasses into his shirt pocket and scrutinized Janine with acute interest.

After acknowledging the sheriff with a stiff smile, she confirmed with a glance that Edna was painfully aware of the officer's presence. Not only had the poor woman paled three shades, she'd also barricaded herself behind the sofa and was wringing her fat little hands. Since Althea and Jules were obviously unhurt, Janine was baffled by Edna's continued distress.

The lawman stepped forward, tipped his broad-brimmed hat and spoke to Janine. "Good evening, ma'am."

"Good evening, Sheriff—" she glanced at the engraved plate pinned below his starched collar "—Rhodes." Pasting on a hospitable expression, she avoided staring at the notebook he'd just opened. "May I offer you some refreshment? Coffee, iced tea?"

"No, thank you." Rhodes flipped a few pages of the small scratch pad, then extracted a ballpoint pen from his pocket. "I'd like to ask a few questions, if you don't mind."

"Questions?" She managed a pleasant smile.

"Yes, ma'am." He frowned at the exposed page. "I understand that you have a tenant named Quinn Coulliard."

Her smile froze. "Yes, Mr. Coulliard is a guest."

"What was his date of arrival?"

Startled by his curtness, Janine glanced toward the sofa and was immediately alarmed by Althea's smug smile.

"Miss Taylor?"

"Hmm?" Janine returned her attention to the sheriff. "Oh. I'm sorry, I don't recall the exact day."

"Could you check your records, please?"

"Yes, I could." She lifted her chin. "But first I'd like an explanation as to what this is about."

"Just routine questions, ma'am." The sheriff angled a covert glance first at Althea, who seemed inordinately pleased with herself, then at Jules, who was engrossed in studying his fingernails while the corner of his mouth curved into a subtle smile.

Janine felt as though she'd swallowed a brick. Something was definitely awry here, and apparently the only uninformed person in the room besides Janine herself was poor Edna, whose tiny blue eyes reflected only bewilderment and fear.

The sheriff cleared his throat. "We have information that Mr. Coulliard arrived on the same evening of the fire at Marjorie Barker's house. Can you confirm that, Miss Taylor?"

Stunned by the implication, Janine was barely able to stammer an indignant reply. "No, I—I can't."

Squaring her shoulders, she told herself that it wasn't entirely a lie. Although Quinn had mentioned that he'd been in town the afternoon before the fire, Janine herself hadn't seen him until the following morning. Therefore she could legitimately disavow any personal knowledge of his actual arrival time.

She took that flawed reasoning a step further. "What's more, I don't feel comfortable answering questions that violate the privacy of my tenants, particularly when I haven't a clue as to why those questions are being asked in the first place.''

"It's part of an ongoing investigation, Miss Taylor.''

"Investigation of what?'' Janine steadied herself on the door jamb. ''The fire was an accident...wasn't it?''

"We're still looking into the Barker case,'' Rhodes replied cautiously. ''There were some irregularities.''

Janine felt ill. She remembered gossip at the memorial service, rumors about how Marjorie's body had been found in bed, hands clasped neatly. But that had been explained. Even the tiny local newspaper had reported that the woman had been asphyxiated by smoke and had apparently died in her sleep long before the fire reached her bedroom.

In fact, Janine recalled being rather surprised by the article. More precisely, she'd been skeptical that Marjorie—or anyone else, for that matter—could sleep through the agonizing process of slow suffocation. Still, she'd accepted the theory because there had been no plausible alternatives. At least none that she'd been willing to consider. Not here. Not in Darby Ridge.

Concealing her mounting turmoil, Janine addressed the sheriff in the most casual tone she could muster. ''Exactly what kind of 'irregularities' are we talking about here?''

Rhodes shifted uncomfortably and spoke to his notebook. ''I can't discuss that, ma'am.''

Before she could question him further, a high-pitched giggle emanated from the sofa. ''I told you,'' Jules announced, barely able to suppress his glee. ''It was murder. I knew it all the time.''

Edna gasped and covered her mouth.

Althea punched Jules in the knee, frowning and shaking her head. The young man nodded and stared at his lap, chuckling softly and fidgeting with his fingernails.

An icy chill slid down Janine's spine as she realized that the sheriff's sudden appearance might not have been routine after all. She spun around and confronted the smirking duo. "My God. What have you two done?"

Feigning innocence, Althea sat down next to Jules and laid a palm on her chest. "Why, just our civic duty, hon."

Sheriff Rhodes slid a disapproving glance toward Althea then faced Janine uncomfortably. "Mr. Delacourt and Ms. Miller have brought certain facts to our attention. Since Mr. Coulliard's arrival coincided with the, uh, tragedy, I thought it prudent to investigate further."

"This is ludicrous." Raising her hands in frustration, Janine started to pace, desperately trying to suppress disquieting memories of Quinn's strange expression at the smoldering ruins of Marjorie Barker's home and the way he'd stared with such eerie fascination at the flames dancing in the parlor fireplace. There was also the unnerving fact that he carried a gun—

She jerked to a stop and pointed an accusatory finger toward the sofa. "I can't believe you would take such foolishness seriously, especially from these two. Good grief, Jules actually believes that the eruption of Mount Saint Helens was a Communist plot—"

Jules interrupted indignantly. "I merely said that it *could* have been."

Ignoring the lame protest, Janine flicked a hand at the gloating woman. "And whenever Althea wants to go shopping in Eugene, she forges medical reports to get sick pay."

Althea crossed her arms and grinned happily.

"I'm ashamed of you both." Disgusted, Janine jammed her fists against her hips. "In fact, I think the nice sheriff would be extremely interested in the details of why each of you has an ax to grind with Mr. Coulliard."

That got Althea's attention. Her eyes narrowed dangerously. "You'd better watch what you say. One false word and I'll *own* this freaking place, get the picture?"

"Oh, I get it loud and clear. But before you hire a lawyer, check out the law, particularly the part where it states that truth is an absolute defense to slander." Janine took satisfaction from the uncertainty clouding the woman's eyes and closed in for the kill. "The bottom line is that Quinn Coulliard kicked Althea out of his bedroom and her ego couldn't handle it, plain and simple."

Althea leapt up, red-faced and furious. "Bend over and kiss it goodbye, lady, because you're going to be sorry you screwed with me." With that, she stalked out of the house, slamming the front door behind her.

"And you—" Janine turned on Jules "—are you actually so childish and petty that you'd seek this kind of revenge because you lost a lousy chess game?"

Jules's mouth thinned. "He cheated."

Completely aggravated, Janine faced the bewildered sheriff and spread her palms in a pleading gesture. "You see? How on earth could your department persecute someone based on such unsubstantiated innuendo?"

Rhodes regarded her warily. "I'm just doing my job, ma'am. When Mr. Delacourt expressed concern about a stranger being in town the night of the fire, we had a few questions, that's all."

"Oh, for pity's sake. Mr. Delacourt—" she gave the name emphasis and cowed Jules with a look "—is a spoiled and vengeful young man with an obviously perverse sense of humor."

"Perverse?" Jules was on his feet, eyes flashing. "How dare you speak of me in such a way, you ill-mannered—"

"Jules!" Edna rounded the sofa and clutched her grandson's arm. "Janine didn't mean that, dear. She was upset."

Shaking off the restraining hand, Jules glared furiously at Janine. "Coulliard is trash. It doesn't matter what happens to him. Why do you care?"

"Why do I . . . ?" Shaking her head, Janine took a step back and regarded her angry young tenant with shocked disbelief. "Quinn Coulliard is a human being, entitled to the same respect and dignity as anyone else in this world."

"He's evil," Jules snapped. "Do you defend Satan's servant over the holy messenger of God?"

Edna's eyes darted frantically. She tugged on her grandson's crisply ironed sleeve. "You mustn't say such things, dear."

Frowning, Jules looked down at his grandmother as though just becoming aware of her presence. "But you told me—"

"Hush, now!" Edna tittered nervously, glancing quickly from Janine to the sheriff and back again. "The Lord has challenged my grandson with a quick temper and a foolish mouth. Jules is still young. In time, he will master his flaws." She prodded him with an elbow. "Now apologize to Janine. You've been quite rude."

Jules's jaw sagged. "I will not!"

"I am not the one who deserves an apology," Janine said. "But if Jules will simply admit that this childish scheme was cooked up solely to embarrass Mr. Coulliard, I'm certain that the sheriff will close the file on this unpleasant incident without pressing false-report charges."

Rhodes cleared his throat. "I'm sorry, Miss Taylor, but that isn't possible."

Surprised, Janine wanted to clarify the sheriff's dire comment but Jules suddenly stepped forward, his eyes glittering strangely. "You hypocritical slut," he murmured, oblivious to whispered warnings from his frenzied grandmother. "You're doing it with him, aren't you?"

"Excuse me?"

"That's it!" Jules crowed with excitement. "You and Coulliard are lovers. That's why you're defending him, because you take him into your bed and let him do nasty things to you." Lifting one lean leg, he easily stepped over the coffee table and confronted her. "Are you naked when you do it? Where do you let him touch—"

There was a blur of motion before Edna's palm cracked across her grandson's cheek. "How dare you besmirch this child of God with such filthy talk?"

A red welt appeared on Jules's stunned face.

Edna continued her shrill diatribe. "Janine is a good Christian woman. She would never defile herself with pleasures of the flesh. *Never!*"

The furious woman drew back a flabby arm and connected another stinging blow that jerked the young man's head around. "You bastard child of sin," she screeched. "You're an abomination to God, unworthy of being in the presence of such purity. How dare you desecrate this chaste girl?" She slapped him again. "How dare you?" And again. *"How dare y—"*

Edna gasped as Jules caught her wrist in midswing. He stared into his grandmother's face with eyes blacker than the pit of hell and spoke through clenched teeth. "Touch me again, and I'll kill you." He flung her hand away, wiped his palm on his trousers and strode angrily out the front door.

With a tiny cry, Edna clutched at her throat and rushed after him.

Janine stood there, frozen with shock, turning only when the sheriff emitted a low whistle. Tipping back his brimmed hat, Rhodes scratched his balding scalp. "Does this sort of thing happen a lot?"

"No." She lowered herself shakily into a nearby chair. "I've never known Edna to raise her voice with her grandson, let alone strike him. She worships Jules."

"Just an observation, ma'am, but the lady seems a lot fonder of you than of her own flesh and blood."

Sadly shaking her head, Janine wanted to dispute that but couldn't defend what she didn't understand.

Rhodes shifted nervously, then pulled up another chair. "If it makes you feel any better, Delacourt was way out of line. I would have stepped in myself, except his grandmother got there first." When Janine looked up sharply, he sheepishly added, "Of course, I wouldn't have hit him, being an officer of the law and all. But I would have told him in no uncertain terms to mind his manners."

She managed a weak smile but was unable to respond, partly because the incident had shaken her to the core and partly because Jules's suggestion of intimacy between her and Quinn had been uncomfortably close to the truth.

Cooling her face with her hands, she took a deep breath, squared her shoulders and faced Rhodes directly. "At least you understand now that Mr. Coulliard has been unfairly accused."

"Well, now..." The sheriff tugged at his collar. "Thing is, we never did put much credence in what Delacourt and Miss Miller said."

"Then why on earth are you here?"

"Like I told you, we're still investigating the Barker fire, so when we were notified that there was a stranger in town, we were duty-bound to investigate."

"Investigate what?" Janine rose angrily. "Good grief, do newcomers leave constitutional protection outside the county line?"

"No, ma'am, but—"

"Then is it department policy to treat everyone like a criminal?"

The sheriff's thick jaw tensed. "Only the ones that are."

She blinked. "Are what?"

"Criminals." Rhodes sighed. "We ran Coulliard's name through the computer."

The significance escaped her. "So?"

"The man is a convicted felon." When Janine suddenly swayed, Rhodes laid a steadying hand on her shoulder. "I'm real sorry, Miss Taylor. I thought you knew."

"No," she whispered sickly. "I didn't know."

But she *should* have known. Given Quinn's secretive manner, Janine had secretly suspected that he was hiding something. The most frightening thing, however, wasn't learning that her suspicions were true; it was that she simply didn't care.

Cloistered in her bedroom, Janine alternately paced and fretted, trying desperately to convince herself that there was a logical explanation for what the sheriff had told her. After all, computers weren't infallible. There must be dozens of Quinn Coulliards in the world.

Grimacing at her own skewed rationale, she sat on the edge of the bed and tried to gather her thoughts. All right, there probably weren't a lot of men with that particular name but what if some frazzled keypunch operator had made an input error? Maybe someone named Quintin Collard had robbed a bank in Des Moines. That would explain everything.

She glanced anxiously at the clock, wondering when Quinn would return so they could clear this mess up. He hadn't shown up at dinnertime—which was probably just as well, since no meal had been served. The last thing on Janine's mind had been feeding people whom she would have preferred to strangle.

Apparently she hadn't been expected to, since none of the tenants had returned. That was fine with her. In fact, Janine hoped that each and every one of them was out searching for new accommodations. That would save her the trouble of giving notice, which by law required a thirty-day wait. On the thirty-first day, of course, she'd have to declare bankruptcy.

God, she missed San Diego.

Sighing, she took the sheriff's business card from the night stand and absently tucked it into her pocket. Even after dropping the bombshell that Quinn had been listed as a felon in the computer data base, Rhodes had continued to insist that the questioning was routine. Then he'd pressed the card into her limp hand and asked her to have Quinn call in the morning. She'd assured him that she'd pass on the message.

And she would, if Quinn ever returned.

The idea that he might not return, that he might be gone forever was more frightening than she could ever have imagined.

By the time Janine heard the front door open, she was frantic with worry. She grabbed the knob and nearly dashed into the hall before realizing that it could be one of her other tenants returning. Since she wasn't ready to face any of them, she pressed an ear to her door and waited.

She heard footsteps on the stairs. After a pause, the muffled sounds grew closer. The soft click was only a few feet away as Quinn's door opened and closed.

Closing her eyes, Janine sagged against the jamb, trembling with relief and renewed trepidation. She moistened her lips, drew on whatever courage she could muster, went into the hall and tapped softly on his door.

After a moment he answered and seemed surprised to see her. "I thought you'd be in bed by now."

"It's not that late." She swallowed hard. "There's something we should discuss. May I come in?"

"Of course." Eyeing her quizzically, he stepped back, allowing her access.

As she stepped inside, the raven hissed, extending its wing in warning. Ignoring the irritated bird, she stood stiffly in the center of the room with her fingers tangled together. She heard the door close softly and knew that Quinn was watching her.

After pulling the sheriff's card from her shirt pocket, she took a deep breath, turned and held out her hand. "You had a visitor this afternoon."

Quinn hesitated before plucking the card from her palm. Except for a slight twitch at the corner of his mouth, his expression remained impassive and said nothing.

Since he appeared to be waiting for an explanation, Janine offered one. "Althea and Jules went to the sheriff this afternoon. They intimated that you were responsible for the fire at Marjorie Barker's. There...are some questions. Sheriff Rhodes would like you to call."

"All right." Quinn dropped the card onto his nightstand. "Is that all?"

She nervously chewed on her lower lip and looked away. "He said something else."

"Something that upset you."

"Yes." A hot mist gathered in her eyes. "He...said you were a criminal."

There was a long silence. "I see."

When the expected denial didn't come, she searched Quinn's face and saw only a bland expression. "It isn't true, is it?"

"What if it was true, Janine? Would that make any difference to you?"

"Yes...no...I don't know." She fingered her bangs in frustration. "I mean, your name came up on a computer. It could have been a mistake."

"It could have been." Quinn sighed. "But it wasn't."

Air rushed from her lungs. "I don't understand. Did you forget to pay taxes or—" she roughly rubbed her forehead "—or steal towels from a hotel?"

"No."

"Maybe you borrowed a few dollars from petty cash."

"Janine—"

"I'm sure you meant to pay it back—"

"Listen to me." He took hold of her shoulders. "The sheriff was right. I was convicted. I went to prison."

"My God." Pulling away, she was overwhelmed by the sensation of being strangled. As she stumbled backward ineffectually yanking at her collar, she realized just how little she really knew about this enigmatic man. She should feel furious, indignant, deceived; she should send him away, eject him from her life forever.

Yet as she gazed into those mesmerizing eyes, the hidden horrors from Quinn's past suddenly didn't matter, because she knew beyond doubt that she'd fallen desperately, irrevocably in love with him.

CHAPTER ELEVEN

Quinn's stomach tightened into a burning knot. He'd always known that his past could catch up with him but had pushed the unpleasant possibility out of his mind, perhaps because he couldn't bear to see this shattered expression in Janine's trusting eyes.

She stood stoically, fighting tears, waiting for the plausible explanation that would restore her faith. He could lie, and she'd believe him because she would want to.

Eventually she'd learn the truth, of course. The sheriff would already have requested the pertinent files from Southern California, but before the gruesome documents arrived he might have enough time to complete what he'd started. At the moment, however, he was sorely tempted to tell Janine exactly what she needed to hear.

In the end, he simply couldn't do it. She had suffered enough deception in her life; soon she would endure even more. But not this time. This time Quinn would be honest—to a point—and hope that she'd understand. It was a risk, of course. If he'd misjudged her, she could cause irreparable harm to others—and to herself.

"Quinn?"

He understood her unspoken question but the answer clogged like mud in his throat. He sat heavily on the bed. "It happened nearly three years ago."

"What happened?"

After a moment's hesitation, he studied his knees to avoid her frightened gaze. "Perhaps I should start from the beginning."

"All right." Janine perched delicately on the chair and watched warily.

Propping his elbows on his thighs, Quinn slumped forward, staring sightlessly at the floor. His mind traveled back in time, focusing on the image of a beautiful blond woman, laughing, energetic, happy to be alive.

She'd held out her pale hand, admiring the twinkling ring as though the microscopic gemstone had been the Hope diamond. "Oh, Quinn, it's magnificent!"

He'd watched anxiously. "It's a bit small but—"

"No!" She'd shaken her head so vigorously that her sunbright hair swept her face and stuck like golden threads. "It's perfect, absolutely perfect. In fact, it's the most perfect thing I've ever had in my entire life!"

Then she'd leaped into his arms giggling, and he'd swung her around the tiny apartment until she'd squealed for mercy. Afterward they'd gone to her bedroom and made sweet, gentle love. He'd whispered that he would always love her. She'd smiled and stroked his face, but had said nothing.

Now, as he remembered that night and all the other nights, Quinn realized that during all their months together Cynthia had never once said that she'd loved him.

The soft sound of the raven shuffling across its perch brought him back to the present. He knew that Janine was watching, waiting. He filled his aching lungs. "As I've already told you, Cynthia and I became engaged shortly after she'd completed the alcohol rehabilitation program."

"Yes, I remember. You also said that the treatment was difficult for her."

That was an understatement. Quinn managed a curt nod, then took a moment to gather his thoughts. "My biggest failure was in not realizing how difficult. She always seemed upbeat and positive so I never looked beyond the forced smile or recognized the pain in her eyes. Cynthia was dying inside, and I didn't even know it."

"You're not clairvoyant."

"No, but I am a professional, or at least I was supposed to be." He took a disgusted swipe at his knee. "I should have recognized the symptoms. Cynthia had no experience dealing with sobriety. From the time she was fifteen, alcohol had taken the sting out of failure, created false courage and generally softened all of life's rough edges. But after only a few months in a controlled environment, she was tossed back into raw reality and expected to cope. She couldn't."

Janine digested that information. "She must have felt very confused and ashamed."

"I honestly don't know. At the time, I was arrogant enough to assume that I understood, but Cynthia never revealed how she felt about what was happening in her life." Quinn didn't add that she'd never revealed her feelings about him, either. That would have made him seem even more simpleminded in Janine's eyes so he maintained an even expression and spoke in a monotone. "As the date of our wedding grew closer, Cynthia became more and more withdrawn. I assumed—" he winced at the word "—that she had a normal case of prenuptial jitters."

"But it was more serious than that, wasn't it?" Janine was leaning forward now. "She knew that once you were married, she wouldn't be able to conceal the fact that she was still drinking."

Quinn wished it had been that simple. Deep down, however, he believed that Cynthia's reluctance was based on the fact that she'd agreed to marry a man she didn't love. That was the reality that had driven her back into the arms of addiction. And that was the reality that Quinn himself hadn't been able to face—until it was too late.

But in answer to Janine's question, he simply rubbed his eyelids and shrugged.

Janine persisted. "Obviously Cynthia's problems were eventually discovered. What happened then?"

An invisible vise tightened his chest. The memories were painful yet he was committed to revealing them. He closed his eyes. "One night about a week before the wedding..."

As he spoke, the words dissolved into images of the past. He envisioned the night he and Cynthia had been preparing dinner in the kitchen of his uptown apartment.

She'd been especially moody that evening, apparently irritated because her car had broken down on the freeway. Earlier, Quinn had received her agitated phone call, then driven to the site, supervised the towing procedure and brought her back to his place, hoping a quiet meal would ease her tension. It hadn't seemed to.

She slammed a cupboard door. "Where's the damned vinegar? How do you expect me to marinade these lousy steaks without a decent red wine vinegar?"

Startled by her uncharacteristic display of temper, Quinn set aside the lettuce he'd been shredding. "At these prices, meat shouldn't be soaked like dried beans. The steaks will be great without marinade."

Not the least bit placated, Cynthia paced the kitchen rubbing—no, scratching—at her arms and face and neck. "I can't eat meat that hasn't been properly prepared. I just can't. It's...uncivilized."

Quinn wiped his hands on a tea towel. "All right. I'll drive to the market and get whatever you need."

She jerked to a stop, then looked over her shoulder. "No. You're tired. It's not fair to send you out again. I'll go."

"It's no trouble." He pulled his car keys from his jeans. "I'll be back in fifteen minutes."

Snagging his wrist, Cynthia faced him, huge blue eyes filled with anxiety. "Please...I could use the fresh air." She plucked the keys from his palm, bit her lip, then gave him a shaky smile. "I'll be right back. Honest."

The emphasis she gave the final word was unsettling. "Of course you will."

Clutching his car keys, Cynthia hurried to the front door and disappeared into the night, leaving Quinn with a queasy sensation that he quickly and neatly suppressed.

Three hours later, Cynthia hadn't returned. Quinn was sick with worry. For the fifth time in as many minutes, he picked up the telephone, held the receiver in midair then carefully re-cradled it. Instinctively he knew that Cynthia was at some bar drinking herself senseless, but for the first two hours he'd refused to acknowledge that. He couldn't face the bitter thought that he'd failed her. By the third hour there'd been no choice but to accept the truth.

He'd called all the hospitals; he'd called all of her friends. In fact, he'd called everyone in the damned city except the police because he was afraid they'd arrest her. Before her stint at the treatment center, Cynthia had had several brushes with the law because of alcohol-related traffic offenses. If the authorities located her and she had indeed been drinking, she'd most certainly end up in jail.

He couldn't allow that to happen. Cynthia was terrified of being confined. Once, she'd been forced to spend two days in the lockup and had nearly had a mental breakdown.

So Quinn sat on the couch, propped his head on his hands and anguished over his limited options. He'd just decided to call a taxicab and canvass the local taverns himself when the front door opened and Cynthia stumbled into the room.

He leaped to his feet and his heart nearly stopped. She looked like she'd been through a war. Her hair stuck out at odd angles, her lipstick had been chewed off and there were black crescents of smudged mascara under her eyes. "S-Something awful h-happened." She hiccuped, sagged against the wall and burst into tears.

Quinn was across the room in three steps and pulled her into his arms. "Are you hurt?"

Sobbing uncontrollably, she shook her head then buried her face in his shirt and continued to weep. Closing his eyes, Quinn let her cry. Since she reeked of liquor, he had a fairly good idea of what had happened. And it made him sick.

When her sobs had receded to an occasional quiver, he spoke softly. "Tell me what happened."

"Y-You'll hate me."

"I could never hate you." He wiped a dirt smear from her forehead. "Tell me."

"I...I..." She sniffed loudly and looked away. "The car. It's all crunched up."

Having assumed as much, he merely nodded. "Are you certain you're all right?"

"Yes." She covered her eyes with her hand. "But you'd b-better look at the car."

"There's time for that."

Vehemently shaking her head, she insisted, "You have to do it now."

A tingling sensation slid down his spine. "All right, if it will make you feel better."

When she remained silent and refused to face him, Quinn decided to do as she'd requested. Hopefully, she'd then be willing to discuss the incident that had so obviously traumatized her.

"I'll be right back." He kissed her cheek, then reluctantly left the apartment and went down to the basement.

The underground garage of the complex was dimly lit; even so, he instantly noticed that his gray sedan was situated nearly sideways across two parking spaces. As he walked closer, he saw a spiderweb of circular cracks on the windshield and felt ill. If Cynthia's head had struck the glass with enough force to do that...

But she had no cuts or bruises and the glass was dented inward.

A heaviness settled in the pit of his stomach. He rounded the undamaged rear of the car and pulled a flashlight from beneath the passenger seat. The beam revealed that the left front fender was dented, the headlight was smashed and the bumper had been pushed into the grillwork. Smeared blood and human hair embedded on the outside of the cracked windshield completed the grisly tale.

Quinn swayed weakly. Dear God. She'd hit someone. Bile rushed into his throat and he was physically sick.

Afterward, he steadied himself against a nearby pillar, took several deep breaths, and when the faintness passed he returned to the apartment to confront Cynthia.

She was as he'd left her, hunched on the couch, absently plucking at her clothes. When he closed the door, she straightened slightly. "It wasn't my fault. He was right in the middle of the street..." She looked tearfully up at him. "He ran out in front of me. I couldn't stop."

Feeling dazed, Quinn sat beside her. "Was he badly hurt?" When she didn't answer, he glanced up and repeated the question.

She shrugged. "I...don't know."

"Didn't the police tell you about his condition? Or the paramedics?"

"I, uh..." Fresh tears slid down her face.

"My God, Cynthia." Quinn gripped her shoulders and spun her around. "You *did* call for help, didn't you?"

"I couldn't," she wailed. "They would have blamed me, can't you see? I couldn't just sit there and let them arrest me. I'd die in jail, Quinn, you know that."

He released her quickly and reached for the telephone.

She frantically grabbed at his wrist. "No! Please, you can't."

"We have to report it." He unpeeled her fingers. "Where did it happen? *Where did you leave him?*"

There was a sharp knock on the front door. Quinn stiffened and looked at Cynthia. She was as pale as death. "D-Don't answer it," she whispered.

He squeezed her hands. "It's all right, honey. We'll get through this together."

As he stood, she whimpered softly. He wavered a moment, then answered the door and saw what he expected.

The taller of the two policemen spoke. "Quinn Coulliard?"

"Yes."

"Are you the registered owner of a gray Buick sedan?" The officer squinted at his notes and rattled off a California license number.

When Quinn acknowledged ownership, the officer's perceptive gaze slid around the apartment. "Witnesses have placed your vehicle at the scene of an accident, sir. Were you driving in the vicinity of Broadway and J Street at any time during the evening?"

Before Quinn could reply, Cynthia blurted, "I knew you couldn't get away with it. You never should have left that poor man."

Stunned beyond rational thought, Quinn whirled to stare at the stranger who was to be his wife.

Cynthia stood ramrod straight, twisting her hands. "I tried to stop him, Officer. I begged him to call for help but he wouldn't listen."

Quinn was dumfounded. "Cynthia...my God... why—?"

Suddenly he was jerked backwards, spun around and shoved roughly against the wall. As his hands were yanked up between his shoulder blades, the chilling words were uttered inches from his ear. *You have the right to remain silent...*

Three years later, Quinn was still haunted by that crushing betrayal. His hands were shaking, his blood ran cold as ice. Blinking numbly, he sucked in a ragged breath, looked up and saw the horror in Janine's eyes.

With her palms pressed against her mouth, she slowly shook her head as a single tear slid down her cheek. She finally curled her fingers into fists, tucking them beneath her chin. "How could she have done such a terrible thing?"

"She was frightened." Quinn rolled his head and tried to suppress the turmoil wrought by having relived the awful memories. "Cynthia was a fragile woman. I believe she understood the consequence of her act but was driven by fear to the point where she lost control of her conscience. There's a point, I suppose, in everyone's life where self-preservation destroys the most altruistic motives."

Janine bit her lip. "But she deliberately betrayed you to save herself. You must have been devastated."

Embarrassed by her overt sympathy, he avoided her gaze. "I was...surprised."

Suddenly Janine stood, folded her arms tightly and paced the small room. "There's no excuse for what she did. When her lies were uncovered, I hope they threw the book at her."

Quinn stared at his hands and said nothing.

She stopped pacing. "Her lies *were* uncovered, weren't they?" When he still didn't respond, she gasped and sat beside him on the bed. "My God. You were convicted. That means—"

Quinn interrupted coldly. "I couldn't prove that Cynthia was lying." His suppressed rage resurfaced, that frigid fury that had been his companion since the day Cynthia's perjured testimony had destroyed his life. "No one who witnessed the accident was certain whether a man or woman was driving or even how many people were in the car. The entire case boiled down to one of credibility."

"And the jury believed an emotionally distraught alcoholic over a man with your professional credentials? Why?"

"Because the prosecutor put forth a rather convincing argument that a psychologist who would take sexual advantage of a vulnerable patient was obviously an unethical cad with the morals of an alley cat."

"But you said that you and Cynthia weren't involved until after she'd left the rehab center."

"We weren't."

"So she lied about that, too?"

"Yes."

Janine laid a comforting hand on his shoulder. "You ... went to prison?"

The question was rhetorical since he'd already admitted as much, but her warm touch was so soothing that he found himself revealing more than he'd planned. "The sentence was three-to-five but thanks to an overcrowded prison system and generous good-time calculations, I was out in two years. It could have been worse."

"I don't see how." Turning her head, Janine discreetly wiped her wet face and felt a frightening surge of resentment toward the woman who had done such a dastardly thing. Her heart went out to Quinn. To be wrongly convicted was a nightmare guaranteed to terrify the most courageous but when added to emotional treason by a trusted lover ... "How could you have forgiven her?"

His reply was cold enough to freeze meat. "I didn't."

She glanced up quickly. "But you excused her behavior."

"No." The sudden sharpness in his voice was startling. "I understood her behavior. I never condoned it, I never excused it." He faced Janine, his dark expression chilling her to the bone. "And I never forgave it."

She sat beside him and took his hand. "You have a right to be angry."

He looked away for a moment, and when he turned toward her again the anger had drained from his eyes. He regarded Janine intently, as if measuring the depth of her soul. After a moment, his gaze dropped to her lap where his hand was cradled between her own small palms. "It's late. You should get some sleep."

She was vaguely aware of her fingers tightening around his hand and surprised herself with a throaty response. "I'm not tired."

Quinn's arm trembled slightly, and she noted a subtle stiffening of his shoulders. For a moment she thought he would send her away. That panicked her, although she wouldn't allow herself to dwell on exactly why. All she knew was that his nearness was intoxicating. His scent filled the room, the heat from his body warmed her skin and softened a secret place deep inside. She wanted to hold his head against her breast, caress away past pain, past betrayals, murmur words of solace and comfort. And more.

She yearned for another taste of the sweetness she'd experienced that night in the ravine when he'd kissed her with breathless emotion and her spirit had soared with an exuberance she'd never known.

As she tentatively caressed Quinn's stiff fingers, he made a sound deep in his throat then stood suddenly, forcing her to release him. "Go back to your room, Janine. I don't need your pity."

Momentarily speechless, she struggled for a response. "What happened to you was tragic and senseless and desperately unfair. I sympathize and share your outrage but how could I or anyone else feel pity for a man with such uncommon strength and determination of spirit?"

Before he found his voice—or she lost her nerve—Janine stood and faced him squarely. "What I feel for you, Quinn

Coulliard, is admiration and...and..." The revelation was cut off as a lump of pure terror suddenly wedged into her throat. If she admitted that she was falling in love with him, would he reject her? Regard her with revulsion? Laugh in her face?

Intuitively she knew that he'd do none of those things but years of abuse had taken a heavy toll. She lowered her gaze, feeling foolish and inadequate yet somehow mustering the courage to confront her deepest fears. "I want to stay with you," she said simply, then stared at her shoes.

After several silent moments, Quinn urged her chin up with his knuckle. "I'm not what you need."

Embarrassed, she tried to maintain eye contact without tearing up. "I'm not asking for a lifetime commitment."

"I know that."

"I just want to spend time with you." Inside she was cringing. Her words sounded trite, repulsively bland when compared to the sensual images in her mind, and she barely recognized the strange voice that spoke with such clear certainty, such brazen intent. "The last time, in the ravine, I wasn't ready for... for intimacy. Now I am."

"Perhaps." His thumb grazed her cheek. "I see the man you want, the man you deserve, reflected in your eyes. I'd give anything in the world to be that man."

"You are."

"No." He shook his head sadly. "I want to be but I'm not. You don't really know me."

"I know enough."

"You know only what I've told you. I could be lying."

"You're not." Janine touched his beautiful face. "I've seen your kindness, the gentle side that you try so diligently to conceal. I know the kind of man you are, Quinn. I know it in here." She lifted his hand and pressed his palm over her heart.

He took a ragged breath but made no move to withdraw his hand. Slowly she met his eyes, searching and finding a desire that matched her own. A stranger blossomed inside her bosom, a woman of passion and love, a woman who forgot past rejection and focused only on a burning need to give, to heal the heart of this wounded man. Her hand slid up the full expanse of his muscular chest, over warm flesh and hard bone and rested against the pulsing cords of his firm throat.

Her own heartbeat escalated, pounding against the masculine palm pressed over her breast. When her tongue darted to moisten her lips, his pulse raced against her fingertips. She felt empowered, confident, seductive, all heady sensations that made her even bolder. Standing on tiptoes, she brushed her lips across his mouth, then the kiss deepened and became more intimate.

Quinn's body quivered. He growled deep in his throat, suddenly embracing her with a fervency that would have been frightening with anyone else. But it wasn't anyone else. It was Quinn Coulliard, her soul mate, the man who had ignited her feminine power and made her feel whole.

Her heart soared. She wrapped her arms around his neck, tangling her fingers in his thick hair, pressing him closer, harder, deeper. He responded instantly by sliding his hands over her bottom and lifting her off her feet. With a gasp of pure pleasure, she instinctively locked her legs around his hips, her mouth seeking his with a wild abandon that she'd experienced only in her dreams.

Suddenly she was floating, swirling, vaguely aware that the walls were turning. She didn't care. A burning passion had ignited her soul as she kissed every inch of his face and neck, tasting, nipping, clutching at his body with her lips and her hands and her legs.

Then his mouth was on her throat, blazing a hot trail where her skin was exposed by the V-neck of her plaid shirt.

With her clasped hands buried beneath his flowing mane
and her ankles locked behind his waist, she threw back her
head and moaned softly.

As her back arched, Quinn's lips moved from bare skin
to blaze a trail over the thin plaid fabric. When his moist
heat permeated her flimsy bra, she whimpered softly. Her
hips moved without conscious thought. She squirmed restlessly, pressing herself sensually against the bulging evidence of his manhood. Tightening his grip on her buttocks,
he rotated her hips to increase the erotic friction of her intimate caress.

Suddenly Janine was crazed, frantic to satisfy the strange
hunger burning inside. The denim barrier frustrated her to
the point of frenzy. Hanging onto his strong neck with one
hand, she clumsily tugged at the metal button on his fly.
When her frantic effort proved fruitless, she was agitated to
tears.

Quinn gently kissed her earlobe. "Shh," he whispered.
"All in good time." With that, he bent forward, lowering
her carefully until she felt the soft mattress at her back.
Standing between her encircling thighs, Quinn unbuttoned
his jeans and shrugged out of his T-shirt. His magnificent
hair, displaced when he pulled the shirt over his head, cas-
caded over his sculpted shoulders like an espresso waterfall.

She gasped, so awed by his masculine beauty that she
barely noticed when he unfastened her own garments. He
parted her shirt as though opening a precious gift and
brushed the fabric back over her shoulders. She yanked out
her arms and tossed the garment aside.

"Lift your hips," he murmured.

Reluctantly releasing her leg-lock around his torso, she
gasped when he slid her jeans down her thighs then knelt to
kiss the exposed flesh. His lips moved just above the sliding
fabric, blazing an erotic trail down to her knees, her calves

and her ankles. After the denim pooled on the floor, he retraced the same path upward then pressed his face against her smooth belly. His hair fell across her skin, a thousand feathery caresses that thrilled her to the core.

"You're so beautiful," he whispered against her quivering flesh. "So perfect. You take my breath away." As he spoke, his hands encircled her slender waist then slowly moved up her rib cage until his thumbs brushed the tips of her breasts. She bit her lip and swallowed a cry, turning slightly when one hand edged under her shoulder blade. His fingers pinched the narrow band of her bra, then the binding loosened and the nylon wisp was swept away.

Air cooled her bare breasts but a moment later his mouth warmed them. Startled by the incredible sensation, Janine reached above her head and tangled her fingers in the bedclothes, moaning aloud as his lips teased each sensitive tip. No one had ever touched her with such tenderness, such reverence. Blissfully closing her eyes, she wondered if it was possible to die of sheer ecstasy.

Then he straightened, leaving her bereft and silently screaming for more. A cold terror settled in the pit of her stomach. She'd done something wrong. He was angry with her, disappointed. Her eyes flew open, and she nearly cried out in relief. He had removed the rest of his clothing and was returning. Apparently he recognized and misread the fear in her eyes, so when he hesitated she opened her arms. His smile sent chills down her spine.

Moving carefully, he nested his hips between her thighs and supported his weight on his elbows. Janine stiffened, clutched at his shoulders and waited for the pain.

But Quinn made no move to enter her. Instead he softly caressed her face. "Are you frightened?"

"No," she lied.

He kissed her sweetly. "I won't hurt you."

She regarded him skeptically. Sex always hurt. A woman's duty was to stoically endure. Her mother had issued the warnings; Charles had proven them true.

With a knowing smile, Quinn brushed a damp strand from her cheek. "I promise that nothing will happen until you want it to."

That confused her. "I want it now."

"Do you?"

She was baffled by the question since they were both completely nude and arranged in the proper position. "Of course."

"Hmm." He kissed a corner of her mouth. "Then perhaps you'll be patient with me. I think I'd like a little more time."

That made no sense whatsoever. Janine had enough experience to know that the masculine equipment pressed against her thigh was as ready as it would ever be. She posed a tentative question. "Time for what?"

"Time for this," he murmured, then slid his lips down to her breasts. At the first flick of his tongue, an electric shock jolted her to the core. She gasped, stunned by the force of her own reaction as the sweet assault continued until her body writhed beneath him and she could barely suck air into her convulsing lungs.

Not an inch of her body was neglected. He explored her secrets with his lips and his hands and fingers until he'd created a burning knot in her belly. Liquid fire seeped from her innermost core, and when he touched her there she cried out in pure joy. She didn't understand what was happening but it was glorious.

Still, she needed more. There was a fiery itch deep inside, driving her to the brink of sweet insanity. She dug her fingernails into his hips, trying to drag him inside her to quench the frenzied fire.

His voice was a soft rasp against her ear. "Are you ready for me, honey?"

At that moment, she'd never been more ready for anything in her life. She was ravenous, starving, doomed to die in agony without the nourishment of his love. But her throat was paralyzed. Unable to verbally respond, she slid her hand between their slick bodies and grasped that which she so desperately wanted.

He sucked in a sharp breath. "I'll take that as a yes."

She moaned in anticipation. Quivering, she thrashed her head anxiously, certain she couldn't endure even another moment of waiting.

"Janine?" From what seemed a great distance, Quinn's voice penetrated into her passion-fogged brain. "You have to let go first."

Dazed, she could only blink helplessly.

He reached down and brought her hand up. Their fingers laced together as he cherished her lips with his mouth, kissing her with a tenderness that brought tears to her eyes.

She sensed a sweet pressure between her legs. His hips moved slowly, increasing her pleasure with each gentle rotation until he had slowly, surely, filled the aching void deep inside. Overwhelmed by the wondrous sensations coursing through her, she moved with him, her hips instinctively swaying rhythmically then frantically as the thrusts became deeper, more urgent.

Then something amazing happened. She was rocked by an explosion deep inside her, an eruption of electric spasms that shook her to the bone. Quinn groaned, embracing her tightly. Colors swirled and lights flashed through her mind as her body vibrated in erotic release.

Slowly, ever so slowly, the dizziness dissipated as she floated back to reality. Breathing hard, she raised a limp hand, peeling a moist lock from her face.

Quinn lay beside her, his eyes closed, an expression of contentment on his face. Her heart swelled with emotion as she nestled in the crook of his arm and laid her cheek against his damp chest. He caressed her bare back, drawing unhurried circles on her skin with his fingertips.

Janine had never in her life felt such a sense of belonging. She was his now, and he was hers. Physically, emotionally, spiritually, they had bonded so intimately that she was certain no couple on the face of the earth had ever experienced such rapture.

Smiling to herself, she tucked her head beneath his chin and cuddled closer. So this was how love felt. No wonder poets wrote odes to its power. She loved Quinn Coulliard with every fiber of her being. Suddenly she heard her own voice uttering the sacred words. "I love you."

Quinn went rigid. An ominous stillness enveloped the room, broken only by the sounds of hushed breathing. Then Quinn stirred and moved away. Instinctively Janine reached out to stop him, to retrieve his soothing warmth. But it was too late. In all ways that mattered, he was already gone.

CHAPTER TWELVE

Dazed and heartsick, Janine scrambled to her knees, dragging the bedclothes with her. "What's wrong?"

"Nothing." Quinn presented his back and pulled on his jeans. "It's late. You should go back to your room and get some sleep."

"I don't understand." She bunched the bedclothes under her chin. "Can't I stay here . . . with you?"

"No."

"But why? Have I done something to displease you?"

When he turned to face her, his eyes were veiled and unreadable. "We're both tired. It's time for you to leave."

She recoiled as though slapped. Suddenly unable to breathe, she found herself picking frantically through the mussed covers for her clothes. "Of course," she mumbled, trying to focus through a blur of tears. "Just . . . let me . . . find . . ."

A denim blob plopped onto the bed. She bit her lip, tasted blood, then snatched up the jeans and clutched them to her breast, humiliated to realize that she couldn't dress without exposing herself.

But then she'd already been exposed, hadn't she?

This was foolish. How *do* consenting adults behave in this kind of situation? What was the proper etiquette? She didn't know. A sob caught in her throat. She didn't know how to be a lover. She didn't even know how to be a woman.

Charles was right. Charles was always right.

The realization that Quinn, too, had been disappointed was shattering, further proof of her inadequacy. Panic-stricken, Janine was desperate to get away, to hide her shame and suffer in private. Without bothering to search for her underwear, she yanked on her jeans, stuffed her arms into the crumpled shirt she'd found on the floor and stumbled toward the door.

As she reached for the knob, Quinn came up behind her and gently took hold of her shoulders. She stopped, staring sightlessly ahead. "Please understand that this isn't your fault," he whispered. "You're the most wonderful woman I've ever known."

Clutching her gaping shirtfront, Janine blinked back tears, and unable to trust her voice she remained silent.

His fingers flexed, hugging her upper arms. "It's my problem, Janine. If this had happened at another time, in another place—" A ragged breath cut off the words and his hands fell away. "I'm no good for you, honey. You deserve better."

Janine felt ill. Even now, he continued to utter kind platitudes. Only this time she was wise enough not to believe them. The fault was hers. She didn't know why—perhaps she never would—but she was completely convinced that in some profound way she had let Quinn down.

A white blur caught her attention, and she numbly realized that her lacy undergarments were nested in his palm. She stiffly retrieved the filmy things, yanked the door open and almost fell into the hallway.

Behind her, the latch shut with a soft click. Instantly Janine slumped forward, burying her face in the soft nylon to muffle her sobs. Hurrying toward her room, she was startled by a sharp gasp. She looked up and was horrified.

There was Edna with her knuckles pressed against her mouth, staring in shocked astonishment as Janine tried frantically to cover herself. As the woman lowered her hands, her expression flickered from disapproval to revulsion and finally pity.

Completely mortified, Janine fumbled with the doorknob, stumbled into her room, collapsed on the bed and wept.

With a furious oath, Quinn smashed his fist into the wall.

Ignoring the raven's indignant screech, he raked his hair, angrily kicked the wadded T-shirt across the floor, then paced the room with increasing agitation.

The first time he'd looked into Janine's guileless eyes, he'd known that he was in trouble. But even though his gut had twisted and his heart had done a double take, he'd sworn to himself that this wouldn't happen.

Another broken promise.

He punched a pillow and flung it across the room. The indignant raven extended its good wing, arched ominously and hissed a warning.

Quinn was too distraught to notice the irritated bird. He was furious with himself for having so little control over his emotions. When he'd heard Janine murmur that she loved him, something deep inside him had cracked. Once, he'd yearned to hear those precious words yet now realized that from Cynthia they'd have meant nothing. From Janine, they meant the world.

It had taken every ounce of his strength to send her away.

He scoured his eyelids as though the futile gesture could erase the haunting image of her wounded expression. It couldn't. Nothing could.

But he'd had no choice. The only way Quinn could protect Janine was to drive her away, to make certain that she couldn't be connected with him when it was finally over. And the end was close now. Too close.

He went to the nightstand and fingered the deputy's business card. Soon all the nasty little secrets would reveal themselves, and Janine would learn the sordid truth.

Quinn sat heavily on the bed, recalling that he'd thought the nightmare was over when he'd been released from prison. But it had just been the beginning. Two days later, Cynthia was dead. It was only a matter of time before Darby Ridge's sheriff discovered *how* she had died.

Quinn had to hurry now. His time had just run out.

Janine put on another pot of coffee, pasted on a phony smile and tried to conduct the morning routine as though her heart hadn't been ripped out. It wasn't easy.

She kept a nervous eye on the stairway and waited for Quinn to come down for breakfast. Although his van was parked outside, he hadn't appeared yet. That was only a partial relief. Janine didn't think she was ready to face him but an uncontrollable segment of her traitorous heart longed simply to see his face. Since the man obviously wanted no part of her, she was disgusted by her own weakness.

Glancing toward the breakfast table, she noted that although Edna and Jules were stiffly seated in their usual places both were quite obviously unhappy. Althea's seat was still empty, so there was one less hostile person to stare icy daggers at Janine's increasingly vulnerable back.

Actually she wasn't particularly bothered by Jules's contemptuous expression and was, in fact, still furious with him for having taken part in spreading the unfounded and totally inexcusable rumor that Quinn had something to do with Marjorie Barker's death.

Edna, however, was another matter. The disillusionment and misery in her eyes sliced Janine to the core. She couldn't blame the woman for being disgusted since she was just as disgusted with herself.

It wasn't that Janine regretted what she and Quinn had shared—she could never regret the most beautiful experience of her life—but afterward everything had unraveled. His disappointed expression had broken her heart.

As fresh moisture gathered in her eyes, Janine grabbed a sponge and absently wiped the spotless counter. She fought the encroaching tears with a silent promise to deal with the pain later, in private. Now, however, she struggled to conduct herself with a modicum of dignity.

A chair scraped away from the table. Janine squared her shoulders and turned in time to meet Jules's frigid gaze. His lip curled in a sneer then he ignored Janine completely and spoke crisply to his grandmother, issuing a harsh command that seemed completely out of character for the usually docile young man. "I'll warm up the car, *Grand'mère*. Don't keep me waiting."

As her grandson strode out of the kitchen, Edna stared forlornly at her half-eaten meal, dropped her napkin and heaved shakily out of the chair.

Janine spoke quickly. "Edna, wait."

The woman paused in the doorway but neither looked at Janine nor made any response.

Swallowing hard, Janine laid the sponge down and nervously crossed the room. "I, ah, want to apologize if you were offended by what you saw last night."

Edna shook her head sadly. "The devil's concubine must seek God's forgiveness, not mine."

Taken aback by the stinging assessment, Janine stammered, "I—I think that's a bit harsh."

The woman's blue eyes were filled with sadness. "Pray for purification, my dear. Ask God for salvation before your soul is condemned to eternal damnation." Then she patted Janine's hand and waddled away.

Stunned, Janine sat at the table and shivered. Even though she was used to Edna's melodramatic zealotry, be-

ing described as the devil's concubine was nonetheless unsettling. She massaged her forehead and was trying to shake
off the disquieting notion that the woman might actually
believe her own pious pronouncement when the doorbell
rang.

Janine moaned. Althea must have stormed off without
her key. With any luck she'd returned to pack her things. If
not, Janine would slap a thirty-day notice in her hand as
encouragement. As for Jules and his grandmother, although Janine didn't feel particularly charitable toward the
grandson, Edna had had nothing to do with the unconscionable scheme and Janine was reluctant to punish the
innocent woman by evicting her grandson.

Perhaps if she offered more time, Edna could locate other
accommodations—

The doorbell rang again and was instantly followed by an
insistent pounding. Since the entire house was vibrating,
Janine leaped up and hurried to the foyer. Expecting to
confront Althea, she angrily yanked open the door and was
stunned to find a somber group of uniformed men on her
porch.

"Sorry to disturb you, ma'am." Sheriff Rhodes tipped his
hat, then nodded to the deputies, who promptly brushed
past Janine and swarmed into the house. One officer headed
toward the kitchen area; another moved down the hall toward her office and two more went directly upstairs.

"What is this?" Janine stepped back as Rhodes entered
the foyer. "What's going on here?"

The sheriff closed the door. "We have a warrant for
Quinn Coulliard's arrest, ma'am. Is he here?"

She managed not to choke, although her voice was edged
by panic. "What is he being charged with?" A loud crash
emanated from the kitchen and was followed by a series of
clanking sounds. "What are they doing to my kitchen?"

Rhodes handed her a folded sheet of paper. "I'm sorry, Miss Taylor."

She stared numbly at the document. "What is this?"

"A warrant to search the premises."

Her head snapped up in astonishment. "Search for what? Do you expect to find a fugitive in my cupboard?"

Before Rhodes could respond, a lanky young deputy appeared at the top of the stairs and announced that the rooms were all locked. Behind him, a second officer was traversing the hall beating on each door and demanding entry.

The sheriff turned to Janine. "I assume you have keys."

Furious but realizing she had no choice, Janine fixed him with an icy stare. "If you will kindly leash your men, sir, I will personally show you to Mr. Coulliard's room."

Rhodes nodded sharply, issued a curt order to the officer on the stairs then followed Janine toward her office, where they found a perplexed deputy fumbling with the doorknob. Janine froze him with a look. When he stepped aside, she took the key from her pocket, unlocked the door and strode directly to her desk.

After retrieving the guest-room master key, she tossed the warrant onto a file cabinet, and ignoring Rhode's outstretched hand, brushed by the startled sheriff to make a beeline for the stairs. She heard footsteps behind her and knew Rhodes was following but continued to hurry down the hall hoping to spare Quinn the indignity of having a uniformed posse burst through the door unannounced.

By the time she reached his room, Rhodes was on the upstairs landing. Janine rapped on the door and called Quinn's name in a stage whisper. When there was no response, she tried again. "The sheriff is here. He has a warrant but I'm sure it's all a mistake." Silence. "Open the door, Quinn. You have to clear this up."

Rhodes came up beside her and silently extended his hand. With a sinking heart, Janine reluctantly dropped the key into his palm, stepped back and was horrified to realize that the other two deputies had drawn their guns.

When Rhodes unsnapped his own holster, she grabbed at his arm. "That's not necessary!"

He brushed her aside. "Please stay back."

Instinctively realizing that Quinn was not inside, Janine simply sagged against the wall as Rhodes unlocked the door then opened it with a swift kick. Instantly all three officers rushed the room and were greeted by an earsplitting shriek.

Her hands flew to her mouth. "Oh, God. Edgar."

Spinning around, she stumbled through the doorway into utter chaos. The hysterical raven was flapping wildly, trying to drive away the intruders. Screeching frantically, the bird faked a swoop toward one lanky deputy, who promptly dived behind the dresser. His partner flattened against the wall, shielding his face with his arms and screaming for someone to shoot the damned bird.

When Rhodes crouched to level his service revolver, Janine emitted a horrified gasp, jumped forward and hung on to his gun arm like a treed opossum. "That bird can't hurt you! Can't you see that the poor thing is injured?"

Rhodes straightened, glanced around, and as his gaze settled on the open window he holstered his weapon. "Looks like Coulliard's gone," he announced to no one in particular.

Janine stared at the billowing curtain, realizing instinctively that the open window had not been Quinn's means of escape. She was certain that he'd used the tunnel but kept that information to herself as Rhodes ordered his troops to search the room.

As the young deputy emerged from behind the dresser, Edgar emitted another raucous screech. The man winced and turned to his partner, jerking his thumb toward the goosenecked perch. "You take that side."

"Me?" The man against the wall seemed horrified by the thought. "You're closer."

"Yeah, but you're the animal lover."

"Birds aren't animals. They're...they're birds." He shuddered. "I hate birds."

The lanky man was unimpressed. "Well, I don't even own a dog—"

Rhodes ended the argument with an unintelligible command, which put both deputies at attention, then he turned to Janine. "Can you take the bird out of here?"

She cleared her throat and slid a nervous glance toward the irritated raven. "I doubt it. I'm afraid Edgar doesn't like me very much, either."

Rhodes considered that. "Does it always stay on that lamp?"

"Yes, I think so."

"Well, I guess we'll find out." Rhodes tugged down his brimmed hat, rounded the bed, then dropped to his knees and crept along the floor.

The raven cocked a yellow eye, watching warily. When the sheriff pushed away the newspapers at the base of the lamp, Edgar arched a wing and hissed. Thankfully, however, the bird remained in place as Rhodes pushed the weighted base until the lamp was safely situated in the far corner.

Satisfied, the sheriff crawled backward, stood and brushed off his hands. "There. Now you—" he gestured toward the younger officer "—search the dresser and bed. Terrence, you take the closet and the rest of the room."

The deputy called Terrence instantly opened the closet and unceremoniously began tossing out the contents. His partner pawed through a dresser drawer, flipping T-shirts and underwear haphazardly over his shoulder until the floor was littered with crumpled garments.

Infuriated by the unnecessary desecration, Janine issued a strenuous protest. "This is positively barbaric. There's no need to destroy the man's possessions."

Rhodes merely shrugged.

Janine was beside herself. "This is all a terrible mistake. As soon as it's been cleared up, you're going to owe Mr. Coulliard an apology for this...this..." Words failed and she encompassed the mess with a frustrated gesture. Finally she stuffed her hands in her pockets and sighed. "What on earth do you expect to find, anyway?"

"Evidence."

"What kind of evidence— Oh, my God! Stop that at once!" Janine stepped over a can of shaving cream, scooped up a toothbrush and travel-size bottle of after-shave, then yanked an empty leather case out of the young deputy's hands. "Surely you can conduct your search without dumping the man's personal supplies on the floor."

Rhodes plucked the items from her hands and returned them to his deputy. "Please, Miss Taylor. We're just doing our job."

"This is outrageous."

"Yes, ma'am." The sheriff grasped her elbow and insistently ushered her out of the room. Once in the hallway, Rhodes released his indignant captive, lifted his hat and wiped his forehead with the back of his hand. "Would you open the other bedrooms, please?"

Janine folded her arms stubbornly. "Absolutely not."

He sighed. "All I need is a quick look-see to make sure Coulliard isn't holed up in one of the other rooms. I won't be conducting an evidence search."

She eyed him skeptically. "You won't touch any of my guests' things?"

"No, ma'am." After a thoughtful moment, he added, "Not unless I have to."

Janine started to quibble, then thought better of it. She knew without doubt that Quinn wasn't in the house, and besides, a cursory glance of the search warrant had indicated that the sheriff was authorized to inspect every square inch of the building if he wanted to. The sheriff obviously planned to inspect the bedrooms whether she liked it or not, so Janine decided that cooperation might make the process quicker and less painful.

With a resigned sigh, she opened the door to her own room. Then over the next few minutes, Janine opened the remaining bedrooms and Rhodes, true to his word, only looked into the closets and checked under the beds without touching any personal possessions.

When he'd finished with the final room, he scratched his head and glanced quizzically out the hall window. She followed his gaze to where Quinn's dusty beige minivan was parked at the end of the gravel drive.

She cleared her throat. "Mr. Coulliard enjoys walking in the woods. You probably just missed him."

The sheriff's knowing smile suggested that he didn't accept the theory that Quinn's absence was coincidental, but before he could respond, the lanky deputy emerged from Quinn's room clutching a familiar, tattered photo. "Terrence found this in the nightstand. It's her, isn't it?"

The sheriff took the photo and inspected it carefully. The two men exchanged a telling look, then Rhodes returned the picture with a curt command. "Bag it."

The young deputy nodded and disappeared back into the room.

Rubbing her hands, Janine nervously stepped forward. "What has that woman got to do with any of this?"

Rhodes regarded her thoughtfully and apparently decided to answer at least some of her questions. "Coulliard's file was faxed from California. That photo was part of it."

"I imagine it would be. She was directly responsible for Mr. Coulliard being convicted of a crime he didn't commit."

The sheriff lazily scratched his earlobe. "Is that what he told you?"

"Yes."

"And you believed him?"

She felt like she'd swallowed a brick. "There was no reason not to."

He regarded her with the pity one feels for the victim of a cruel hoax. "Exactly what did he tell you about her?"

"Well, that she was his fiancée and her name was Cynthia Zabrow..." She paused and, reassured by Rhode's confirming nod, continued to carefully relate what Quinn had told her. When she'd finished, she faced him squarely. "I assume the file indicates that throughout the trial Mr. Coulliard consistently declared his innocence."

He was unimpressed. "Most people do."

"I believe him."

"I can see that." He regarded her for a moment. "Did he tell you the rest of it?"

Nonplussed by the man's intense stare, Janine absently smoothed her clothing. "I know that he was unfairly convicted and unjustly imprisoned."

"And Miss Zabrow...did he happen to mention what happened to her?"

Janine continued to fiddle with a loose thread. "I didn't ask, actually."

"Maybe you should have."

She looked up. "What is that supposed to mean?"

Rhodes sighed and laid a hand on her shoulder. "The day after Coulliard was released from prison, he went to see Miss Zabrow. According to witnesses, they had one hell—begging your pardon—of a row."

Although that information was admittedly disturbing, Janine forced a noncommittal shrug. "He'd just lost nearly two years of his life because of her perjured testimony. I can't blame him for being testy."

Without commenting on that, he tucked his hands into his pockets. "Right after that fight, there was a fire at Miss Zabrow's apartment."

Janine sucked in a quick breath. "A...fire?"

"Yes, ma'am." He scrutinized her reaction. "The funny thing was that Miss Zabrow was found in bed, her hands folded across her chest, just like she'd been asleep—Miss Taylor? Are you all right?"

The hall started to undulate. Laying a palm over her eyes, she shook her head weakly. Rhodes slid a solicitous arm around her shoulders. Without the strength to push him away, she permitted him to guide her down the hall and into her bedroom. As she sat limply on the edge of the bed, the tears started. "I...don't believe it."

"I'm sorry, Miss Taylor. I don't blame you for being upset but it's true, all right. Coulliard's fiancée and Marjorie Barker died exactly the same way."

"A coincidence," she whispered.

He pulled up a chair. "That's not likely. Both had smoke in their lungs, indicating that they were alive when the fire started but neither one of them had made even the slightest effort to get away. According to pathologists, the body's involuntary responses to suffocation should have kicked in and the victims should have made some attempt to escape. Once could be an anomaly. Twice adds up to murder."

"No." She shook her head violently, understanding the facts yet completely dismissing them. "It doesn't make sense. There's no reason, no motive..."

"Miss Zabrow's testimony sent Coulliard to prison," Rhodes said firmly. "In my book, that's motive enough."

"But Quinn didn't even know Marjorie Barker. Why on earth would he kill her?"

"I don't know, but when I catch up with him I plan to find out." Standing, he adjusted his hat. "I have to get back to my men. Are you going to be okay?"

"Yes." The word almost choked her.

After the sheriff left, Janine gave in to burgeoning hysteria. There had to be some mistake. It was that Quintin Collard person. He was the real killer. And the California authorities must have sent the wrong file, or if they sent the right one, Rhodes must have misread the information...

With a distraught whimper, she clutched the bedclothes and mentally recounted the mounting evidence. She didn't want to believe that a man as tender and loving as Quinn had the capacity for murder but the circumstances surrounding Cynthia's death had dealt an almost mortal blow to her faith.

Outside, the wind moaned like a human cry, an eerie echo of Quinn's own whispered warning. *Trust no one... especially me.*

As that veiled warning took on a more sinister tone, Janine was frightened, confused and certain of only one thing: If the man she loved *was* a cold-blooded killer, she could be his next victim.

CHAPTER THIRTEEN

It was late afternoon before the deputies completed their search, and Janine was thankful that the guests had been out during the chaos. Edna's shift at the clinic hadn't ended until four and Jules had apparently spent the day in Eugene. Althea, still nursing her snit, had spent the night elsewhere and still hadn't returned.

Unfortunately, however, Jules and his grandmother had driven up as the deputies were leaving and required a lengthy and unpleasant explanation that she would have preferred to avoid. Upon hearing that a warrant had been issued for Quinn's arrest—Janine scrupulously avoided details—Jules had smirked silently while Edna graciously announced that she and her grandson would dine in town before church that evening. Janine had been grateful for a reprieve from attempting to prepare a meal in a kitchen that looked like a war zone.

After they'd left, Janine had spent nearly two hours restoring order to the ransacked pantry and returning dishes, utensils and cookware to cupboards that had been emptied by the marauding officers.

Now it was past sundown, and she was finally able to drag herself upstairs to determine what, if anything, could be done to repair the havoc wreaked in Quinn's devastated bedroom. When she flipped on the light, the raven emitted the menacing hiss that she now recognized as pure bluster.

"Give it a rest," she muttered to the ruffled bird, then sat tiredly on the chair and surveyed the damage. Empty drawers were piled on the floor, crumpled clothing was strewn everywhere and even the bed had been stripped of linens and thoroughly inspected. The upended mattress was still propped against a wall.

A cool breeze swirled through the open window, lifting the fine hairs at her nape. The fresh air felt delicious but she had no time to appreciate the lovely spring night. As foolish as it seemed, she didn't want Quinn to see that his privacy had been so callously violated. Even if he never returned—a thought too distressing to seriously consider— she was much too fastidious to accept such a disheveled mess in her home. So she had work to do.

With a pained sigh, she started by wrestling the mattress back on top of the box spring. After she'd muscled the awkward thing into position, she threw the trampled bedclothes into the hallway and retrieved fresh sheets from the linen closet.

When the bed had been neatly made, she began the tedious process of restocking the closet and folding the garments that had been heaped on the floor. Janine still didn't understand what the deputies had been looking for and suspected that they didn't, either.

One officer had been particularly excited about a supply of gasoline kept for the backup generator. Rhodes, however, had pointed out that no trace of liquid accelerant had been found at the fire scene so the deflated deputy had returned the confiscated fuel container to the basement.

So as far as Janine knew, the only "evidence" produced by the massive effort had been the dog-eared photograph of Cynthia and a brush containing samples of Quinn's hair. What the deputies hadn't found, however, was most bothersome.

Quinn's revolver was missing.

She assumed, of course, that he'd taken the weapon with him and was unsettled to know that he was armed. Still, she hadn't told Rhodes about the gun for the same reason that she hadn't mentioned the secret tunnel—she simply couldn't bring herself to believe that Quinn was a killer and had rationalized the mounting evidence as purely circumstantial.

Initially her faith had been severely tested when she'd learned the details of Cynthia's death, but as the day progressed, she'd mentally twisted the facts to justify other possibilities. Now she sat cross-legged on the floor, carefully smoothed a white T-shirt and tried to convince herself that, although perjured testimony could be considered a motive for murder, the woman might have had other enemies as well.

Perhaps the hit-and-run victim's family had discovered that Cynthia, not Quinn, had been behind the wheel. But that was difficult to believe. If there had been any evidence to that effect, Quinn would never have been convicted.

Janine laid down the folded shirt and massaged her stiff neck, considering other possibilities. Even if the grieving kin believed the court version, they may have still held Cynthia partially responsible because she'd admitted being at the scene.

Now that made sense. In fact, the more Janine stretched credibility, the more loopholes she found. But the main flaw in Rhodes's logic was the Marjorie Barker connection. There was no motive and not a shred of evidence that Quinn had even met Marjorie.

There were, of course, certain psychopathic personalities for whom the thrill of the kill was motive enough but Janine dismissed that horrible idea. Quinn Coulliard was no psychopath. In spite of having been cruelly betrayed by his fiancée, he was a man of compassion and great tenderness. She'd seen his gentle side. She'd touched it, been moved by it. Even now her skin tingled with the memory of how his sweet caresses had ignited the fiery passion in her soul.

She fingered the folded T-shirt, then lifted it to her face and inhaled the faint scent lingering in the soft cotton. Quinn's essence enveloped her, invaded her, aroused her. The images sharpened. She remembered the electric feel of his fingertips sliding across her bare skin, the pounding of her heart as his lips brushed down her throat and beyond. Closing her eyes, she clutched the fragrant fabric to her breast and remembered every joyous moment of their love-making.

And then she remembered how he'd sent her away.

Instantly sobered, Janine wiped her moist eyes, shook off the bittersweet memories and quickly completed her task. She put away the folded garments and forcefully closed the dresser drawer. The sharp slam startled Edgar. The raven screeched and flapped frantically, repeatedly beating his wing against the wall.

Janine tried to soothe the nervous bird. "It's okay," she murmured, moving slowly toward the narrow corner where Rhodes had shoved the gooseneck perch. "Be a good bird and I'll put the lamp back where it belongs, okay?" At her approach, Edgar's back feathers lifted ominously and his beak parted in a silent threat.

She hesitated. "Let's make a deal here. I'll move your perch if you promise not to put holes in my skin. Does that sound like a good plan?" When she reached slowly toward the lamp stem, however, the raven aimed a sharp peck at her wrist. Yanking her hand away, she took a quick step back and rubbed the stinging welt. "You are an ungrateful brat."

Edgar cawed irritably.

"Look, you're not the only one who's had a lousy day so let's cut each other some slack, all right?" Janine frowned and massaged her eyelids. Now she was negotiating with a bird. It was ludicrous, absolutely ludicrous, but the worst part was that for a brief, insane moment, she'd actually been waiting for a reply.

Shaking her head, she dropped to her knees as Rhodes had done and crept forward until she could touch the lamp. But the sheriff had simply slid the weighted base forward into the corner. Janine had to grasp the stem and drag the lamp against the carpet grain as she crawled awkwardly backward. For Edgar, the trip was not a smooth one. The bird screeched with every jerk, and the lamp swayed dangerously.

She muttered under her breath as the circular base tipped enough to dig into the nylon fibers. She tugged gently, then with a bit more force. The lamp tilted. Janine ducked. Edgar shrieked.

As she shielded her head with one arm, the terrified raven leaped straight up and fluttered onto the dresser as the goosenecked perch crashed to the floor.

Stunned, she peeked under her elbow, then sat back on her heels and moaned in frustration. Shards of the shattered light bulb were scattered across the floor and the lamp base had split in half. She should have left well enough alone. Now the poor bird was terrified, and its perch was in pieces.

Hoping to repair the damage, she inspected a flat metal circle that had separated from the base, glanced toward the convex portion that was still attached to the stem and noticed a brown paper triangle sticking out. A closer look revealed that a manila envelope had been curved to the proper shape and taped inside the lamp base.

The hairs on her nape tingled.

With trembling fingers, she removed the envelope, opened it and shook out the contents. A dozen yellowed news clippings fluttered to the floor. Dazed, she shifted through them until a newsprint photo caught her eye. Her stomach twisted as she recognized Cynthia Zabrow's image. The faded headline read Spurned Lover Questioned In Arson Death.

The accompanying article verified what Rhodes had revealed earlier, adding that although the police considered Quinn as their prime suspect they'd lacked sufficient evidence for an arrest.

The remaining articles documented several other fatal fires, which had taken place over the past seven years in such widespread locales as Boston, Seattle, Boise and some dinky Nevada town that Janine had never heard of. From the meager information provided, she didn't see any connection between the gruesome incidents but apparently someone did.

Someone? She slumped forward, propping her forehead on one fist. No matter how valiantly she tried to absolve Quinn of responsibility, there was no doubt that the clippings belonged to him, and it didn't take a genius to figure out that he'd hidden them to conceal the information they contained.

But except for the article about Cynthia, the other incidents seemed to have no relationship to Quinn whatsoever. Perplexed, she arranged them in chronological order and noticed that one article from Southern California that seemed particularly out of place.

It was an upbeat story about a bookstore owner sponsoring a church camp for disadvantaged youngsters. The accompanying photograph showed the chaotic clutter of about a dozen manned fund-raising tables. In the foreground the event sponsor was hugging a smiling blond volunteer.

As human interest stories went, this one seemed rather mundane, but as she scanned the first paragraph a familiar name leaped out like a death scream. With her heart pounding in denial, she reread the piece again and again and again until dazed numbness turned to stark horror.

Anxiously scrutinizing the faded photo, Janine was stunned to recognize Marjorie Barker as the bookstore owner. The volunteer she was so fervently embracing was the woman in Quinn's tattered photograph—Cynthia Zabrow.

The clipping fluttered from Janine's limp fingers. The article offered more than photographic evidence that Cynthia and Marjorie had been acquainted. It also provided the missing link connecting Quinn Coulliard to murder.

Illuminating the keyhole with a penlight, Quinn inserted a homemade lock pick and felt the tumblers slip. With a final glance toward the darkened street—and the pin-striped pickup he'd borrowed from the lumberyard parking lot—he slipped inside the brick building and crept down the deserted hallway.

Following dim light pools cast by small ceiling domes, Quinn cautiously traversed the main corridor. When the passageway emptied into an expansive lobby, he flattened against the wall and peered around the corner.

The guard station was across the room, not far from the building's double-doored entry area. A security guard lounged behind the counter, feet propped on the desk, sipping a soft drink and engrossed in watching a sports event on the tiny television nested in his lap.

Considering the guard's distraction to be a stroke of luck, Quinn stealthily moved to the clinic's suite directory situated in the center of the lobby. Concealed from the guard station by the massive glassed board, he scanned the list and located a name he recognized from a business card in Jules's room: Aaron Orbach, M.D.—Adult Adolescent Psychiatry, Suite 207.

Keeping a watchful eye on the preoccupied guard, he backtracked quietly, slipped into the main corridor and headed toward the marked doorway he'd passed on the way in. With a final glance down the darkened hall, he slipped inside the stairwell. The passageway was cramped and lighted only with small bulbs at the landing. He switched on his trusty penlight and followed the slender beam to the second floor.

After emerging into a narrow hallway studded with doors, Quinn found Suite 207 and examined the lock. Because the tenants relied on guards, the building's entrance doors hadn't been wired to an alarm system. He fervently hoped that such lackadaisical security measures extended to the individual medical offices. Tripping an alarm could be a fatal mistake but he'd run out of options. The sheriff was on to him now. He had nothing to lose.

Wiping away her tears, Janine choked back another sob and struggled with an agonizing decision. Should she hide the clippings? Burn them? Turn them over to the sheriff?

No. She couldn't betray Quinn.

Even if he's a murderer?

"He isn't," she whispered aloud. "He couldn't be."

The evidence says otherwise.

"Damn the evidence!" She angrily swiped at the pile, scattering paper bits randomly over the floor. Clutching her abdomen, she slowly rocked back and forth and tried to convince herself that she was overreacting. After all, a few stupid articles filled with vague innuendo and disjointed supposition weren't proof of anything. So what if Quinn's fiancée had known Marjorie Barker? Cynthia probably had had a lot of friends Quinn had never met. The fact that both Cynthia and Marjorie had suffered similar fates was pure coincidence...

With a distraught whimper, Janine covered her face with both hands. In her desperation to absolve Quinn of responsibility for the heinous crimes, she'd mentally created a defense so lame that even she didn't believe it.

Finally she sniffed, wiped her cheek on her sleeve and realized that she'd been deluding herself. Facts were facts. People had died, and despite her silent denials evidence indicated that Quinn had been involved. If Janine concealed everything she now knew, there could be other deaths. She couldn't stand idly by and allow that to happen. She had to turn the documents over to the sheriff. There was no other choice, but the decision broke her heart.

Taking a deep breath, she gathered the clippings and was hastily stuffing them into the envelope when the raven cawed a warning. Janine glanced over her shoulder and frowned. "What's wrong now?"

As the agitated bird hopped and flapped, she heard something peculiar. Actually it was more vibration than sound. She hesitated, then laid her palms on the floor and waited. A moment later, she felt another minute vibration, which was followed by a faint creaking, like footsteps on a warped floorboard.

Or the sound of rusty hinges.

Janine froze. Only she and Quinn knew about the hidden panel. After a few more moments, she heard another sound but this time it seemed to be coming from downstairs. She relaxed slightly, assuming one of her tenants must have come in and the creaking sound had been nothing more than a warped stair.

Still, it was odd that she'd heard the stair squeak *before* she'd heard the downstairs noise. She shook off a disquieting sensation. Perhaps someone had returned earlier and come upstairs when she'd been too preoccupied to notice, then decided to get a snack from the kitchen and returned to the lower floor.

She rose and quietly crossed the room. She put her ear to the door and heard footsteps in the hallway. Someone was definitely upstairs. Gathering her courage, she carefully opened the door and looked down the deserted hallway. She stepped out, berating herself for being so skittish.

But what if it was Quinn? If she confronted him with what she'd found, would she be in danger? As she glanced back at the manila envelope, a tiny voice in her brain whispered that Quinn would never hurt her.

Mentally fortified, she managed to croak out a greeting. "Hello?" Silence. "Is anyone there?" When there still was no reply, she moved cautiously toward the landing. "Edna? Jules? Is that you?"

Emerging at the point where the two upstairs hallways joined, her gaze was riveted on the hidden panel. It was closed tight and she saw no fresh mud on the carpet. A quick glance downstairs confirmed that the front door was still locked. There was no evidence that Quinn—or anyone else—had returned.

Her breath slid out slowly. Apparently her shattered nerves had magnified normal settling sounds from the crumbling old structure into something sinister. Feeling supremely stupid, she massaged a stiff shoulder and rolled her neck. Every inch of her body ached, and now her head was beginning to throb.

She glanced at her watch. Although it was barely past nine, she was utterly exhausted and the thought of dragging herself to the sheriff's station was less than appealing. Something urged her to go, anyway, but after a brief mental argument, she decided that tomorrow would be soon enough. Perhaps the respite would allow time for some kind of miraculous reprieve—

A shadow loomed from behind her.

Whirling, Janine touched her throat, then steadied herself against the wall and tried to catch her breath. "You scared me half to death." When there was no response, she was instantly concerned. "Is something wrong?" Extending her hand, she took a step forward. "What is it? Tell me what's happened."

Edna's eyes were filled with misery. "Armageddon," she whispered. "It has begun."

* * *

After jimmying the locked file cabinet, Quinn slid the pick into his pocket and used the penlight to search through Orbach's patient records. He'd already found the meticulously labeled session tapes, but since it would take hours to review the recordings, he hoped that Orbach had written summaries of his findings.

As Quinn flipped through the marked folders, his professional conscience cringed. Violating the confidentiality of a psychiatrist and patient was not only against the law, it ruffled the moral grain of his deepest convictions. But when he found the file he'd been seeking, conscience was overwhelmed by urgency.

Scrutinizing the pages, he recognized that Orbach's notes provided a thoughtful analysis but the diagnosis was sketchy and inconclusive: Patient delusional with psychoneurotic conversion syndrome. Psychopathically repressed, symptomatic schizophrenia suggestive of possible MPD.

The last entry irritated him. Although Multiple Personality Disorder was quite real, it had become a psychobabble buzzword for any behavior that couldn't be categorized by a neatly defined psychosis. Other than that diagnostic aberration, however, Quinn saw nothing unexpected until he turned to the patient history and scanned the chronological records. Then he nearly dropped the penlight.

As he studied the revealing entries, his blood iced and a nauseating numbness settled in the pit of his stomach. His quest was finally over but the result shocked him to the core.

He shoved the file back in the drawer, rushed out of the building and prayed that this time he wouldn't be too late.

"What on earth are you talking about?" Janine asked anxiously. "Has something happened to Jules?"

At the mention of her grandson, the color drained from Edna's face. "I'm afraid for you, child."

"Me? Why?"

The woman moaned and shook her head. "There's danger, such terrible danger."

"What...kind of danger?"

"The danger of losing your immortal soul."

"Oh, for crying out loud." Since Janine was already as edgy as a treed cat, she was unwilling to endure another round of gloomy prognostications. "I'm sorry but I really am quite tired. In fact, I was just on my way to bed so unless there's something I can do for you—"

"God loves you," Edna blurted, clutching her handbag like a shield. "He, in his infinite wisdom, has chosen to absolve you of blasphemy and moral turpitude. He has bestowed upon you the blessing of eternal life, a place of glory in His holy kingdom."

"I'm pleased to know that. Now if you'll excuse me..."

With a movement too quick for such a squat woman, Edna blocked Janine's path. Her blue eyes bulged with terror. "Please...you must listen. The beast is coming."

"What beast? I don't understand what on earth—" Janine suddenly had a horrible thought. Edna had expressed the same raw terror after learning that Jules and Althea had been alone together. Later, embracing Althea with perplexing ferocity, the older woman had nearly wept with relief. And then there was that night in the kitchen, when Jules's eyes had glittered so strangely....

Janine cleared her throat. "Exactly where *is* Jules?"

Rolling her eyes heavenward, Edna let out a wail that made Janine's hair stand on end. "The devil's disciple has been sent to defile purity and devour innocent souls. It is the end of the world, child. You must save yourself from the clutches of evil."

Janine instantly placated the terrified woman. "I will, Edna. I promise."

Tears of relief seeped from her wrinkled eyes. "Praise the Lord," she murmured. "God is merciful."

Janine backed toward the stairs. "In fact, I'm going to leave right now and I want you to come with me."

Tiny blue eyes blinked in bewilderment. "There is no escape except through the grace of God. You have sinned, given your body in lust."

Stunned, Janine stammered, "Excuse me?"

"That foul man—" Edna wiggled a frantic finger toward Quinn's room "—has besmirched a woman of God. He must be punished."

Although baffled by the odd response, Janine decided not to quibble with such nonsensical rambling. The woman's terror seemed quite genuine, and since Jules could arrive at any moment, Janine was anxious to leave.

Grasping the older woman's arm, Janine glanced over the railing to the deserted foyer. "We'll talk about that later. Right now we need to go downstairs and get into my car."

Edna yanked away. "You cannot run from destiny."

"First you warn me to leave and then you say I can't get away." Janine's head was spinning as frustration turned to annoyance. "If this is some kind of melodramatic hoax designed to get my attention, it's definitely succeeded. I want to know what's going on, and I want to know now."

Edna's gaze softened. With a tolerant smile, she lovingly caressed Janine's cheek. "It wasn't your fault, you know. Too many souls have been led astray by temptation but it's not too late. I can save you."

"Save me from whom?" Janine's nerves and patience simultaneously snapped. She shook the startled woman's shoulders. "Answer me and no more double-talk. Is Jules dangerous? Are you afraid of him?"

Edna gaped in astonishment. "Afraid of my own grandson? How utterly ridiculous!"

Persisting, Janine tightened her grasp on the woman's flabby arms. "Should *I* or anyone else be afraid of him?"

"Of course not!" As Edna indignantly pulled away, her frizzy curls brushed Janine's chin. "Jules is a good boy. He wouldn't hurt a flea."

The sincerity of her strenuous protest added to Janine's doubt and confusion. But since Edna had seemed so obviously terrified of someone, Janine still wasn't convinced that the source of that fear hadn't been her grandson. "Where is Jules now?"

"Why, he's in church, child, praying for your soul." Her saggy jowls creased with her smile. "You know how much he loves you."

The information that Jules regarded Janine with affection wasn't particularly comforting. She did, however, relax slightly and regarded Edna's odd behavior with a more jaundiced eye. The woman's ominous status as self-appointed prophet of doom was certainly common knowledge; therefore it was reasonable to conclude that the dire monitions had been based on metaphysical foreboding rather than the human peril Janine had first imagined. There was no legitimate danger—at least not on this earthly plane.

Janine was irritated with herself for jumping at shadows, seeing danger everywhere and envisioning just about everyone she'd ever met as a potential murderer. It was all ridiculous, obviously the product of an overactive imagination and a sleep-deprived brain.

A gentle hand touched her arm. "Are you all right, dear? You look quite peaked."

She offered a stiff smile. "I'm just a little tired, that's all."

"Of course you are." The woman clucked sympathetically, then took Janine's elbow and guided her down the hall. "What you need is a good night's rest."

Janine offered no resistance. Stepping around the bed-clothes heaped in the hall, she turned to say good-night but Edna brushed by and entered Janine's bedroom. The woman waddled to the bed, placed her handbag on the nightstand and began turning down the covers, chattering cheerfully about love and forgiveness and the power of eternal salvation.

All Janine wanted, however, was to be left alone. "That's not necessary, Edna."

"I enjoy doing for you, dear." She fluffed a fat pillow, then arranged it lovingly on the bed. "Marie Louise loved the way I turned down her bed. She could never sleep well unless I tucked her in."

"Marie Louise is your daughter?"

"Yes." A faraway look glazed the woman's blue eyes. "She's with the Lord now."

"I'm sorry."

A peculiar expression crossed Edna's face. "The Heavenly Father's call is an occasion of great joy." Then she blinked, smiled sweetly and patted the bed. "Come, child. Rest. Sleep. Dream. Pray for the purification of *ekpyresis*."

At the word "purification" Janine instantly went rigid and her mind flashed back to a college course on ancient Greek mythology. Her lungs contracted, squeezing her breath away.

She remembered. Dear God, she remembered. *Ekpyresis* was an old Greek theological term meaning spiritual purification through fire. In that heart-stopping moment, Janine realized that she *had* to get out of that room. Her frantic gaze darted around the room, but as she eased toward the door Edna blocked the exit.

"You mustn't go, dear." The woman seemed puzzled and strangely hurt by Janine's attempt to leave. "Your bed is ready."

"I—I'm not tired anymore. I have work to finish. Downstairs."

"Poor dear. You work much too hard." Eyes filled with sympathy, Edna reached for her handbag. "You need rest. I have something that will help."

The woman reached into her purse. When she extracted a hypodermic syringe, Janine's horrified gaze was riveted on the white plunger, an exact duplicate of the plastic tube she'd found in the tunnel.

Then Edna advanced with serenity on her lips and madness in her eyes.

CHAPTER FOURTEEN

Janine backed away until her skull touched plaster. With a cry of despair, she held up her palm. "Don't come any closer."

Edna's eyes widened in surprise. "Why are you frightened, child?"

"I—I've never liked needles." Inching along the wall, Janine swallowed her surging panic and focused on the closed bedroom door. A few more feet and she'd be in a position to leap over the bed and get away.

"A mild tranquilizer will help you sleep." Edna smiled calmly. "I'm a nurse, dear. I know what you need."

When the woman stepped forward, Janine dashed for the bed and rolled over the mattress, but as her feet hit the floor Edna's chunky frame barricaded the door. "You mustn't disobey," she admonished, obviously annoyed by Janine's refusal to cooperate.

Quickly scanning the room, Janine realized that leaping out of a second-story window was not a viable option, so if she was going to escape unscathed, she had to use the door.

Flexing her fingers, she scrutinized her deranged adversary. Edna outweighed her by fifty pounds but youth and strength should give Janine an advantage—assuming that she could keep the syringe a safe distance away while she wrestled the hefty woman to the ground. A physical altercation was risky, of course, but the odds were in Janine's favor, and besides, she didn't seem to have another choice.

She squared her shoulders and met Edna's glassy stare. "Please stand aside. I don't want to hurt you."

With a perplexed frown, Edna murmured, "Oh, my." Then she casually reached into her open handbag and pulled out a small revolver. "You're making this quite difficult. I'm very disappointed in you."

With the lethal barrel pointed straight at her heart, Janine's escape plan evaporated much like steam. There was no way out now. She was trapped. All she could do now was distract Edna and hope for a miracle.

"Did Marjorie make it difficult for you?" Janine blurted, frantically scanning the room for something—anything— that could be used as a weapon. "Or Cynthia?"

Edna's glazed expression melted into one of exquisite pain. "No," she whispered. "They were such good girls. They always did as they were told."

Janine felt sick, realizing that because of Edna's medical background the women had probably trusted her and submitted willingly to her "treatment." She also suspected that the injections must have contained a drug powerful enough to induce a comatose condition so the victims couldn't be roused by the suffocating smoke.

Janine shuddered. "If you were so fond of Marjorie and Cynthia, why did you kill them?"

"Kill them?" The woman's head snapped up. "Oh, my dear Lord, I *saved* them."

"Saved them from what?"

"Evil, child. *Evil!*" Eyes bulging, Edna shook the gun like an admonishing finger. "They were decent, God-fearing women but they succumbed to temptation, allowed themselves to become the devil's whores. I gave them salvation, eternal life in the kingdom of their Creator."

Suddenly Janine noticed that Edna held the syringe in her right hand, and because the gun was wobbling unsteadily it seemed doubtful that she was a southpaw marksman. Besides, the woman was obviously as cunning as she was crazy, and since she'd taken great pains to conceal the previous murders as accidental, Janine wondered if the weapon was intended only as an intimidation tactic.

She decided to call the bluff. "If you shoot me, the authorities will know it wasn't an accident."

"Your demon lover will be blamed," Edna snapped. "It's God's will."

Janine's heart sank. The crazy old woman was right. The sheriff would arrest Quinn in a heartbeat and once a jury learned of his connection with the other victims, he'd almost certainly be convicted. She wanted to weep in despair.

Edna held out the syringe. "Give me your arm, dear. We must hurry."

Janine jerked away and suddenly realized why the woman was intent on using drugs when a bullet would have been quicker. "But you're not going to kill me, are you? I have to be alive when the flames come or my soul won't be purified."

Edna chortled gleefully and stepped onto the braided throw rug. "That's right, dear! You'll be saved, absolved of earthly sins. *Ekpyresis.*"

Janine focused on the oval mat. "Tell me, Edna, how many people have you saved lately?"

The woman blinked but said nothing.

"Let's see, there was Marjorie and Cynthia and uh..." As Janine struggled to recall names from the clippings, she remembered the first victim, the one in Boston, had been named Marie. Although the surname had been unfamiliar, she played an instinctive hunch. "And then there was your daughter, Marie Louise. You saved her too, didn't you?"

The wrinkled mouth quivered. "I had to. She'd been tainted by Satan, neglecting her poor son and allowing her body to be soiled by lust."

"But she was your child, your own flesh and blood. Didn't you love her?"

"Love her? Oh, dear Lord, I adored her. That's why I had to save her, don't you see?" Edna's fat hands trembled violently. "I loved my daughter dearly. I loved them all."

"Even Cynthia?"

Blinking back tears, Edna smiled sadly. "Dear sweet Cynthia. She was a saint, rising from the ashes of demon rum to divine purity. She and Marjorie did God's work, creating a place of prayer for children of the streets. It was miraculous, a gift of love that touched the Lord's heart."

Knowing that Edna was referring to the youth camp described in one of the news clippings, Janine also had a fairly good idea of how Quinn's unfortunate ex-fiancée had eventually fallen from grace. "But Cynthia succumbed to sin, didn't she? She started drinking again."

The woman's eyes clouded. "It was the devil's work."

"What about Marjorie?"

"Marjorie was my dearest friend. I cherished her."

As the disturbing pattern became evident, Janine realized that the common thread linking past incidents was a warped affection for the victims. "So after Marjorie moved back to Darby Ridge, you came here to be close to her?"

"Yes, of course."

"And when Marjorie had an affair with Althea's boyfriend, you must have been quite upset."

"Her sin was an abomination to the Lord."

Having already ascertained that her own fate was sealed the night Edna caught her leaving Quinn's room, Janine sickly realized that the deranged woman might be planning even more purifications. "What about Althea?"

Edna scoffed at the notion. "Althea Miller is an unconscionable harlot, unworthy of salvation."

Exhaling slowly, Janine uttered silent thanks that Althea wasn't on the insane hit list. But her relief was short-lived when Edna became agitated and repeatedly glanced at the door as though expecting unwanted company. Finally she raised the syringe and leveled the gun at Janine's chest, assuring her that there would be no pain when the fire came.

Realizing that time had run out, Janine emitted a tiny whimper and pretended to feel faint. She sat heavily on the edge of the bed then swayed forward until her forehead touched her knees and her fingers brushed the rag rug.

From the corner of her eye, she watched Edna's feet. When the woman took a hesitant step, Janine's fingers curled around the braided binding.

Edna bent solicitously. "Please lie down, dear. God will take you home—"

Janine yanked the rug away. The woman flipped backward and landed with a thud, winded and gasping for breath. Janine leaped over the writhing woman, flung open the door and dashed down the hall.

The moment she reached the stair landing, she smelled smoke. As Edna emerged from the bedroom, waving the gun and shrieking furiously, Janine sprinted downstairs and headed straight to the front door.

As she struggled with the dead bolt, she glanced into the parlor and was stunned to see newspapers piled on the hearth and scattered around the room. The fireplace screen had been propped open, allowing popping embers to ignite the papers. As she watched in horror, the parlor curtains went up in flames.

A bullet slammed into the jamb inches from Janine's head.

She whirled and saw Edna at the top of the stairs wildly screaming gibberish about divine wrath and the gates of hell. As the woman aimed the revolver, Janine ducked and spun around. The bullet stung her scalp, knocking her off balance. She stumbled against a wall, then lurched forward and staggered into the kitchen.

The room wobbled, growing dark as her eyesight faded. Her head throbbed. She moaned, touched her temple then stared stupidly at the sticky stain on her fingers. Dazed and disoriented, blinded by blood, she wasn't certain where the danger was or which way to go. She clutched the counter, trying to feel her way along the smooth Formica toward the back door.

A blurry figure loomed in the doorway and Edna's shrill voice reverberated through the room. "The Lord is a vengeful God and His wrath a mighty sword."

As the frenzied woman raised a hand, Janine instinctively lurched away, shielding her face with her arms. She stumbled and fell, then crawled blindly across the floor, unwilling to abjectly surrender to a fate that seemed inevitable.

As she dragged herself forward, Janine was vaguely aware of peculiar noises in the room, an odd, strangled gurgle followed immediately by sounds of struggle. Wiping her eyes, she squinted toward the doorway and saw Edna wrestling with someone. Someone large.

"Quinn," she croaked. "Edna has a g—"

A sharp retort stung her ears. The kitchen window shattered and the pungent smell of gunpowder mingled with wafting smoke. Then the entire house shook violently the revolver clattered to the floor and the parlor exploded into flames.

A nuclear heat blasted into the kitchen, searing Janine's lungs. Still lying on the floor, she rolled away from the burning wind. A moment later, two denim-clad legs appeared and she was lifted by strong arms.

As Quinn carried her toward the back door, the dining room glowed like orange neon and a thick black cloud spilled into the kitchen. A squat figure stood in the doorway, enveloped by smoke. Like an evangelist at the gates of hell, Edna raised her arms and proclaimed, "Satan fell like

lightning from heaven. With fire did God smite His enemies.''

Quinn shouted at her. ''The place is going up. Save yourself!''

With a shrill cackle, Edna dashed back into the raging
inferno and was enveloped by the devouring flames.

Quinn muttered a sharp oath, kicked open the door and
carried Janine into the backyard. She greedily gulped fresh
air, coughed convulsively, then filled her lungs with another wheezing breath. Damp earth touched her back and a
cool palm brushed her cheek. ''Are you all right, honey?''

With some effort, she opened one eye and squinted into
his anxious face. ''I, uh—'' A coughing spasm cut off her
words but she managed a jerky nod.

A cool breeze brushed her cheek, and she realized that
Quinn had gone. She propped herself up on one elbow and
was stunned to see that he was braving the blasting flames
in a futile attempt to reenter the building. ''No, Quinn!''
Janine struggled to her feet. ''It's too late! You can't help
her.''

A second explosion knocked out the laundry-room wall
and blew Quinn off the porch. He landed twenty feet away.

Terrified, Janine stumbled to his side and cradled his
soot-stained face in her lap. ''Oh, God, Quinn.'' Wiping his
singed brows, she inspected him anxiously. His hair was
badly scorched. One side of his face was blistered. ''Can you
hear me?''

He blinked, winced and for a dazed moment didn't seem
to recognize Janine. Then he stared past her toward the
second story and his eyes widened in shock.

At the same moment, Janine heard the familiar screech,
barely audible over the roar of the fire. She looked up, saw
the smoke pouring from the window of Quinn's room and
uttered a cry of dismay when she recognized the terrified
creature frantically hopping along the windowsill.

Quinn rolled off her lap and struggled to stand but was still shaken by the force of the blast. Janine leaped to her feet and quickly positioned herself under the window. Shading her eyes against the fiery glare, she shouted, "Edgar! Jump!" She clapped her hands to capture the frenzied bird's attention. "Come on, Edgar! You can do it!"

The raven cocked its head, looked down at Janine and then focused on a nearby oak tree. Flapping madly, Edgar flung himself at the nearest limb, tumbled down through the branches until the squawking, ruffled heap landed in Janine's outstretched arms.

Instantly Quinn appeared, grasped Janine's waist and hustled her across the yard. When they reached the redwood picnic table, she collapsed on the bench, clutching the raven to her breast.

Quinn dropped to his knees in front of her, framing her face with his palms. He closed his eyes, lowered his head and shuddered. After a moment he inhaled deeply, and when he looked up again his expression was an odd combination of despair and profound relief. "I—" his voice broke and he coughed away the weakness "—I thought I'd lost you."

Still holding the passive raven with one hand, Janine caressed his burned hair. "And I thought I'd lost *you*."

He gently wiped blood from her brow. "You're hurt."

She caressed his jaw, taking care not to touch his blistered flesh. "So are you."

Telltale moisture gathered in his eyes. "I thought you were safe. I swear to God, honey, I didn't know until to—"

"Shh." Her fingertip brushed his lips, silencing him. "You saved my life. If not for you, I'd be dead now."

"It's all my fault. I was so damned arrogant, thought I had everything all figured out...." Words failed him. Quinn shook his head miserably, then moved up to the bench and embraced her.

A distant siren wailed.

Absently stroking the passive raven, Janine laid her head on Quinn's shoulder and they silently watched as the historic Victorian was completely engulfed in flames.

Two hours later, red-and-blue emergency lights strobed over a charred heap of smoldering embers, all that remained of Janine's boardinghouse. Fire fighters rerolled their massive hoses. Deputies, medical personnel and curious onlookers shuffled though the yard, whispering to each other and sneaking compulsive glances at the carnage.

Earlier, in the midst of the chaos, Jules had returned, and upon discovering his grandmother's fate had to be physically restrained from dashing into the flames. The distraught young man had finally collapsed in Quinn's arms, sobbing hysterically. Because of Quinn's effectiveness in calming Jules, the sheriff had been content to keep a watchful eye on the elusive "fugitive" without immediately placing him under arrest.

Althea, who'd also been drawn by the blaze, stood in the middle of the yard like a horrified statue, neither moving nor speaking until the roaring inferno had subsided into a cloud of sizzling steam. Then she found Janine, and the two women had embraced silently.

Now Jules was lying on a stretcher beside an open ambulance, his pathetic sobs punctuated by an occasional grief-stricken wail. In spite of everything, he had loved his grandmother. Edna had been a sick woman, but to the terrified young man his grandmother's death was yet another cruel abandonment.

Quinn stood beside the stretcher, gripping Jules's hand and waving away the frustrated paramedic who was attempting to tend his burns. Althea moved from her seat on the ambulance bumper to the stretcher. "Let them take care of you," she told Quinn. "I'll stay with Jules." She laid a gentle palm on the young man's forehead, leaned over and whispered, "Everything will be all right, hon. Auntie Althea's here. I won't let anyone hurt you."

Quinn hesitated, then turned away and went to Janine. He touched the white gauze taped above her ear then opened his arms. She eagerly fell into his warm embrace, hugging him fiercely and offering a silent prayer of gratitude that the man she loved had been spared a fiery death.

But her heart was filled with guilt and shame at having doubted him in the first place. Like the court that had imprisoned him unjustly, Janine had convicted Quinn in her mind even though her heart had known he was incapable of such heinous acts.

Now she was deeply conflicted, torn between maintaining a wall of silence and being honest with a man who deserved nothing if not the truth—a truth that would hurt him deeply. When Quinn learned that Janine had planned to give damning evidence to the sheriff, he might hate her but that was a risk she had to take. Lies of omission would eventually evolve into an invisible wall of mistrust that could never be overcome. She had to reveal everything and hope that he understood the lapse of faith instead of considering it an unforgivable betrayal.

Wiping her sooty face, Janine reluctantly stepped away and stared at the front of his shirt sharpening her determination. Just as she opened her mouth, however, a masculine voice captured her attention.

"Excuse me." Sheriff Rhodes acknowledged Janine awkwardly before speaking directly to Quinn. "As you suggested, we've contacted Delacourt's psychiatrist. He's on his way here."

Quinn nodded. "Good."

Rhodes pulled the familiar notepad from his breast pocket. "Miss Taylor, I understand you were inside when the fire started. I have some questions, if you're up to it."

Quinn slid a protective arm around Janine's shoulders. "Can't this wait? Janine has been through a lot."

Rhodes frowned. "I suppose, but..."

Janine touched Quinn's arm. "It's all right, really." She turned to the sheriff. "What do you want to know?"

"For starters, how did the fire—" Rhodes waved a hand toward the smoking ruins "—start?"

Holding on to Quinn for support, Janine took a shaky breath. "It was Edna Fabish. She killed Marjorie Barker and tonight..." Janine closed her eyes as Quinn encouraged her with a comforting squeeze. "Tonight she tried to kill me."

With Rhodes frowning skeptically, Janine explained how Edna had used a hypodermic tranquilizer to immobilize her victims for the final purification. "And since there were pieces of a syringe in the tunnel, I knew that—"

Rhodes's hand froze over the notepad. "What tunnel?"

At that point, Quinn intervened. "There's a passageway leading from the house to the ravine below the lumberyard. When I used it tonight, I found a couple of suitcases by the exit. They're probably packed with Edna's personal things."

The sheriff's narrowed gaze slid from Quinn to Janine and back again. "I guess that explains why you were gone when my men and I arrived this morning. But I still got that warrant in my pocket, Coulliard."

Quinn didn't blink. "I'm sure you do."

"I should cuff you right this minute and haul your butt to the station."

Janine went rigid but Quinn simply nodded. "I understand."

Rhodes tapped his pen on the notepad's spiral binding. Finally he emitted a pained sigh. "Aw, hell. Just finish the damned story, and I'll figure out what to do with you later."

With both the sheriff and Janine listening intently, Quinn explained how he'd spotted the sheriff's vehicles from his bedroom window, then slipped into the tunnel and escaped. "I borrowed a truck from the lumberyard parking lot—"

"A blue pickup with lambskin seat covers and a load of rolled wire in the bed?" Rhodes moaned and uttered a succinct oath. "That was Fred Watson's truck. He's been pounding his fist on my desk all afternoon."

Quinn shrugged. "Perhaps in the future Mr. Watson will avoid leaving his keys in the ignition."

"So now we can add auto theft to that warrant." Scribbling madly, Rhodes spoke without looking up. "Where's the vehicle now?"

"Back in the parking lot."

"Why'd you take it in the first place?"

"I had to get to Eugene."

"What in hell is in Eugene?"

"Jules's psychiatrist." Quinn rubbed the back of his neck and nodded at the deputy's notepad. "You might as well put breaking and entering on the list."

Janine, who had been listening in stunned silence, suddenly found her voice and grabbed the sleeve of his leather jacket. "Oh, God, Quinn, what did you do?"

"I went to the mental health clinic and searched Jules's psychiatric files." His eyes softened, pleading for understanding. "I thought he was the one who'd killed Cynthia and all the others."

Rhodes's head jerked up. "How many others?"

Ignoring the perplexed sheriff, Janine spoke to Quinn. "The people in the clippings?"

"Clippings?" Rhodes blinked in bewilderment. "What clippings?"

Quinn frowned. "You found them?"

"The lamp fell over and the base came apart," she explained hastily. "I know I shouldn't have opened the envelope and I honestly didn't mean to pry—"

A sharp whistle cut off her words. Taken aback, she turned just as Rhodes took his fingers away from his mouth. "Now that I have your attention," he said politely, "perhaps you'll start at the beginning and *tell me what in hell is going on here.*"

Quinn glanced warily at Janine, then faced the sheriff. "Have you read the files from California?" When Rhodes indicated that he had, Quinn's jaw twitched. "Then I won't reiterate the details of my ex-fiancée's death except to say that I had a gut feeling that the fire was no accident, so I started my own investigation."

Rhodes scoffed at the concept that an untrained civilian could uncover evidence that had eluded police, but when Quinn's story continued, both Janine and the sheriff listened in rapt fascination as an eerie set of circumstances was revealed.

Quinn explained that after the trial Cynthia had apparently been tormented by guilt and had turned to religion, joining a congregation that included Edna, Jules and Marjorie Barker. Quinn's focus shifted to Jules because it soon became apparent that the young man was severely disturbed.

After traveling to Boston, he'd discovered that when Jules was sixteen his mother had suffered a fate almost identical to Cynthia's, right down to the hands-folded position. Within days of the incident, Edna had taken her grandson and left town.

At that point, Quinn had been certain Jules was the killer so he'd scrupulously reconstructed the young man's movements over the following years. After researching old news reports, he saw a pattern of similar fire fatalities, which had occurred in locations in or near towns where Edna had worked. Shortly after each incident, the woman had resigned her position and moved on but the cycle had always begun again.

Rhodes folded his thick arms and eyed Quinn skeptically. "With a whole passel of dead folks lying around, it's not likely that some police officer wouldn't have made a connection."

"All the deaths were ruled accidental," Quinn pointed out. "So the cases were closed without being entered in the computer network."

The sheriff cringed and glanced away, apparently embarrassed by the flaw in communications between law-enforcement agencies. He cleared his throat. "That all sounds well and good but I just keep coming back to the fact that you were in town when Marjorie Barker died. How'd you know to come here?"

"A hunch," Quinn replied. "The last fire on my list was one that happened about eighteen months ago in Seattle. By the time I got there, Edna and Jules were gone but I'd kept tabs on their friends and knew that Marjorie Barker had sold her bookstore, then moved back to her hometown."

The sheriff rubbed his chin thoughtfully. "So that's why you came to Darby Ridge?"

"Yes, but I was too late." Quinn gazed sadly toward the smoldering ruins of the boardinghouse. "After that, I was determined that Jules wouldn't get the chance to hurt anyone else."

The air rushed from Janine's lungs all at once. Now the veiled warnings and comments about Jules's fragile psyche made perfect sense. She also realized that Quinn's absences had coincided with Jules's schedule. "All those times you left the boardinghouse, you were following Jules?"

"Yes."

"But sometimes when Jules was out, you stayed at the boardinghouse."

"Since I'd never figured out what his motive was, I couldn't predict who he'd victimize next but I was determined that it wasn't going to be you. I tried to make sure you were never alone with him. Unfortunately I also concluded that he wasn't a danger to anyone as long as he was with his grandmother. That's why—'' His voice broke. Obviously shaken, he blew out a breath, closed his eyes and took a moment to compose himself. When he looked up again, his eyes were filled with silent misery. "That's why I went to Eugene tonight. I knew the church service wouldn't end until ten and assumed that they'd be together until then. I swear to God, honey, I thought you'd be safe."

"I know. It's not your fault." Janine squeezed his arm, then glanced at the sheriff. "Have you spoken to Jules about when his grandmother left the church?"

"I tried," Rhodes replied. "The most I could get from his babbling was something about his grandmother needing air about halfway through the service."

Quinn gestured toward the ravine. "Edna must have walked the two blocks from the church to the lumberyard, climbed down the embankment and used the tunnel."

"I heard the panel open," Janine told him. "At first I thought it was just the house settling, then there were noises downstairs. I guess that must have been when Edna was lighting the fireplace and spreading newspapers around the parlor." Since that was also the moment that Janine had decided to turn Quinn in to the sheriff, she avoided his gaze and spoke directly to Rhodes. "The newspaper articles I found will substantiate everything he's told you. I'm sure we can get copies."

"Yes, ma'am." Although Rhodes's skepticism hadn't disappeared completely, his interest was definitely piqued. "One thing I can't quite figure, Coulliard, is why you went to the trouble of digging up that information but didn't turn it over to the authorities."

"I tried, but I the evidence was too circumstantial to be taken seriously. I didn't believe that Jules would be prosecuted unless I could provide absolute proof."

Rhodes rocked back on his heels. "Is that why you broke into the doc's office? For proof?"

"Yes, but since anything I found was privileged information, it was more an act of desperation than intelligent reason." Quinn rubbed his face. "As it turned out, I learned a great deal more than I'd expected."

The sheriff glanced furtively around then lowered his voice to a conspiratorial whisper. "So what's wrong with Delacourt, anyway? Some kind of Freudian thing?"

"I'm sorry, I can't reveal that." Quinn hesitated before carefully adding, "But I can say that Jules spent considerable time in mental institutions and was hospitalized when two of the fires took place."

"So that's when you realized that Edna must be involved?" Janine asked.

"Yes."

Rhodes was unconvinced. "But if Jules knew about the murders, he could still be charged as a conspirator."

"I don't believe he had any knowledge of what his grandmother was doing," Quinn insisted. "With the exception of Marjorie Barker's death, I doubt Jules was even aware of the other fires. Edna was a cunning, manipulative woman. She completely controlled her grandson's access to information and even managed to convince the poor kid that his mother had simply walked away. Edna took her grandson away without even notifying the school. To this day Jules truly believes that his mother is still alive."

When the sheriff started to respond, he was interrupted by a deputy Janine recognized as one of the men who had searched the boardinghouse. Terrence angled a nervous glance toward Quinn but spoke directly to his boss. "Do you want me to, uh, escort Mr. Coulliard to the squad car?"

Pursing his lips, Rhodes returned the notepad to his pocket. He stared at his shoes for a long moment, then squared his shoulders and responded brusquely. "No. Mr.

Coulliard will come by the station tomorrow and clear things up."

The deputy's Adam's apple bobbed. He mumbled an acknowledgment and quickly left.

Rhodes gave Quinn a hard stare. "*Be there,* Coulliard. I'd hate to look like a fool."

Janine felt Quinn's muscles relax. "I will. Thank you."

"Don't be thanking me yet. I'll call Fred and explain what happened to his truck but he'll probably want to press charges."

"I understand."

"And I doubt that Delacourt's shrink is going to be happy about having his files rifled." Rhodes pushed back his hat. "There'll be a lot of questions, Coulliard. I'm betting on you to come up with the right answers." With that final caveat, the sheriff nodded to Janine and disappeared into the loitering crowd.

Quinn's arm tightened around Janine's shoulders. "He's right, honey. This isn't over yet."

"I know that." Janine squeezed her eyes shut, then spun and faced him decisively. "Quinn, I have to tell you something."

He regarded her cautiously. "What is it?"

"When I found those clippings..." She licked her lips then took a deep breath and blurted the awful truth. "I was planning to give them to the sheriff."

To her shock, he simply nodded. "Of course."

"You don't understand. I was actually going to turn you in. I thought—" she shivered as Quinn wiped a tear from her cheek "—I thought you were...guilty."

"I don't blame you." He slid his thumb under her chin, urging her to look at him. "From the first moment I arrived, I did everything possible to push you away and make you mistrust me."

"But why?"

"Because you affected me. There was something about you that touched my heart and invaded my mind. I tried to convince myself that you were just a sweet distraction but deep down I knew that you were so much more." His thumb traced her jaw then slid down to caress her throat. "Even after we made love, I still wouldn't let myself admit it."

Janine was completely bewildered. "Admit what?"

Quinn averted his gaze for a moment, then lifted his chin and looked directly into her eyes. "Admit that I'd fallen in love with you."

With a hushed gasp, she touched her throat and swayed. "But you were disappointed in me. You...you sent me away."

"Oh, God, honey, I was never disappointed in you." He gripped her shoulders urgently. "I was angry at myself for having taken advantage of you when I knew I had nothing to offer you."

"Nothing to offer?" For a moment her voice failed, and she simply stared in disbelief. Finally she managed to stammer, "You are kind and gentle and decent, not the mention the most selfless and courageous man I've ever known."

He winced at the praise. "I'm also arrogant and stubborn."

She smiled. "Nobody's perfect."

"You are." He kissed her forehead, then held her at arm's length. "You deserve better, Janine. Even if I manage to wriggle out of my latest legal problems, I'm still a convicted felon."

"I don't care."

"And if I can't put food on the table because no one will hire me?"

"I'm an excellent gardener. We'll grow our own food." When he started to protest again, she captured his face firmly between her palms. "You just don't get it, do you? None of that matters. I love you, Quinn. It's that simple."

He gazed at her in abject wonder. "You really mean that, don't you?"

"I could deny what I feel but that wouldn't change anything." Her lip quivered and she fought a humiliating surge of tears. "I admit that I'm frightened of being hurt again. But you are the missing piece of my soul, Quinn. I don't know what to do about that."

He took a shaky breath and whispered, "What do you want to do about it?"

"This." Bracing herself on his shoulders, she stood on tiptoes to kiss him sweetly then murmured, "How do you feel about that, Doctor?"

He stroked her hair and wrapped a strand around his finger to urge her even closer. "I'd rather show you than tell you."

"Private therapy?" She fiddled with the front of his shirt. "Sounds expensive. How much will it cost me?"

"Can you afford a lifetime commitment?"

"And then some." Janine laid her head on Quinn's shoulder. Everything she owned was gone but the material loss meant nothing. Her heart was filled with the riches of love. In all things that mattered, she was the wealthiest woman in the world.

EPILOGUE

Stretching comfortably on a woven chaise, Janine watched a half dozen laughing youngsters splash in the backyard pool of their suburban San Diego home. She lounged contentedly in the shade of a massive magnolia, enjoying the sunshine and the joyful squeals of the children who now shared her life.

Across the yard stood the huge house purchased a year earlier, a wonderful old structure with rambling hallways and an eccentric personality that reminded her of the stately Victorian, that bittersweet place that had eventually provided regeneration and renewed hope for most of its final inhabitants.

Janine hadn't rebuilt the boardinghouse. Restoring the historic flavor of the magnificent structure would have been impossible, so after the rubble was cleared the land had been deeded back to the town. The site was a park now, a nurturing place where families could picnic and enjoy the new hiking trails winding through the wilderness ravine. Returning to its natural state seemed a fitting redemption for a place which for decades had stoically endured the worst of human behavior.

As Janine reminisced, a childish voice broke into her thoughts. "Mrs. Coulliard!"

Shading her eyes, Janine watched a bouncing eight-year-old clamor down the porch steps and bound across the yard, waving a white envelope. The girl skidded to a stop and wiped her sweaty little face. "The mail came. Mr. Coulliard said I should give this one to you right away."

"Thank you, Sally." Janine's smile broadened as she recognized Althea's rushed handwriting.

Sally fidgeted. "Can I go swimming now?"

"Is your counseling session over?"

"Uh-huh."

"And your morning chores?"

The blond head bobbed vigorously.

"All right, sweetie, but when you change into your swimsuit, don't throw your clothes all over the bedroom. Hang them up neatly, okay?"

With a gleeful chortle, the child scampered into the house and Janine anxiously opened the letter.

Hi, guys!

Well, it's finally happened. Good old Al has found the man of her dreams. His name is Walter Chubb and yes, the name fits—but you know what? I've discovered that paunchy bald guys can be a hell of a lot sexier than those sophisticated Euro-types. Walt even thinks I look good without makeup. Can you beat that? He's crazy about me, so you'd better start making plans for a trip north. I'm not getting married unless Quinn agrees to give me away—something he'd been trying to do for years.

Oh, I stopped by the shrink house last week and Jules is doing just fab. He sends regards and wonders if you'd ship another batch of peanut butter cookies—says the sugar content helps him focus on the sociological aspects of reconstructive psychotherapy. Personally, I think the guy just likes your cookies.

Anyway, Doc says Jules might be up for a weekend pass pretty soon and Auntie Althea will be waiting. He might even be a full outpatient by next year. Great, huh? But don't you guys worry about him. Walter and I talked it over and when Jules finally gets out of the booby hatch, he'll always have a home with us.

By the way, Walter and I will be in San Diego next month—the old poop has never been to Sea World—and we were hoping to stop by and check out your new place. A halfway house for troubled kids, huh? Sounds so noble it makes me gag. But I love you both, anyway (especially YOU, Quinn. If you ever decide you got the wrong woman, give me a call. Walter will understand.)

Tootles, guys. See you soon. Hugs and Smoochies,

Althea

Chuckling softly, Janine refolded the letter and tucked it in her pocket. When the afternoon sessions were over, Quinn would enjoy reading it. He always got a kick out of Althea's letters and the "you got the wrong woman" part had become a standard joke between them. Janine didn't mind.

Over the past two years, she and her former tenant had become close friends. Janine admired Althea's resilience and was still in awe of her dramatic transformation since the night of the fire. When Jules had been committed to the psychiatric facility, Althea had moved to Eugene and visited him daily.

According to Dr. Orbach, with whom Quinn had established a personal and professional relationship, Jules's excellent progress was directly linked to Althea's staunch support and unwavering friendship. Thriving in her new role as protector/nurturer, the once-lonely woman had turned her life around.

Leaning back, Janine stared at the cloudless sky and considered how far they'd all come since that time in Darby Ridge. Within a week of the boardinghouse fire, she and

Quinn had been married. The Reverend Mr. Weems had performed a lovely service, and the old Presbyterian Church had been packed to the rafters with well-wishers. As for Quinn's legal problems, Fred Watson had been happy to get his truck back with a tank full of gas, and since Dr. Orbach concluded that the end result of Quinn's trespass had been in his patient's best interests, no charges were ever filed.

After Janine and Quinn had moved to San Diego, he'd petitioned for and won reinstatement of his psychotherapy license. The fire-insurance money had gone to renovate this wonderful old house into a haven for neglected and abused children. Now Quinn helped their troubled young residents understand and deal with their hidden rage while Janine mothered them and tended to their physical needs. It was a perfect partnership, a perfect marriage, and the birth of their first child in two months would herald the beginning of their perfect family.

As Janine dreamily stroked her swollen tummy, a raucous screech emanated from the stately magnolia and the branches rustled impatiently. She pulled a peeled apple slice from a plastic bag and a sleek black bird instantly soared from the tree, gracefully circled the chaise, then landed on her shoulder.

Janine laid the fruit on a nearby table. "Here you go, Edgar. Enjoy."

With a delighted caw, Edgar fluttered over and ripped a beakful of the juicy white pulp just as Quinn's office door opened. He emerged with his arm draped around the skinny shoulders of a sullen, dreadlocked youngster.

She sat up eagerly, her heart swelling with pride and with happiness as her husband's mesmerizing gaze swept the yard, then settled on Janine and softened with palpable love. He winked, blew her a kiss, gestured at his watch to signify that he had only one more session. With a final longing glance, he returned to his office.

Janine leaned back in the chair, smiling in contentment. She was happy; she was loved; and she was still the richest woman in the world.

* * * * *

Relive the romance. . .
Harlequin and Silhouette are proud to present

A program of collections of three complete novels by the most requested authors with the most requested themes.

Available in June:

They're not what they seem. . . .

Three complete novels in one special collection:

BETWEEN THE RAINDROPS by Mary Lynn Baxter
MOMENTARY MARRIAGE by Annette Broadrick
THE ICE CREAM MAN by Kathleen Korbel

Available wherever ⬦*Silhouette*®

books are sold.

SREQ694

Three new stories celebrating
motherhood and love

Birds, Bees and Babies'94

NORA ROBERTS
ANN MAJOR
DALLAS SCHULZE

A collection of three stories, all by
award-winning authors, selected
especially to reflect the love all
families share. Silhouette's fifth annual
romantic tribute to mothers is sure
to touch your heart.

Available in May,
BIRDS, BEES AND BABIES 1994 is a
perfect gift for yourself or a loved one
to celebrate the joy of motherhood.

**Available at your favorite
retail outlet.**

Only from  *Silhouette*®

—where passion lives.

BBB94

CAN YOU STAND THE HEAT?

Silhouette

SUMMER Sizzlers '94

You're in for a serious heat wave with Silhouette's latest selection of sizzling summer reading. This sensuous collection of three short stories provides the perfect vacation escape! And what better authors to relax with than

ANNETTE BROADRICK
JACKIE MERRITT
JUSTINE DAVIS

And that's not all....

With the purchase of *Silhouette Summer Sizzlers '94*, you can send in for a FREE Summer Sizzlers beach bag!

SUMMER JUST GOT HOTTER— WITH SILHOUETTE BOOKS!

Rugged and lean...and the best-looking, sweetest-talking men to be found in the entire Lone Star state!

In July 1994, Silhouette is very proud to bring you Diana Palmer's first three LONG, TALL TEXANS. CALHOUN, JUSTIN and TYLER—the three cowboys who started the legend. Now they're back by popular demand in one classic volume—and they're ready to lasso your heart! Beautifully repackaged for this special event, this collection is sure to be a longtime keepsake!

"Diana Palmer makes a reader want to find a Texan of her own to love!"   —*Affaire de Coeur*

LONG, TALL TEXANS—the first three— reunited in this special roundup!

Available in July, wherever Silhouette books are sold.

SILHOUETTE... Where Passion Lives

Don't miss these Silhouette favorites by some of our most
distinguished authors! And now, you can receive a discount by
ordering two or more titles!

D#05706	HOMETOWN MAN by Jo Ann Algermissen	$2.89 ☐
D#05795	DEREK by Leslie Davis Guccione	$2.99 ☐
D#05802	THE SEDUCER by Linda Turner	$2.99 ☐
D#05804	ESCAPADES by Cathie Linz	$2.99 ☐
IM#07478	DEEP IN THE HEART by Elley Crain	$3.39 ☐
IM#07507	STANDOFF by Lee Magner	$3.50 ☐
IM#07537	DAUGHTER OF THE DAWN by Christine Flynn	$3.50 ☐
IM#07539	A GENTLEMAN AND A SCHOLAR by Alexandra Sellers	$3.50 ☐
SE#09829	MORE THAN HE BARGAINED FOR by Carole Halston	$3.50 ☐
SE#09833	BORN INNOCENT by Christine Rimmer	$3.50 ☐
SE#09840	A LOVE LIKE ROMEO AND JULIET by Natalie Bishop	$3.50 ☐
SE#09844	RETURN ENGAGEMENT by Elizabeth Bevarly	$3.50 ☐
RS#08952	INSTANT FATHER by Lucy Gordon	$2.75 ☐
RS#08957	THE PRODIGAL HUSBAND by Pamela Dalton	$2.75 ☐
RS#08960	DARK PRINCE by Elizabeth Krueger	$2.75 ☐
RS#08972	POOR LITTLE RICH GIRL by Joan Smith	$2.75 ☐
SS#27003	STRANGER IN THE MIST by Lee Karr	$3.50 ☐
SS#27009	BREAK THE NIGHT by Anne Stuart	$3.50 ☐
SS#27016	WHAT WAITS BELOW by Jane Toombs	$3.50 ☐
SS#27020	DREAM A DEADLY DREAM by Allie Harrison	$3.50 ☐

(limited quantities available on certain titles)

	AMOUNT	$_____
DEDUCT:	10% DISCOUNT FOR 2+ BOOKS	$_____
	POSTAGE & HANDLING	$_____
	($1.00 for one book, 50¢ for each additional)	
	APPLICABLE TAXES*	$_____
	TOTAL PAYABLE	$_____
	(check or money order—please do not send cash)	

To order, complete this form and send it, along with a check or money order
for the total above, payable to Silhouette Books, to: **In the U.S.:** 3010 Walden
Avenue, P.O. Box 9077, Buffalo, NY 14269-9077; **In Canada:** P.O. Box 636,
Fort Erie, Ontario, L2A 5X3.

Name: _____

Address: _____ City: _____

State/Prov.: _____ Zip/Postal Code: _____

*New York residents remit applicable sales taxes.
Canadian residents remit applicable GST and provincial taxes.

V *Silhouette*®

SBACK-AJ